THE
ANCESTORS

A TALE FROM OUTSIDE TIME & SPACE

A NOVEL BY
WM. BARNARD

A LAMP POST BOOK

THE ANCESTORS: A TALE FROM OUTSIDE TIME & SPACE
BY WM. BARNARD

ISBN 10: 1-60039-217-2
ISBN 13: 978-1-60039-217-7
ebook ISBN: 978-1-60039-730-1

www.lamppostpubs.com

This book is dedicated to all those who diligently pursue the Truth.

CHAPTER 1

The incessant buzzing of a mosquito bouncing inside my ear canal caused me to slap myself out of a deep slumber. Dazed, I sat up in the sweat-drenched back seat of our open air jeep, startled to discover a throng of children surrounding the vehicle. Having fallen asleep hours ago back near the border of Sudan, I had no idea how long it had taken us to arrive to this tiny remote village in Northern Uganda.

Now that the half-naked children knew I was actually alive, they surged forward, pushing up against every side of the jeep in an effort to get closer. The light pink skin of their outstretched palms contrasted against their extremely dark faces as they motioned for whatever handouts I might offer. Their continued pleas in broken English went unheeded as I tried to rub my eyes awake with one hand while waving them off with the other. With their requests growing increasingly louder, a man under the rusted hood

1

of a nearby truck shouted something in the local dialect and their voices immediately dropped off. All but one young boy walked away dejected.

The man shook his head, glancing over at me before fixing his gaze back at the engine, apparently still puzzled as to what was wrong with the truck. It seemed that his attempt to silence the kids was not merely out of respect to me, but so he could contemplate the mechanical problem in quiet.

Standing up in the back of the jeep, I scanned the area for my photographer and our two guides while the remaining child leaned silently against the spare tire on the back. The smell of burning trash directed my eyes to a small fire pit about a hundred yards away where I recognized the back of Bob's hulking frame. Dwarfing our companions, Bob had his camera bag strapped to his back and appeared engaged in a conversation with some elders of the tribe.

Late the night before, we had come close to pulling right into the middle of a tribal skirmish. In order to avoid becoming casualties of misdirected bullets, our guides had pulled an immediate U-turn and had begun driving back south. I could only assume now that we had stopped driving because we were a good distance away from the conflict. The previous day's threatening black storm clouds had been replaced this morning with a crisp blue backdrop and I hoped it somehow was a sign that we were relatively safe.

My parched throat caused me to start searching for the plastic bottle of water that I had stashed the night before. Relieved to locate it at the bottom of my rucksack, I guzzled half of it before I caught the eye of the shirtless boy who still stood in front of me. With his head now cocked to the side, I could sense that his quick study of me had left him perplexed.

"What's your name?" I asked.

"Cuto. Who are you?" He replied, revealing two missing top teeth.

"My name's Zach."

"Where are you from?"

"I'm from the United States. How do you know how to speak English?"

"Some missionaries from America come here to teach us. They show us how to make clean water." He pointed over to a nearby well that had some kind of filtration system attached to it. "What are you doing here?"

"I'm a writer. We're trying to interview some children who used to be soldiers with the L.R.A. We were supposed to meet up with a few boys in a displacement camp last night, but had to turn around."

"You want to talk to kids who got away?"

"Yes. Do you know any children that live around here who have escaped?"

"My cousin Adroa across the lake."

"Near here?" I said, becoming hopeful.

"Yes, but he moved to the city for work."

"Oh. Have you ever seen the L.R.A., or other armies fighting in this area?"

"No, sometimes we hear shooting. But we never see the L.R.A. They come in the night and steal the kids away."

"Are you afraid they will get you one day?" I asked him gently.

Cuto didn't answer and his gaze fell down toward his feet.

Having to live under this constant threat had obviously robbed him of his childhood, and made me wonder why some of my colleagues ever chose to be war correspondents.

I regretted bringing up the subject with him and tried to think quickly of something to distract his thoughts. Pulling out one of the five soccer balls from an old army duffel bag, I bounced the small gift to him off my knee and into his eager arms. All of my last minute efforts to get to the sports store back home in time were instantly rewarded by the unforgettable look on Cuto's beaming face.

"I can keep?" Cuto asked, his voice rising.

"It's all yours," I smiled back.

"Thank you. Thank you very much, Mr. Zach," he said, beginning to juggle it successfully off his knees for a minute before inadvertently kicking it too hard and having to give chase.

Watching him run freely, I remembered how Bob and I were moved to compassion when we first heard about the plight of children like Cuto in this central Africa region. Since 1987, the L.R.A. (Lord's Resistance Army) had notoriously kidnapped children and brainwashed them into believing that their rebel militia was ordained from God. While many world leaders were well aware of the L.R.A.'s criminal acts, I hoped our story would help create an international outcry that would motivate the United Nations to take action and intervene.

As Cuto returned to the jeep with the ball, I dug down into my backpack so I could offer him a candy bar. Like most kids, Cuto saw no need to savor the treat but ripped off the wrapper and quickly engulfed the half-melted Snickers bar before I could even finish half of mine.

It was always a joy to watch how quickly the demeanor of a child could change from the pure pleasure of chocolate, and Cuto did not disappoint. The resulting sugar rush made him talk a mile-a-minute while he repeatedly bounced the soccer ball off his forehead.

"Do you like to fish, Mr. Zach?"

"I used to. I haven't been in a while. Do you?"

"Oh yes. Very much. We have some big fish in our lake."

"How far is it from here?"

"Very close. Do you want to go? I will show where I saw a ship come down from the sky and go into the water."

"You saw a plane crash? I asked, stepping out of the jeep.

"No, no, Mr. Zach. It was changing colors and then landed very slowly and down into the water," he said with a toothless grin that only a kid can pull off as cute.

Odd as the account about the aircraft sounded, only his continued yanking on my hand compelled me to look further into it. As Cuto lead me to the local shaman's home on the outskirts of the village, we walked by a collection of small, circular mud huts that ostensibly lacked electricity or plumbing. Two women balancing water jugs skillfully on top of their heads approached us, looking bewildered and no doubt wondering what this white man was doing in their village.

At times, my travels to isolated locations such as this didn't feel like I had simply gone overseas, but had instead landed on an entirely different planet. While growing up, I had always dreamed of going outside of California to see the world, but now seeing it for the past several years made me painfully aware of the immense amount of human suffering.

When I reflected on the vast difference of my lifestyle compared to those who struggled to survive from day to day, it always made my return home to the daily grind of Southern California seem like a day at Disneyland.

⊕   ⊕   ⊕

CUTO CONTINUED TO DEFTLY DRIBBLE the ball off his bare feet until we came to a slightly larger hut with an unusual doorway. While most of the entrances to the huts had traditional blankets covering them, the shaman's hut held a large faded beach towel with the cartoon image of Homer Simpson gripping a Duff Beer.

Even with this American Icon hanging from the door, I began to imagine the "bush doctor" coming out to suspiciously inspect me, wearing nothing but a loincloth and a necklace of animal teeth. Cuto scooped the ball into the air with his left foot and caught it on the run as he scampered into the hut.

Seconds later, the shaman burst out from behind the beach towel, flinging Homer to the side and causing me to take a step back. With the young boy at first tightly clutching his arm, Cuto finally let go as the man stretched out his arm toward me.

5

"Hello, my name is Mukama," he said, politely waiting to shake my hand. The shaman stood six foot tall and wiry, and his choice of a white polo shirt and beige slacks made me laugh at my naivety for stereotyping him as the witch doctor from a National Geographic special.

"Nice to meet you, Mukama. I'm Zach. Your friend here tells me he saw some kind of strange air craft crash into a local lake."

"Not crash. Just flying in and out of the water," he smiled pensively.

"You mean landing on the water and then taking off?"

"No, into the water. Submerged completely. It's quite bizarre."

"You've seen this yourself?" I asked, tilting my head as if that would help me comprehend what he just said.

"Yes; actually more than once in the last couple of weeks."

The story only got stranger. According to Mukama, this particular ship not only possessed the ability to alter its colors, but could even change shapes as it hovered over the lake.

"Do you want to go to the lake where I saw it?" Cuto asked, his eyes getting bigger.

"Sure. But wait a second; I need to find out what's going on with my photographer."

Bob always gravitated toward those afflicted by adversity and as I jogged towards the jeep, I found him taking a photo of a man who apparently lost his leg from a previous war. Despite the man's tragedy, he stood proudly for the photo, leaning against a crude wooden crutch and wearing his injury as a badge of honor.

After I told Bob to grab his gear and follow me, he gave me the latest update as we walked briskly back towards the shaman's hut.

"Our guides think we might have enough gas to make it to a town about forty-five minutes south of here where we could refuel and try to get an update on any tribal conflicts. At this point, I don't think it would be a bad idea to start working on an alternative plan to fly out of Sudan instead if our route back to Kampala becomes too dangerous."

"That sounds precarious in itself," I stated.

"Well, it's looking like a pretty risky proposition either way now."

When I relayed to Bob the story about the mysterious aircraft, he arched his left eyebrow.

"So Zach, you want me to lug all this gear down here so I can take photos of some little green men?"

"Didn't you mention something back home about wanting an adventure?"

My comment brought out Bob's trademark smirk, and as he shifted the weight of his camera bag he let out an exaggerated grunt. "Well, who knows, a photo like this just may top my lifelong dream of capturing a Big Foot on film."

"That's what I like about you Bob. You're always looking to dream big." I shot back, which caused him to chuckle.

Working for several magazines through the years, Bob had enjoyed traveling the world for different shoots, but I sensed that time away from home was putting too much strain on his wife and young son, and this might be his last overseas job. Even though we were both thirty-three, I was still single, free to pursue my quest for that one big story that would leave my mark on the world.

After meeting up with Cuto and Mukama, we headed into a wooded area surrounding the village that mainly consisted of giant eucalyptus trees before ending up on a twisting path beside a small creek. We all walked side by side until a dramatic increase in a variety of trees and shrubs caused the trail to narrow, forcing us to follow single file.

Now under the dark canopy of a dense forest, the shaman shared how he had perfected his English.

"One of the former missionaries that stayed here was Dr. Brent Gallagher. He set up a scholarship so I could go to the University of North Carolina and become a doctor. Unfortunately when my father died, I had to leave school early and come back to assist my family."

"I'm sorry to hear that," I offered.

"I'm hoping by next year I can go back to finish up. It would really help my tribe if we had a doctor in the village. The nearest one right now is almost an hour from here."

I couldn't put my finger as to why his accent seemed somewhat different until it finally dawned on me: Mukama's native tongue was now mixed with a Southern drawl.

The oppressive humidity seemed to increase with each step as we huffed down the trail for fifteen-minutes before coming upon a milk-chocolate colored lake, which appeared to be about a half mile across. Bob immediately began snapping shots of some local fishermen who were casting nets on the other side of the lake from their small wooden dinghy.

Mukama pointed over to a small outcropping of rocks and said, "That is where we were fishing from last Tuesday when we saw an enormous orange triangular ship land in the middle of the lake. But right before it went it to the water, it turned into a bright green sphere."

Mukama's retelling of the account caused Bob's eyebrow to elevate a couple notches higher than usual on the skeptic scale and he shot me a sarcastic "okay" sign with his fingers. Now completely disinterested, Bob wandered off to snap photos of a colorful tropical bird that was perched in a nearby tree.

Hoping he had not seen Bob's dismissal of his account, I tried to keep Mukama occupied with my questions.

"So Mukama, are there less fish in the water now or do the fish caught taste any different after you saw the aircraft?

He stroked his chin and thought for a moment before answering. "No, I don't think so. Not that I noticed anyway…"

Right as he replied, a thundering splash startled us as a radiant object soared out of the center of the lake. Stopping abruptly about a quarter of a mile above the lake, the glowing orb hovered above us for what seemed like just a few seconds before it darted away horizontally.

"Holy smoke!" Bob yelled.

Pulling his camera back down and peering into the view finder, he exclaimed, "Yes! I got it."

Too stunned to even move at first, I could not believe Bob had been collected enough to take a photo. Eager to see what he had captured, we all ran over to look at the film. Unfortunately, the photo only revealed a small sphere of light and we would have to wait until we got back so we could enlarge the photo. However, as the small brown waves began lapping up onto the banks of the lake, we were given clear evidence that we just stumbled upon something extraordinary.

"See? I told you," Mukama smiled directly at Bob.

Bob shook his head and laughed. "Yeah, you sure did." Turning to me, he asked, "What in the world do you think that was, Zach?"

Before I could answer, we all flinched as the distinctive blast of a mortar shell reverberated through the woods.

Mukama's thin face strained as he shouted, "We need to go back!"

While I had been in South American countries that were battling rebel forces, I had never been thrust into an actual combat zone. With a surge of adrenaline pumping through my veins, I immediately thought about the very real possibility that another reporter would be writing how my first encounter with live fire ended up being my last.

As we quickly rushed toward the village, the rattling of machine gun fire echoed through the dense trees causing us to pick up our pace. Despite standing only half our height, Cuto sprinted ahead while tightly clutching his brand new ball.

I tried to lighten Bob's load by carrying one of his bags, but the jog was taking a toll on his two hundred and seventy pound frame. Bob's labored attempts to breathe made me concerned that he might not make it back without having a heart attack, but stopping to rest simply wasn't an option.

Nearing the tree line that bordered the village, we could hear sounds of heavy machinery and the surging of truck engines. Mukama told us to crouch down behind an embankment while he crept up ahead to spy out the commotion.

He jogged back looking calmer and said, "Don't worry. There are Federal troops in our village now."

A cloud of red dust from the approaching convoy of military vehicles greeted us as we exited the woods. Our guides spotted us as they stood on the hood of our jeep and frantically waved us over to where they had relocated the vehicle.

When we arrived back over to the jeep, Bob bent over and held his knees. The back of his shirt was soaked in sweat and his face had grown extremely pale. While relieved to stop our run, he now appeared to be on the verge of vomiting. Our rest proved short-lived when we heard more shells exploding, this time much closer. The driver started the engine and hurried us to get our gear in the jeep.

Speeding away from the direction of the convoy, our jeep shot past several children running to their huts for refuge. When we finally passed Mukama's home, I saw Cuto standing alone, his shoulders slumped forward. Several yards away his new soccer ball lay abandoned.

I continued staring back at Cuto until I could barely make out his small frame. Even though I knew I was powerless to change his situation, I still couldn't prevent the sense of guilt that came over me as we drove away in the safety of our jeep.

⊕   ⊕   ⊕

OUR TWO NATIVE GUIDES WERE on loan from African Tours, which normally caters to wealthy Americans and Europeans who want to go on a safari and observe lions roaming the plains. While they didn't verbalize it, we could sense their increasing edginess about continuing our search for former child soldiers to interview.

Akiki, who looked to be in his mid-twenties, sat shotgun and turned around to face us before saying, "This is somewhat strange. The L.R.A. usually tries to sneak into the villages during the night. But once in a while they will launch artillery shells in the daytime and try to get the children to run into the forest so they can ambush them. I'm sure once they see that government troops have arrived they will retreat further into the forest."

"That's good. Hopefully they'll be safe now," I said, leaning forward.

Appearing to be twice the age of Akiki, our driver Kikongo had remained relatively quiet the entire trip, but now felt the need to chime in. "The problem is, most of the villagers don't trust the Ugandan military, either. It's not as bad as it was, but for many years there was widespread abuse. The people in this area have a very long memory."

His comment sounded like it came from personal experience and made me slump back into my seat.

About twenty minutes outside of the village on the way to Gulu, our driver's hat blew off, causing him to slow down so he could turn around and retrieve it. Realizing this was good time to take a pit stop, we all piled out of the jeep so we could relieve ourselves while Kigongo drove back up about a hundred yards where the hat lay in the middle of the road.

Standing several feet from me, Bob jerked his neck upward when we heard a faint whistling sound dropping from the treetops.

⊕　　⊕　　⊕

THE NEXT THING I KNEW, I was waking up in medical clinic in Juba. Tilting my head to the side, I found Bob lying bare-chested on a cot beside me, his neck and shoulder covered in bandages that were encrusted with blood.

"Bob?" I grunted, struggling to get my bearings straight.

"He's asleep. He just passed out when they were sewing him up,"

Kikongo said, standing at the other side of the room. "They were able to stop the bleeding and said he will be fine now."

"Did we get attacked?"

"Yes. A mortar landed right near you in the woods. The shrapnel tore up his shoulder and it barely missed the carotid artery in his neck," he said, moving closer to my cot. "The doctor told me you both have busted ear drums. You were bleeding out of one of them, which is why you have a bandage on your head."

"Is that why I feel dizzy and my ears are ringing?"

"I'm sure it is. The doctor gave you medicine for the pain and to help prevent any nausea."

"What about, um…" I said trying to remember the name of our other guide.

"Akiki is getting stitches right now to stop his bleeding, but he needs surgery immediately and they cannot do that here. He's in really bad shape."

"Oh, man."

"I hope Bob will not get angry with me, but I had to trade his camera equipment to pay the clinic."

"Don't worry about it. I'm sure he'll understand."

"My company is sending one of their tour planes tomorrow morning to fly all of you back to Kampala and then you can catch a flight back home."

"Thank you, Kikongo."

"There's something you should know. Bob must have known the mortar was coming in because I saw him dive on top of you right before the blast. I think because he's such a large man that he must have knocked you out when he landed on you. He was bleeding all over the place, but he still carried you and Akiki to the jeep. So really, you should be thanking Bob," he said before turning and leaving the room.

WE TRAVELED FOR OVER THIRTEEN hours straight, and as the initial shock of what had happened began to wear off, I had more time to digest what Kikongo had told me.

While words are inadequate to describe what it's like to discover that someone personally risked their life to save yours, staring at Bob as he slept next to me on the plane caused an immense sense of pride to well up within me, knowing that I had such a friend.

After landing safely in Paris, a cab escorted us to the famous *Pitié-Salpêtrière* Hospital. X-rays revealed shrapnel embedded deeply in Bob's shoulder and the doctor made arrangements for surgery within the next hour. As the nurses prepared to wheel him away on a gurney, I leaned over and grabbed Bob by the arm.

"Kikongo told me what you did back by the road," I said.

"Did what?"

"How you threw yourself on me and saved my life."

"I've wanted to tackle you for a long time, Zach." Bob smiled.

"I'm sure you have. But seriously," I said and looked him in the eyes. "I know this is kinda awkward for you, but I want to thank you."

"It's not awkward at all Zach. You're my boy. I'd do it again in a heartbeat."

The male nurse undoubtedly had no idea what we were saying and shot me an impatient look, so I quickly said, "Hey, I'll be here when you get out."

"Just tell them I like my morphine black. No sugar, no cream," he winked at me as they began to roll him down the corridor. Turning the other way, I walked toward the exit to grab some breakfast.

Four hours after I learned that the surgery was a success, I called Bob's wife Cheryl as he had instructed me and finally gave her the brief details of what had happened in Uganda.

Before handing the phone to him, I tried to get her to calm down, but finally gave in and said, "Look Cheryl, he's awake now so you can talk to him yourself."

"Honey, slow down already. Listen to me. This is why I didn't call you earlier..." Bob tried to interject.

From ten feet away, I could hear her interrupt him through the receiver and Bob rolled his eyes at me. Figuring this would be a good time to walk down the hall to the water fountain, I left the room so Bob could defuse the situation with his wife. When I returned to the room, I stayed by the door to let him wrap up the call.

"Look, I told you. We're just a little banged up, but we're fine. Nothing to worry about. We're out of the woods now and we'll be home in few days at the most. I'm not going to miss seeing little Scotty's first steps, trust me."

Sensing that I could hear him from the doorway, Bob tried to lighten the mood.

"Now honey, you know you don't have to worry about me since I have the strength of ten men. You should, however, be worried about Zach. He's always been a little frail, you know."

Grabbing the plastic rod that held the dividing sheet, I zipped it back so I could face Bob.

"Ha! Now Cheryl knows for sure that you're indulging in the fruit of Europe's best pharmacy," I yelled loud enough so she could hear me.

Bob sneered before continuing, "You see? Zach's fine. I'm fine. Now make sure you give Scotty a big hug from Daddy and tell everyone we appreciate their positive thoughts and prayers. I love you, baby, and I'll see you soon."

Cheryl must have finally relented, acknowledging we were no longer in any danger and allowing Bob to get off the phone. As soon as he hung up, his head dropped slightly, and he let his tongue hang out of his mouth. Relieved that he could stop putting on a front, Bob grunted, "Ugh. I feel like a run-over dog."

While it may have seemed odd to some when Bob used his sense of humor to make light of serious situations, I knew he had to be shaken by the thought that he came close to never seeing his family again.

Before speaking again, he slowly exhaled. "Man, we got lucky, Zach."

"Yeah, I know you're right. And I know I should just be grateful that we escaped with our lives, but I'm still super disappointed that we didn't even get our story," I said, smacking my lips.

"I hear you. I took a ton of great photos. I was also looking forward to blowing up that picture of that crazy aircraft, but now they're all gone."

"When you were going under the knife, I went down to a small café and did a little research. There've been rumors that in exchange for the large amounts of financial aid from China, the Ugandan government has been allowing the Chinese to conduct military operations and test secret aircraft."

"Man, now that would have been a great story to come across if we could've confirmed that photo."

"Tell me about it," I said, shaking my head.

He paused as he winced in pain. "Well... there will be other stories. I just thank God that we got out of there."

"I'm pretty sure God got out of there a long time ago."

⊕   ⊕   ⊕

RIGHT BEFORE SUNRISE AS I enjoyed a Vicodin induced deep sleep, the uninterrupted alarm of Bob's heart monitor blared loud enough to wake me up in time to witness a flurry of nurses and doctors converge into our room. Despite not speaking French, I could still discern that his condition was dire from the tone and speed of the head doctor's voice.

The next sound confirmed my worst fear.

Ka-thump.

The distinctive noise of a defibrillator trying to revive Bob almost caused my own heart to stop beating. Now frozen with fear, I watched the feet of the nurses shuffle quickly around his bed. Over the next ten minutes, I periodically held my breath, hoping I would soon hear intermittent beeps from the monitor indicating a resuscitated heart.

As the voices hushed, I knew the results before the doctor stepped around the divider and stood next to my rollaway bed.

"I am sorry monsieur, but we could not save your friend."

"What? Why? I thought they said everything was okay," I muttered in shock.

"There will have to be an autopsy to say for certain, but most likely his heart seized up because it was unable to fight off the staph infection," he said solemnly. Not knowing what else to say, he bowed his head, turned quietly and walked away as I stared blankly where he had just stood.

While I had heard the doctor clearly and now listened to nurses clicking off equipment, I kept trying to deny that this was real. Part of me wanted to get up and see if I could somehow wake him. Instead I lay paralyzed, only moving my hand on to the painful lump in my throat when I heard them wheel his corpse out of the room.

Now conceding that I would never see my friend again, my whole body began to shudder. Thinking about his young son and what I would say to Cheryl, I closed my eyes, pulling the pillow up over my face to soak up the steady stream of tears.

CHAPTER 2

Essence Magazine occupies the entire twenty-fourth floor of a newly built high rise overlooking downtown San Diego and her famous harbor. The complete building has the appearance of being constructed completely of glass and from my office window you can see all the way south to the beaches of Tijuana. While starting my day to such a majestic vista usually left me feeling inspired, the view had no effect on my somber mood when I returned to my workplace a week after Bob's funeral.

Deep in mourning, Bob's wife Cheryl still declined to speak with me as she had convinced herself that I somehow manipulated Bob into taking the trip to Africa and held me responsible for the death of her husband.

Fortunately, Essence's senior editor, Harry Edwards was sensitive to my emotional stress level and suggested I take on some more lighthearted subjects. I had agreed in hopes that these diversions would help take my mind off recent events, but daily reminders, like walking by Bob's vacant desk, continued to confront me.

I found concentrating for long periods of time extremely difficult and for the first time in my career struggled daily with writers block. My efforts felt almost robotic as I approached assignments on hot air balloon racing and an ex-football star's new wine making business. The stories were so crummy that the magazine declined to run them.

Naturally Harry had begun to wonder when I'd come out of my mental funk and be ready to take on some stories of more substance. When he called me into his office a few weeks after I had returned from Africa, I could already sense what he wanted.

"Look, Zach, I know you lost all the photos from your Africa trip, but do you think a story is salvageable? I'm not trying to rush you, but..." Harry subtly stopped to wipe the lenses of his designer frames.

"Geez, I don't know, Harry. I really hadn't wanted to even think about it. But I guess I could try..." I said, hoping he would realize I was just trying to appease him.

"Like I said, when you're ready; I'm confident some good could come out of all this, especially if you write about what you went there for," Harry said, leaning back against his giant red leather chair with his arms now resting on his protruding waistline.

Not knowing if Harry even recognized he was contradicting himself, I pinched the end of my cropped hair behind my ear nervously and said, "Well, we did see something crazy over there and Bob actually took a photo of it, but..."

Only at this moment did I realize that I hadn't even talked with anyone else about the strange aircraft Bob and I had seen.

Harry waited for me to continue, but got impatient. "Well, what was it?"

Exhaling a big breath, I finally confessed. "Well, you're not gonna believe this, but we saw something like a U.F.O. I think it could be some aircraft the Chinese are testing."

"Zach, I need something tangible here. Not some wild theories with absolutely no photos to back it up. Even if you had some photo, you know we stay away from any of that paranormal garbage. Surely you got to have something…"

"Yeah, I know. I don't know why I even mentioned it. It was just so strange," I said, staring at the back of his computer monitor.

Pulling his chair closer, he looked down at the papers covering his antique mahogany desk and paused to choose his words carefully. "Look, you know the bosses will always try to see a return on their investment. If you are unable to produce a story about the L.R.A, I can live with it. You put your butt on the line over there and we appreciate that. You just let me know when you're ready."

"Okay. I will," I said, consciously looking away from Harry. *Maybe I should explain to Harry that I have already tried to sit down several times and write the story,* I thought. Instead, I stood up quickly and rushed out of his office.

While I understood Harry had a job to do, it still irked me that they were trying to work me for a story that got my friend killed. Unfortunately, it had only caused me to start dwelling again on all the depressing things I had seen and experienced lately.

For the most part of my career, with the exception of my recent assignment in Uganda, I had been able to detach myself from the suffering of those I wrote about. Even though this caused me to feel somewhat shallow at times, it was the only way I had thought I could stay objective as a journalist.

In the same way, I now wished I could simply disconnect from my emotions. My remedy was the same thing I had been doing every evening after work for the last two weeks; I grabbed my jacket and headed over to Murphy's Pub.

THE FAMOUS BLUES SONG, "STORMY Monday," appropriately greeted me as I walked through the side door and down the short corridor leading into the dark tavern.

"Hey Zach, you're starting early today?" yelled Jim Murphy as he washed some shot glasses from the end of the bar. A brother of the owner, Jim had managed the place ever since I had started frequenting the pub several years ago.

"What kind of beer you drinking today?" he asked.

"Actually Jim, set me up with a couple shots of tequila."

"Wow! What's the occasion?" Jim reached on the top shelf for a decorative bottle holding the golden liquor.

"Nothing. Just want something different," I said, not wanting to get into why I had shown up midday. Normally a place where I came to relax and enjoy the company of friends, Murphy's had now become merely a source of refuge. Setting up at the bar seemed to be the only time of the day I was able to dull my heartache, even if it was for only a few hours.

Setting down two shot glasses in front of me, Jim asked, "When's Johnny getting back from his surfing trip to Indonesia?"

"Supposedly late Sunday night."

I downed one shot with ease, but the second one caused me to cough. I slapped my chest before wheezing, "I think now I'm ready for some beer. Pour me a pitcher of Bass, Jim. I'm gonna rack up some balls over at the closest table."

The fluorescent light hanging over the pool table advertising the "King of Beers" made it the brightest place in the otherwise dimly lit pub. While the State had outlawed smoking from bars and restaurants over a decade ago, the residual smoke of previous years had permanently penetrated the walls and carpet, now blending with the perfect complement of stale beer.

I moved over to practice various bank shots on the ragged green felt for half an hour before my friend Todd Gilmore arrived.

Sporting the usual untucked Zane's Electrician uniform shirt and faded blue jeans, his brown curly hair hung from the edges of a Padres baseball cap. Certain that I had never met a genuinely nicer guy, I had my theory confirmed when Todd changed out the circuit breakers on my house a few months back, charging me a twelve pack of beer.

I hadn't seen Todd in the last couple of weeks around the pub and his presence helped briefly lift my spirits.

"Hey, you up for a game? I got another pitcher on the way," I shouted at him.

"Definitely," Todd said, pulling up a stool next to the pool table.

"Johnny's coming back this weekend, huh?"

"That's the story I heard," I said.

"You know, you hear a ton of people claim they're gonna start living life to the fullest after going through a tough ordeal, but Johnny really has stuck to that mantra after he beat throat cancer."

"Yeah, you gotta give it to him. This is like his third surf vacation this year," I said, focusing on the cue ball before smacking it.

"I'm glad that he got to get down there. I'd love to be able to take off and just surf for a couple of months."

"I was just thinking about how simple life was back in school when I surfed every morning and worked nights as a bellman."

"Life definitely seemed easier when we were younger," Todd said, chuckling.

Jim brought us a new pitcher and another mug. As I poured Todd a beer, I said, "Well, word on the street is that you're going to be jumping into the fire soon."

Todd flashed a huge smile while eyeing his options on the pool table. "Yeah, after I finish up coaching Little League, Jenny and I are getting hitched up next June. Looks like we are actually gonna get to Maui for our honeymoon."

He glanced at his watch and said, "She should be here soon."

"So does it already feel like you got a ball and chain strapped to your leg?" I asked before taking a couple of hefty swigs off my beer.

"Not at all. I'm really looking forward to it. Jenny is super cool and we've already been living together for almost two years anyway so she knows all my bad habits," he said, laughing.

"Good for you, Todd. I'm happy for you."

"You're going to be there, right?"

"Of course, my man. I wouldn't miss it." I reached over and clinked Todd's mug in a spontaneous toast.

"So is Jenny coming here with Heather?" I asked.

"I'm not sure. She might be working a night shift."

I had met Jenny's attractive sister a couple of times before and had been really impressed with her. Easy to build rapport with, Heather not only possessed a great sense of humor, but she seemed to truly care about people. Regretting not asking for her phone number last time we hung out, I had been hoping to cross paths with her again soon.

Shortly after Jenny arrived, I told her of my interest in Heather and she said, "You should have asked earlier. She's been dating this doctor from her hospital for the last couple of weeks and they seemed to be really hitting it off."

"Of, course. Just my luck," I said smiling and trying to hide my disappointment.

"I'm getting another drink. You guys want anything?" I asked.

They both declined so I headed over to the bar with no intentions of coming back and being a third wheel. I must have ended up drinking my body weight in booze because the rest of the evening became an absolute blur. I don't recall when I left the pub or how I managed to lose the valuable watch my grandfather had given me. And I certainly don't have any recollection of going to sleep in a strange bed. Unfortunately, my foggy memory would prove to be the least of my worries.

CHAPTER 3

The white walls of the room melded with the white uniform in front of me as I strained to focus my eyes.

"Zach, can you hear me?" I recognized my sister Vanessa's voice, but still didn't see her face.

Pain seared through the top of my head while a nurse fiddled with the IV tower next to my bed. My eyelids fought to stay open and only when I tried to rub them did I become conscious of the sling on my left arm. Along with the increased pulsating pain from my swelling head, I became queasy from the sickening smell of antiseptic in the air.

"Geez, what happened to me?" I said hoarsely, my face cringing as I burped and tasted bile.

"You slammed your car into a lamppost about a mile from your house. You have thirty-five stitches in your head. The doctor said you were lucky…"

"Extremely lucky, Mr. Miller." A doctor in a white lab coat announced as he entered the room. Shining his miniature flashlight into my eyes to check the dilation, he asked, "How are you feeling this morning?"

"My head is killing me," I complained, hoping he wouldn't continue to feel the need to use such a loud tone.

"You have suffered a major concussion, so you're likely to experience some headaches for at least a couple of weeks. You also have a sprained left arm, but fortunately that's the extent of your injuries."

"That's good." I mumbled.

"It's quite ironic, Mr. Miller, that the very reason you wrecked was the same reason you sustained less injuries as the alcohol kept your muscles re-laxed when you crashed. I'm sure you know that I'm not advocating drink-ing and driving – I'm just trying to explain how lucky you are to not have been more seriously hurt. I'll be back in a few minutes," he said, grabbing a clipboard from the foot of the bed before walking out.

With her strawberry blonde hair tied in a ponytail, Vanessa wore no make-up as usual, which helped to expose the dark circles under her hazel eyes. Standing up from her chair near the foot of my bed, she moved over to my right side so she could grab my good arm.

"Zach, you know I've been worried about your drinking for a while and I hope this all really sinks in that you need to give it up," she whis-pered, attempting to keep our conversation from being overheard from any nurses that walked in.

"Vanessa, I never drive loaded."

"You did last night," Vanessa said, her cheeks now flushing red.

"Look, I don't..."

"Don't even start trying to BS me, Zach!" She cut me off and then lowered her voice again. "Do you want to end up like Dad? Do you want me to have to bury you, too?"

Biting her lip as it began to tremble, she looked up at the ceiling before rushing out of the room and down the hall.

I glanced around at some of the machinery that surrounded my bed before she returned to the room a few minutes later with moistened eyes and holding a wadded Kleenex. No longer looking angry, she sat down on the edge of the chair facing me from the foot of the bed.

"Zach, I know you might not believe this, but God was looking out for you last night." Her voice was slightly shuddering.

I let out a deep sigh and closed my eyes.

"He's been looking out for you your whole life," she finished, innately knowing that was all the preaching I could handle right then.

MY HEADACHES SLOWLY SUBSIDED OVER the next week, but my real problems were just beginning. I had already been essentially unproductive over the last month and now I had to call my work and let them know I probably wouldn't be able to write for at least a couple more weeks. While informed by my lawyer that I faced some hefty fines for the DUI charges, I also owed money on the loan for my only vehicle, which lay totaled in the junkyard. The news only got better when my insurance agent notified me that they were going to cancel my policy because of the serious violation.

Struggling to remain positive and be thankful that I at least still had my health and my job, I dropped by the office to give my boss an update on what I had heard.

"Zach, thanks for stopping by. How are you feeling?" Harry said, avoiding eye contact and fidgeting with the knot on his crimson necktie.

"Just sore right now," I said, sitting down in front of his desk. "I wanted you to know that getting to work will not be a problem. While my license isn't suspended yet, my attorney is going to arrange it so that I will have a permit to drive to work; and since my job calls for a varied schedule at a variety of places, I could basically say to any officer who happened to pull me over that I was on my way to work."

Harry hesitated before speaking, abruptly getting up from his seat to go over and close his office door. As he gently walked back and sat down at his desk, an uneasy feeling rose up in my stomach when I saw his need for privacy.

"Zach, I have to tell you something. This isn't coming from me, but because you essentially left your job last Monday, the magazine has decided to suspend you without pay. By the end of this week they will reach a decision on whether there are sufficient grounds for termination."

Staring right past him, I knew right then my life had just stopped on a dime.

"Zach?" He tried to get my attention as I sat unresponsive to his last statement.

"What? I just cannot believe this." I shook my head still trying to grasp what he just said.

"I know, I know. I got the call from H.R. this morning and I tried to make a stand for you but..." He flipped his palms upward implying there was nothing else he could do.

"Harry, I, uh, have never even heard of anything like this."

"Me neither, Zach. I don't totally understand the decision," he said, trying to sound as empathetic as possible.

Although unsure if Harry was being truthful about the suspension coming from Human Resources, I really didn't care who had made the decision at this point.

"You know what, Harry? Let's just see how many awards this magazine wins in the future because I'll never, and I mean never, write another one for you or your donkey bosses!" I stood up so quickly that Harry flinched backwards in his chair.

"Zach..." Harry said trying to calm me down.

I marched toward the door, but a photo from a few years back of the

MLJ awards ceremony caught my eye, stopping me in my tracks. Hung in a cherry wood frame, the picture had captured Harry with his arm around my shoulder as I held up my plaque for Journalist of the Year.

Glaring at the photo of the huge smile on his chubby face, I began to grind my teeth and wanted to slam it with my fist. Instead, my foot played the fool and I kicked right below the frame, causing the picture to hop off the hook and crash to the floor.

While my punting skills had served me well back on the high school soccer team, my strong leg now betrayed me as my shoe plunged completely through the wall. The dry wall immediately clutched onto my ankle, somehow trapping me and I struggled to set myself free.

Grabbing onto the door handle with my good hand, I inadvertently yanked it open which allowed all my co-workers to not only hear me shouting profanities, but now everyone could see my herky-jerky dance with the door.

"Great! Just great!" I screamed as I struggled to hold onto the moving door.

"Security, can you come up to my office immediately," Harry said timidly into his speakerphone just as I retrieved my chalk-covered shoe.

Stooping down to knock the white dust off my pant leg and put my shoe back on, I kept my gaze on the floor as I could sense everyone on the twenty-fourth floor rubbernecking for a better vantage point of the commotion.

With my face flushed red, I dodged the numerous stares as I hurried over to my desk, grabbing my day planner and laptop before heading to the staircase to avoid being escorted out by the rental cops. After pushing open an exit door with my back, I suddenly became lightheaded and had to grab the handrail as I slowly made my way down the stairwell. While I had tried to be careful to keep my hurt arm from moving, a bolt of pain now shot down my elbow from the exertion.

Back on the street level, I walked a couple blocks to where I parked

my compact rental car, and was welcomed by a bright yellow parking ticket under the windshield wiper. I removed it, my eyes scrolling down the
scribbled handwriting before I found the bottom line. *Seventy-five dollars!*
I said to myself. Crumpling the citation into a ball, I slung into the empty
passenger's seat.

After pulling into the street, I took some deep breaths to try and get my
anger to subside, but it only took a few minutes before downtown traffic
poured more gas onto my fury.

Thoughtlessly engaged on a cell phone, a young lady driving a brand
new BMW cut me off, and almost clipped my front end. I slammed on the
horn and yelled several select words as I caught her glance in the rearview
mirror. She returned my exchange by flippantly waving back at me while
continuing her conversation. When she barely skated through the yellow
light at the intersection in front of me, I was left to test my rental car's
braking system, skidding to a halt.

I continued to bang on my steering wheel until I noticed two teenage
boys parked to the right of me, mocking my behavior. Looking away to
my left, I hit the button to roll up the windows while rapidly tapping my
foot in anticipation of the light change.

"I can only imagine the wonderful surprises the rest of this day has for
me," I said out loud, stomping the gas pedal when the light finally turned
green.

By the time I pulled into my driveway, my head was throbbing and
I felt sick to my stomach. Ignoring the blinking light on my answering
machine, I made a beeline to the refrigerator to grab a beer before sinking
into my black leather couch. I clutched the TV remote, hoping to find a
show that would somehow divert my thoughts from all my impending bills
with no steady source of income to pay them. After flipping up and down
through at least a hundred channels of nothingness, I shut off the TV and
hurled the remote onto my coffee table. I headed to the fridge to grab another beer when the phone rang, providing a brief detour.

Noticing the caller ID, I answered glumly, "What's up Johnny?"

"Just calling to see how you're doing."

"My head is spinning. I just got fired."

"No way! What happened?"

"I'm not even sure. I just talked to Harry about thirty minutes ago." I let out a huge breath and tried to keep my anger from rising again.

"Man, you're having a string of bad luck. I was actually going to see if you felt up to going down to Las Playas for some tacos. I told Todd and Jenny I would come by there and show them my photos of Indo, but it doesn't sound like you are up to it."

"Nah, definitely not."

"Okay, hopefully we can catch up later in the week."

"Yeah, I'll talk to you later," I said, wanting to get off the phone.

"Okay, Zach. Take care, man."

We hung up and I grabbed two more beers. Setting the bottles on the coffee table before me, I stared at them for a few minutes until finally popping one open. For the first time in my career, I contemplated whether I even wanted to stay in the journalism game. Back in school, I held lofty dreams of changing the world with the mighty pen. But ten years later, I now felt like a weary traveler in the hot desert heat, wondering if those aspirations of my youth were merely a mirage.

CHAPTER 4

The hammering noise did not belong in this place. Sitting on my surfboard out at sea, I looked back toward the empty tropical island trying to figure out the source of this racket that made absolutely no sense among the gently swaying cocoa palms and crashing surf. Fortunately, the maddening sound stopped right when I started paddling for a giant swell on the horizon. As I spun around and jumped to my feet, the banging noise returned, distracting me and causing me to fall all the way from the top of the crest. The ensuing slam caused me to twitch forcibly, waking me up against my will. With my perfect dream of a tropical paradise vanquished, I gazed at my bedroom ceiling, realizing the noise was someone knocking on my door.

Wishing I could have at least finished out the dream and surfed that last wave, I slowly stumbled to my feet, wiping the slobber off the side of my mouth and made my way down the hallway. When I finally opened the door, I instantly threw up a hand in front of my face as the sunlight knocked me back a step. While I couldn't see his face, the outline of his posture told me that it was Johnny.

"Hey, what's up?" I nodded, withdrawing from the brightness and moving over to the couch where I collapsed down into the cushions.

A quick glance at my unshaven face and the numerous beer bottles littered all over the coffee table was all Johnny needed to see that I hadn't been out in days.

"Wow, Zach. You look rough," Johnny said solemnly as he rubbed the back of his head.

"Yeah, I know," I said, letting out a yawn.

The intense Indonesian sun had bronzed Johnny's skin and had turned his sandy blonde hair almost platinum white. Knowing he felt awkward about what to say next, I asked him if he had brought over the photos.

"Yeah, yeah," he said hurriedly, reaching into his jacket pocket and handing me two packets of freshly developed pictures.

"These are pretty good shots, Johnny. Were the waves this big the whole time you were there?"

"The whole time. The best thing after surfing all day was coming in and getting a massage for five bucks. Zach, you gotta get down there."

"Yeah, I need to add that to my bucket list. But I'm not going anywhere unless I come up with some cash flow soon," I said, scratching the stubble on my chin.

"You should go just down to Mexico for a weekend or something. We could go camping, do some fishing. You need to get away. I mean, I've never seen you like this."

"It's a trip. Just the other day I was thinking about you, how after you beat cancer your whole view on life really changed; how you said you were not going to take things for granted anymore. And you did. You started taking advantage of all the opportunities life has to offer. I know that's how

I should be living, too, that I should be trying to seize the day and all that. But honestly I can't help…" I let out a breath and stared up at the ceiling, trying to think of the right words.

"I feel this immense burden because Bob ended up dying to protect me. I feel like I need to be doing something big, something significant, but right now I just can't motivate myself to do anything."

"Zach, you're just in a rut. You'll get out of it. You've made a real impact with your writing."

"I don't know if you can say I've made an impact. All I do is write about what I see. Everything I write about is meaningless."

"Meaningless? If you wouldn't have done the research and written that story about alternative ways to treat cancer in Mexico, I would have probably ended up taking chemotherapy cocktails and getting even sicker. The treatment I got in Tijuana changed my life."

Johnny stood up. "Alright, get dressed. We're going to the beach. Somewhere. We need to get you out of this house already."

"Okay, you're right, you're right," I said, pushing myself slowly off the couch.

On the way over to Ollie's' Bar & Grille in Ocean Beach, Johnny revealed that he had almost been killed in Indonesia.

"So I'm flying around Kuta on a motorcycle, which they call ducks for some reason, hoping I can arrange for a ferry over to G-land. This Australian guy tells me to go outside the city a few miles and I can get hooked up with the best deal. It's getting dark, but I'm just cruising along when a huge truck veers into my lane. I yank to the left, go flying through this ditch and end up skidding to a stop at the edge of this huge cliff. I get off my bike and I'm just freaking out. I look over the cliff and it's straight down. At least 500 feet."

"Yikes."

"And that was just day one. Things only got crazier," he said as we pulled into the parking lot.

Even though Ollie's had a solid crowd for lunch, our waitress brought our fish tacos faster than expected. The seasoned yellowtail tuna on our plates caused Johnny to share another story.

"They have some huge tuna over there. One day, me and this local kid are out spear fishing off a reef. I nabbed this good sized red snapper and was about to put it in my bag, when out of nowhere, this six foot bull shark is about ten feet to my left, heading right for me."

"What did you do?"

"I did what any brave fisherman would do. I shoved the fish away from me and ducked. And bam! Like a lightning bolt, that shark just engulfed my snapper. I darted away, swam to the top like I was Aqua Man and went right in. The kid I was with, probably twelve years old tops, comes strolling in like ten minutes later with like a thirty pound mahi-mahi, thing was like half his weight. When I asked him if he saw what happened to me, he just laughed all nonchalantly and said, 'Oh, yes.'."

While it was obvious Johnny enjoyed sharing his travels, I would catch his eyes drifting off as if he was already planning his next route of escape. I'm sure his adventures helped him avoid the thoughts of coming out of remission and ultimately, confronting his own mortality.

We ended up walking through the annual street fair and over to the old pier before heading back to my neighborhood. While getting out of the house provided a much-needed distraction, sitting on my couch later that night in the dark caused me to quickly become despondent again. With the half empty beer cupped in my hand growing warmer by the minute, I slid it across the coffee table and trudged off to bed early.

When I woke up the next day, I knew immediately I needed to do something productive and try to get out of this negative mindset. Having procrastinated long enough, I wanted to get my old motorcycle working again so I could get rid of my rental car. Simply changing the spark plugs and oil seemed to do the trick, and my bike fired up on the first kick-start. Hurrying inside, I grabbed my helmet, but the phone rang and delayed my test run.

"Hey, Vanessa, what's up?"

"Just crazy busy here at the precinct, as usual. I'm working on that case about the missing teenage girl from La Mesa."

"Oh yeah, I heard about that. I actually saw your old Lieutenant on the news talking about it. Does it look pretty bleak for her?"

"It's kinda hard to say right now. Anyway, I just wanted to call real quick to see how you were feeling."

"Still pretty sore, but I'm not wearing the sling anymore. And I am officially unemployed."

"What in the world happened?" she said, surprised.

"Harry's a weasel. He tried to tell me that it was "Human Resource's" decision to suspend me, which of course usually leads to firing, so I just basically told him I quit."

"So what are you going to do now?"

"I'm not sure. Obviously in this economy it's not going to be easy to find a full-time gig that's the right fit for me. There may be some freelance opportunities with the *New York Times* that I might explore. I've been trying to figure out who I might want to work for, but..." I let out a deep breath. "Boy, it's weird. I haven't even felt like writing since I got back from Africa. Just feel burned out right now so I might just take a break."

"You should, Zach; you've been through a lot lately."

"I'm looking to get away with Johnny soon, maybe down to Baja. But I'm kinda torn because I also think I should hurry up and try to get back in the swing of things. I don't know. I just need to find something that will get me inspired to write again."

"You will. It just may take some time. Look...I wanted to ask if you might want to go to church this Sunday with me." Before I could answer she tried to back pedal. "Just try it out, see what you can get out of it..."

"Vanessa, I have no interest in going to some church."

"Well, actually it's not about going to some building. It's about trying to cultivate a relationship with God."

"Okay, whatever. Let me lay it out for you. When you got into this whole religious thing, I thought it was good for you since you and Ted just broke up. And if that's what works for you, that's great. But stop trying to convince me that Jesus is the only way."

"I'm not the one who said Jesus is the only way; He did. The problem is that you don't think that there is such a thing as absolute truth."

"You keep talking to me about absolute truth, but you are talking to someone who has been around the world. I've seen plenty of people who don't know Jesus from their elbow, and they're completely happy. Whether it is Krishna, Allah, whatever, if it makes you happy, if it gets you into your little nirvana, then Buddha bless you."

"All those religions you just spoke about are mutually exclusive by the very things they proclaim, so how can they all be the same? The Bible is the only book that you can actually prove is God's word..."

"God's word?" I said, shaking my helmet before slamming it onto my tile countertop.

"How can you sit there and make such a ludicrous statement? The most misinterpreted piece of literature on the face of the planet is more like it. Why don't we start with religion at its finest and talk about the Lord's Resistance Army? How they use 'God's word' to enslave children into their army and turn them into killing machines? And by the way, where is your God when all this is happening, just sitting on a cloud playing a harp?"

"Well, I don't pretend to know why God allows certain things..."

"Nice cop out," I interrupted. "Seriously, you need to really think about the things you believe in. It not only goes against science, but it's grossly bigoted."

"Look, Zach, I didn't call to make you upset," she said, trying now to be careful about her word choice.

"Then stop your preaching! I've heard you spout this 'Jesus saves!' bit for two years now, and I don't want to hear it anymore," I said, pacing the kitchen floor.

"Okay, but you know it's because I care about you and…"

"Look, my bike has been running this whole time out in the garage. I need to go."

"Alright then," she said, uneasily.

After an awkward pause, my lips rumbled as I let out a deep breath and said, "Look, I'll call you later."

"Okay, bye."

Returning outside to the garage, I slapped the electric door opener and snatched up my sunglasses lying on a makeshift workbench. The engine sounded good as I revved up the throttle several times while the garage door opened slowly. Even though I just remembered that my helmet still sat in the kitchen, the exhaust smoke caused me to gag so I sped out of the driveway without it.

As I made my way over to a nearby canyon, I gunned it through some S turns and quickly realized how much I missed the power of my bike. With the sun shining down on my face, the cool wind that whipped across my body seemed to breathe life back into me and I began to feel free. For the first time in almost a month, I found myself truly smiling.

SOMETHING AS SIMPLE AS FIXING my motorcycle and the resulting ride had somehow left me feeling refreshed and rejuvenated. Even though I wasn't sure what I would be doing next in my life, this afternoon had been a start in the right direction.

After parking the bike in the garage, I walked back into the kitchen just in time to receive the most peculiar phone call of my life.

"Zach Miller?" an unfamiliar voice asked.

"Yes?"

"You don't know me. My name is Andre and I've been told to contact you about a piece of work that comes along once in a lifetime. You've been chosen not only for your journalistic integrity, but because of your open-mindedness when approaching a subject matter."

"I'm sorry, who did you say you're representing?" I said, somewhat baffled, but flattered.

"Before I can divulge that information, I will need to ask you a few questions," Andre said, matter-of-factly.

"Well, *Mister...*" I emphasized, trying to elicit a last name.

"Andre," he said, flatly.

"Your name is Andre Andre?" I tried sounding fascinated that he actually had the same first and last name. My sarcasm had no effect on Andre as he continued talking in the same dry tone.

"For now, I can only tell you Andre. It is not me who you will want to meet with, but rather they that have sent me. There will be a meeting of tremendous historical significance, and you will be given a message that will change the way we look at life itself. This story will easily be sold to every media outlet in the world. But please allow me to ask you a couple of questions."

"Okay. Go ahead," I agreed, and began to think of who could be playing a prank on me.

"Would you be available starting next week to spend possibly as long as a month at a secluded ranch to record the events?"

"I could, possibly."

"And could you also agree not to contact anyone outside the ranch until all of the research is completed?"

"No contact with anyone?" I said, looking over at my laptop.

"There will be several people staying at the facility throughout the next couple of weeks who you will be interviewing, but during your stay we would need you to agree to be cut-off from communicating with the outside world."

"Yeah, I guess, unless there was some emergency?"

"Of course, if you had an emergency medical condition, we would certainly help you get to a hospital. What I'm implying is that you would be cut-off from hearing from any friends and family, so you would be unaware if you needed to return due to a crisis concerning one of them."

I paused for a moment to think. "Well, sure. No one is sick and dying right now, so I guess that wouldn't be a problem."

"Have you ever been, or are you currently, involved with any political parties or movements?

"Never have, never will."

"Are you affiliated with any religious organizations?"

"No. I agree with Marx that religion is the opiate of the masses," I added.

"Alright, Mr. Miller, I appreciate your time and we will contact you in the next couple of days."

"Okay, Andre. So what's the deal? You can't tell me anything else?"

"I can only tell you that if you choose to be the one who brings this story to the world, you'll not only bring honor to yourself, but will receive blessings beyond your wildest imaginations. Have a great day, Mr. Miller."

I assumed he hung up when I heard a click, but kept the phone next to my ear.

"Well then. This is turning into the weirdest week of my life," I said out loud. "And now that I'm talking to myself it must mean I should check myself into the Hotel California and throw away the key. Better yet…" I called Johnny.

"Hey, where you at?

"I'm going through the drive-thru to pick up a burrito."

"I just got the craziest phone call."

"From who?"

"I'm not even sure."

"What do you mean?" The drive thru speaker blared loudly in the background, interrupting us so I waited for Johnny to finish his order before continuing.

"Hey, why don't we just meet at the pub and I'll tell you the rest?"

"I thought you were going to stay away from there after what happened," Johnny said, sounding his concern.

"Well, I'm having a change of heart."

"Yeah, well, I wouldn't mind having a few beers, but I don't want stay too long."

"Wow. What's gotten into you all the sudden?"

"Look, it's okay for me because I'm a professional drinker and I have to look after my enormous stock investments in Anheuser Busch. But you, Zach, have a great talent and I don't want to see you throw it away."

"Did I mention that I'm buying?"

"I'll be there in ten minutes," Johnny said, and hung up.

CHAPTER 5

"Do you know what the best tasting beer in the world is?" Johnny asked.

"I have a feeling I'm about to be enlightened," I answered, tossing a ten-dollar bill to the bartender.

"Free." Johnny said, taking a huge drag from his frosted glass.

I hid my grin behind my beer, adding, "It's utterly amazing you haven't written a book to record all these words of wisdom."

"Oh, you know that's coming," Johnny laughed and our mugs clanged in a toast.

Sitting bar side next to some empty stools, we had come in right after the Tuesday night happy hour crowd got their fill of beef taquitos, nachos supreme and two dollar beers. As I relayed to Johnny the details of the bizarre phone call I had received earlier, Murphy's had become completely vacant, except for a few college kids who were playing darts in the opposite corner.

"So, Zach, who do you think is offering this assignment?"

"Not a clue. I was imagining it could be some biotech company that wants to announce a great discovery. I just don't know why they would want me instead of someone from their PR firm."

"Maybe so people will see it's unbiased if it's coming from you."

"Yeah, that could be it. It's really kind of weird when there is this big shroud of secrecy."

"Well, that could make it all the more exciting."

"I obviously have the time to do it now," I said, letting out a burp. "It could be good for me to have an assignment where I can go into it not knowing anything, you know? Just to give me a fresh set of eyes. I feel I've done some of my best work when I've had basically no real knowledge of a subject."

"Hmm…" Johnny said as he took another sip off his beer. "That's weird. It seems like it should be just the opposite."

"Sometimes, when I'm forced to write about something I don't have much background in, it can end up producing a work that's not so mechanical, not so textbook," I tried to explain. "Anyway, I hope I can get some more information to help me decide whether I want to do it or not. Do you want to shoot some pool?"

"Can you afford to lose any more money from me, is the question you should ask."

"Look, tough guy. Just try not to leave any skids on the table and try to keep the cue ball from hitting any patrons this time," I jabbed.

THE SHRILLING BLAST OF THE doorbell pierced my skull, and I reached over the side of the bed with my eyes half-closed to search the floor for my pants. Leaning downward caused me to immediately roll onto my back and grab my throbbing head.

Why is drinking with Johnny so rarely a painless experience? Oh man, it's already eleven-thirty, I thought as I glanced at the bright red numbers on my alarm clock.

Ding-Dong.

I was now certain I had pinpointed the most annoying sound in the universe.

Who in the world is ringing my doorbell? None of my friends ever ring the bell.

Looking out my bedroom window, I saw two men standing by the front door. When the doorbell echoed again, I envisioned cursing those two Jehovah Witnesses out and asking them if they were ready to meet Jehovah today. I then noticed that neither of them toted the ubiquitous literature, which gave me hope that these two weren't here to proselytize me after all. After clambering down the hallway, I opened the door cautiously with the chain lock still attached and peered out through the small gap.

"Yeah?" I said through narrowed eyes.

"Zach Miller?" A short, stocky Filipino man asked.

"That's me," I said, recognizing the voice but not the face.

"I'm Andre. I spoke to you on the phone yesterday."

"I thought you were going to call me back."

"Well, due to the urgency of our upcoming meeting, one of my employers wanted to come over so you can meet him personally, and he can give you some more details of our proposal. He's sitting in that car, but if this isn't a good time, you're certainly not obligated to meet with him."

Normally, I would have told these guys to hit the road; having strangers just show up at my door has yet to prove rewarding. But now curiosity replaced my irritation, so I told them to give me a couple of minutes. Hurrying to my bathroom, I stuck my head under the sink faucet to wash down some aspirin and then I splashed my face.

Back at my front door, I found a man who could have passed for a Santa Claus stunt double. Instead of his usual red attire, St. Nick sported a Hawaiian print shirt and khaki slacks.

"Zach Miller, it is an honor to meet you. My name is John Norstrent," he said in a deep, but gentle tone.

"Oh, hi, it's nice to meet you," I tried to say politely, but wandered if he could sense my hesitancy.

"Can we sit down and talk? I have a very exciting proposition for you."

In my sleepy haze I stared at his long, white beard that hung at least a foot below his chin and gave him the aura of a wise, old sage. My attempts to grow a beard had always resulted in patchy scruff, so naturally I coveted this real deal man-beard.

"Ah, yeah, sure, just let me get these papers off my couch and we can sit in here," I said, glad I had at least taken time yesterday to clear all the evidence of my recent binge drinking.

After sitting down on the couch, Norstrent leaned forward and looked directly at me. "I'm assuming, Mr. Miller, because you noted that taking on this freelance project was indeed a possibility, that you are still available."

"Free at the moment."

"Well, as Andre alluded to in his phone call, we can only reveal so much information to you as to not compromise our position. You would be staying at the personal residence of one of my dearest friends where you'll meet with several people who will bring you their stories. You will be sworn to secrecy during this month, until the story's published, so the entire public is made aware of it at the same time. If you decide to pursue it, I have no doubts whatsoever that you will find it one of the most remarkable events in the history of the planet."

John paused, looked over and smiled at Andre before looking back at me. "I'm a retired Navy pilot and was more than skeptical when I heard some of these things from an old friend. But now I've seen them with my own eyes and in total soundness of mind can say that I'm one hundred percent convinced. The people I want to introduce you to bring a message of truly tangible hope for all of mankind. These individuals will show you that they don't merely have some philosophical idea about bringing peace and unity to our planet, but have the means, the real vehicles to bring it to fruition. To bring this story to the world will undoubtedly prove to be the highlight of your already illustrious career. Not only financially, but this journey will do wonders for your soul."

"Well, I'm sorry… What's your name again?" I said, really wanting to know.

"John Norstrent. Please call me Jack," he said, smiling.

"Jack, you definitely make it, whatever this is all about, sound very interesting. When would I have to give you a definite answer?"

"We would like to know by Friday; the sooner the better. You are our first choice to write this. We think your reputation gives the credibility we're looking for and the public really desires."

"Okay, let me think about it for the next couple of days and I'll give you a call."

"Actually, Zach, we'll call you on Friday around noon, if that's okay with you."

"Sure, that's fine." I got up as Jack was rising.

"Until we meet again," Jack said with an outreached hand and the same warm grin with which he had greeted me. Giving me a firm hand-shake, I noticed a huge gold ring on his finger with a strange, but beautiful gemstone set in the middle.

"Wow, that's quite a unique ring there, Jack. I've never seen anything like it."

He held it up so I could take a closer look. "Thanks. It's my flight school graduation ring. I replaced the original stone with this one. It's called rainbow titanium quartz. They do something with the titanium that causes the crystal to make all the colors look metallic."

"I've never even heard of one."

"I hadn't either. My friend makes them and said it had healing properties and would cure my insomnia."

"Did it?"

"I haven't had a bad night of sleep in years," he said.

"That's interesting," I said, thinking placebo effect.

"It's just one of those things that show us how little we truly know. Well, we got to get on the road." Jack turned to leave.

"Hey, uh, whatever happens, thanks for the offer."

Jack just smiled, nodding as he headed out the door.

Later that same night, I started looking over some of the concepts for freelance stories I had been interested in writing over the past couple of years, but never had the time to work on. While confident that these stories would draw interest from some publications that had responded to my emails, I simply didn't feel motivated to write any of them at the moment. Even though I felt I was emerging from the dark cloud that had enveloped me since Africa, I instinctively knew I still didn't possess enough passion to pursue any of these potential stories and my half-hearted efforts would produce something less than prolific.

Reclining back in my chair and contemplating the things Jack had said earlier that morning, I became even more intrigued about his proposal. While I had to admit the secrecy played a role in my interest, his claims that this story would have an incredible effect on people everywhere had really captivated my imagination. I definitely didn't want to end up reading "The Story" that made headlines everywhere, knowing I had declined the opportunity.

AFTER ANSWERING HIS PHONE, JOHNNY told me to wait for a second, and I heard a ball rolling down a wooden lane before crashing into some helpless bowling pins.

"That's right. That's how we do it," Johnny bragged after apparently throwing a strike.

Before I could even inform him on why I called, he began to offer his usual insightful commentary.

"I've been thinking a lot about that mystery assignment that guy offered you. It has to be about a group of physicists who have finally figured out the exact number for Pi. With this new number, all kinds of secrets of the universe will be unlocked. And with this new knowledge, someone will finally invent the zero calorie beer."

"Wow. You've had several days to come up with something funny and that's all you got? Needless to say, I'm pretty disappointed," I deadpanned.

"Yeah, I know you expect more from me. I'm sorry to let you down." Johnny did his best to sound remorseful.

"It's okay. I'm more than used to it by now. Look, I called to let you that I'm going to go ahead and do the story. They're actually going to pick me up this Monday."

"Geez, that's pretty quick. Have you really taken the time to think about it? I don't know if I'd be taking a job with all these unknowns. I mean, weren't you just complaining the other night about all your bills starting to stack up?"

"Since when have you gone all conservative?"

"Just trying to give you the sound advice of a good friend."

"You know, 'friend' is such a strong word..."

Johnny wheezed out a laugh. "That's cute. I'll have to remember that one."

"Seriously though, I'm going to need you to keep an eye on my place, take care of the mail, the usual."

"For a small fee, right?"

"Let's just say that I have a feeling when I get back I might be able to even take care of your bar tab down at Murphy's."

"You must think you're gonna win a Pulitzer because I plan to spend some real quality time over there with that kinda payment plan."

I laughed to myself as I thought about how large my bill could end up being with this kind of arrangement with Johnny. "Look, I gotta try to get things squared away so I can be ready to leave."

"Johnny, you're up." Todd's voice echoed in the background.

"Yeah, I gotta get back to putting the beat down on Todd and Chris. The beer-gods have been smiling on me over here and lavishing some free rounds."

"Cool. Thanks a lot, Johnny."

"No problem, my man. I'll talk to you when you get back."

CHAPTER 6

Just as I brought my laptop outside and gently set it on the rest of my gear on the sidewalk, a customized van pulled into my driveway. As the driver slowly waddled out of the van, I was taken aback at his enormous size. Despite lacking a neck, he still stood close to seven feet tall and I wondered if my hands would even touch if I reached around to bear hug him. When he asked me if I needed help with my bags, I almost laughed out loud; the deep, husky voice I expected to come out of this behemoth of a man instead squeaked in a high pitch like that of a young teenage boy.

Handing him my duffel bag, I grabbed my camera bag and laptop, and we walked to the back of the van to load up. From the opposite side I heard the sliding door open and a short, wiry Asian man came walking around to the back with a cell phone pressed against his ear.

"Yes, he's loading up his bags right now," he said before hanging up and reaching out his hand to me. "Zach Miller, nice to meet you. I'm Peter. I'll be one of your hosts during your stay. Jump in the back with me; we have some refreshments back here if you want."

Before ducking into the side of the van, I noticed that the back seats had been removed and the only place to sit was on a futon spread out on the floor.

"Mr. Miller, we request that you wear this to protect our location," Peter said as he handed me a shiny, blue blindfold.

"Well, Peter, that makes me a tad nervous," I said, stepping back outside.

"I understand. But these are my instructions."

"I thought you guys said it would take six to seven hours to get there. Why do I need to wear it the whole time?"

"Look, I'm just trying to do my job. Believe me, you'll come to see why we need such secrecy once you arrive," he said, handing me the blindfold.

"Okay," I said apprehensively and climbed back inside. Sitting on the futon, I stared at the smooth material of the blindfold as I rubbed it in my hand. It looked like the ones I had seen on airplanes and I could only guess as to where someone even buys such a device.

Pulling the elastic band over my head, my world went black as I slowly slid the blindfold over my eyes. My mind began sprinting as I speculated the very real possibility that I had just stepped into some elaborate trap.

I tried to ease my concerns by breaking down the situation; it didn't seem logical that these people would be interested in kidnapping me since I wasn't from a wealthy family. It also didn't make sense that they would wait for me to agree to get into their van if they were going to abduct me. My little background search on John Norstrent had uncovered a decorated Korean War pilot who currently owned recycling plants in San Diego and Phoenix.

Convincing myself that I didn't face any imminent danger, I began to

relax and enjoy the jazz music that played softly on the radio, even though
I had no idea where I was headed and what I would find once we got there.

"Hey, this place got a pool?' I asked casually.

"Oh yeah. Jacuzzi, tennis courts; It's a nice spread," Peter said, his voice
turning more distinct as he turned towards me. "But you'll probably be
so engaged in the coming week's activities that you'll find little time or
interest in any of that. You could actually go horseback riding because the
owner has a whole stable full of horses."

"So, there is some sort of head honcho I'm going to meet."

Peter's chuckle echoed off the windshield told me he had resumed his
gaze on the road ahead. "Sort of, yeah. There is, how should I put it, 'an
organizer of events' and he's the one you'll be probably spending the most
time with. There will be several extremely interesting people there for you
to interact with and they'll give you plenty of material for your story."

"Yeah, I'm just anxious, you know, to see what this whole mystery is
all about."

"I'm sure you are. Trust me when I say it will be well worth the wait,"
he said confidently, and I could hear him texting someone on his phone.

Trying to peek out from under the blindfold to figure out which way
we headed, I discovered that the tinted side windows made it virtually
impossible to see anything. At first I had a feeling we had been traveling
north, but soon lost my sense of direction once my body began swaying
back and forth due to the curves in the road. The gentle and constant hum
of the tires eventually lulled me to sleep, and when I awoke I had no idea
how much time had elapsed.

Coughing to clear my throat, I asked Peter, "Hey, what time is it?

"It's just after eight. We'll be there pretty soon."

Now continuously ascending upward, the popping inside my ears made
it obvious that we had arrived in a mountain range. Without warning, we
swung to the side as the van cut a sharp ninety-degree turn, gravel now
ricocheting loudly off the bottom as we sped down a side road. Twenty

50

minutes later, we stopped abruptly and the giant driver began speaking to someone outside, informing him that he had the writer in the back. After receiving clearance, we continued driving for another fifteen minutes or so before Peter grabbed my shoulder. Removing the blindfold, he said, "We're here."

As my eyes adjusted, I saw a large ranch-style house where smoke billowed out of a stone chimney. The front screen door screeched as a small woman wearing a brightly colored apron came out onto the wooden porch and waved at us. Immediately I wondered how anything "monumental" like Jack had promised could take place at such a quiet, quaint looking residence, and if this wouldn't end up being a colossal waste of time.

Lumbering out of the vehicle and stopping momentarily to stretch, I inhaled a deep breath of the clean country air and gazed straight up into the black sky. Without any city lights to obscure the view, the stars sparkled like fine diamonds in a jewelers showcase. A cool breeze blew gently across my back, removing the last bit of tension from my body.

We walked over to the house where Peter introduced me to Gloria Hunter, the owner of the ranch. He quickly excused himself, noting that he and the driver would be retiring to a large guest house in the back.

Graciously welcoming me into her house, Gloria explained that her husband would return soon from the store. A mix of Mexican and Native American décor throughout her house made it even more comfortable on the inside than it had looked from the driveway. Leading me back down a hallway, she showed me to the small bedroom where I would be staying and I dropped off my bags on an antique wooden desk in the corner.

The aroma of chili peppers roasting on the stove filled the entire house and I gladly accepted Gloria's invitation to join her at the dinner table for the enchiladas she had prepared earlier. While I guessed that my hostess had to be in her late fifties, Gloria raced around the kitchen with the energy of someone half her age. Her sweet voice and kind demeanor made it impossible to imagine anyone not liking her.

As I finished up the delicious homemade meal, she explained how she had recently retired from nursing when I noticed her beautiful necklace.

"Hey, is that a rainbow quartz at the end of your chain?"

"Yes. It's actually called titanium rainbow quartz. How did you know that?"

"I saw the same stone on Jack's ring."

"I made that for him. He didn't believe me when I told him about the power in that quartz, but now he sleeps like a baby." She smiled.

"What kind of power?" I said, trying not to show my skepticism.

"All kinds: healing energy, promoting healthy thoughts, helping us get in touch with our spiritual side. I have friends who claim it helps them with creativity. You should try it."

While not convinced, I still inquired, "How do you make them?" but a phone call interrupted our conversation. When I heard her start speaking in Spanish and sensed that the conversation was personal, I decided to head to my room and give her some privacy. I tried to stay occupied by reading until Mr. Hunter returned home, but lying on the warm bed caused me to become too comfortable and I crashed out.

A shrieking rooster jolted me out of my deep slumber and I instantly experienced that odd feeling when you awake in a strange bed. When the bird rudely rang in yet another unwanted wake-up call, this city boy started to wonder if I could handle the country noise. The sun had just started to rise and as I pushed the curtains aside, I saw the enormous black tailed gamecock strutting arrogantly right outside my room. Blaring car alarms and bumping stereos I could deal with, but this constant cockle-doo-doo was driving me crazy.

The smell of *huevos rancheros* wafting under my door soon replaced my agitation with a healthy anticipation of Senora Hunter's cooking. Ambling down the hall light footed, not knowing who I might encounter, I only found Gloria leaning over into the back of the fridge.

Trying not to scare her, I softly said, *"Buenos dias."*

"Oh, *buenos dias*," she replied, smiling and adding, "Please sit down and have some breakfast."

A selection of fruit as well as a large plate mixed with black beans, eggs and homemade *salsa fresca* sat at the end of long wooden table.

"Sure. Thanks." Pulling out a chair and sitting down, I felt someone's presence behind me.

I turned just as a large man entered the room wearing a cowboy hat with an eagle's feather nestled in its side. Towering over me with broad shoulders, Bill stood at least six and half feet tall. His tanned leather skin, flattened nose and two long strands of black and gray braided hair hinted at his ancient heritage.

I stood up as he extended his enormous hand and said, "Hi, Zach. Bill Hunter. Sorry I couldn't be here to greet you last night. I had some unexpected business come up."

"Hey, uh, that's okay," I stammered at his thundering voice, but managed to smile back. "Gloria treated me to some incredible enchiladas."

"Well, we do make a point to eat good around here. Sleep well?" Bill asked, grabbing a plate off the table.

"Yeah, great." I said, wondering why he looked familiar.

"Let's eat and then I'll show you around my ranch."

Nodding back, I strained to recall where I might have seen him before. Several years ago, I had done a story on an Indian Reservation gaming scandal that involved several tribe members and Bill resembled one of the elders. His name didn't ring a bell, however, and I couldn't imagine him inviting me to the ranch if he had been involved, since the story was less than favorable to the tribe. With my memory still fuzzy during breakfast, I knew it would probably stay so unless I consciously stopped thinking about it when we headed outside.

A forest of pines blanketed the rolling hills and surrounded the property with a dark mint green, while majestic snow-capped peaks lined the horizon. Concluding that we stood west of the Sierras, I knew pinpointing exactly where we were would prove difficult since the famous mountain range ran almost the entire length of the state of California.

During the tour of his estate, I observed several men walking horses, repairing a fence, and working on farm machinery. A twenty foot tall pole barn, approximately fifty by seventy feet wide, looked newly assembled, and stood next to a smaller, dilapidated wooden shed that leaned slightly to the side.

My chauffeur from the previous night waved at me from the nearby guest house as he and Peter brought in supplies. After he kept the conversation mainly about the workings of his ranch, Bill finally began to explain why I had been selected to write this story.

"Zach, do you believe that we only use ten percent of our brains?" he asked, removing his cowboy hat to dust it off.

"Well, that's what they say."

"It actually makes sense when you think about all the things we don't understand. But look at the things we've accomplished with using only using ten percent," Bill said, smiling before putting his hat back on.

"I never really thought about it from that angle."

"For some reason, the things I'm going to tell you are hard for our so-called intellect to comprehend. The great thing is that at the end of your stay, you won't have to just take my word for it. You'll actually witness it for yourself. That's why we wanted you to come out here, to see experience everything firsthand. My ancestors have lived in this region for thousands of years and this knowledge has been in our tribe forever. It's only in these dire times that we've had the vision to share this great knowledge. Our Mother Earth is hurting and there must be a healing of our planet; if not, She and everyone who lives on the earth will perish. Zach, do you recognize the dark days that face this planet?"

"I would say that things don't look too positive in a lot of places."

"With the environment suffering as it is now, and the population explosion we are about to encounter, there is a consensus among scientists that this planet will not survive another fifty years."

"Yeah, I've heard that."

"And with man using only ten percent of that brain, I'd say we could use some help," he chuckled.

Bill crouched down, picking up a handful of dirt before slowly letting it slide out through his fingers. "Zach, where do you think we all came from?"

"Well, considering the fossil and DNA records, it seems logical that we evolved most recently from a species related to apes."

"Have you thought about why apes never evolved?" he paused when he saw that his rhetoric caused my eyebrow to arch. "You may have a hard time digesting this, but I'm going to tell you where we actually came from. And I'm sure you're skeptical. So was I at first, but this will make more sense once you hear and see everything during your stay."

Bill paused again before standing up and looking me right in the eyes. "Thousands of years ago, extraterrestrials brought us here after they had cultivated this planet for us. My tribe believes we are all descendants of the 'Keepers of the Sky' and that these aliens are in reality our brothers. But this isn't just some tribal lore, Zach; I have personal contact with them."

My eyes automatically narrowed after hearing such an outrageous claim from a seemingly normal guy, and I began scanning the ground for a response.

"I guess what you're saying is all very possible. I pride myself in being able to articulate my thoughts, but, uh, whew," I said, letting out a puff of air. "I mean, I actually saw something a couple of months ago in Africa I can't explain."

Bill smiled back and nodded. "I know you did. In Uganda, right?"

"How did you know that?" My eyes widened.

"The Ancestors were revealing themselves to you, preparing you for this very time. How else do you think we picked you to write this story?"

"I don't know. Everything you just said is really kinda blowing my mind."

"Well, Zach, here's my suggestion to you right now: Don't even worry about what to say or even think. Just take in what you experience the next couple of weeks and then I reckon you'll have plenty to say. And write," he said, and we continued walking along a barb-wired fence.

"Okay, but I just had a question run through my mind. You say you have contact with these aliens. How so?"

"Well, most of the time, and this may seem extremely odd to you, I speak with them telepathically. This is an art that has been passed on to me from my elders."

"You said most of the time?"

"Well, this is the part that will completely convince you. I have physical contact with them from time to time and you'll be able to observe that for yourself."

"What? You," I stuttered and froze where I stood, "you mean here?"

Bill stopped and turned to me. "That's exactly what I mean."

"When?" I gasped.

"Sometime later this week, I believe. We're waiting for others who've been anticipating this day to arrive from all over the world."

While Bill seemed completely confident in his claim, I continued to wonder if what he just promised would really come to pass.

"Zach," he said calmly. "You are a chosen one. You will bring the world proof of our ancestors' existence and the great message of real hope they have for the future of this planet. You will see they have the perfect plan to restore our Mother Earth."

After a moment of silence, I managed to only babble, "Wow. This is pretty overwhelming to say the least."

"That's why I want you to try to relax and absorb it all over the next week. You'll have most of your questions answered before you leave. *If* you keep an open mind and open heart. I mean, the real questions," he emphasized. "Like why you're here, and what life is all about."

"What is this message of hope you keep talking about?"

"I can see the journalist in you is starting to come out." Bill smiled while rubbing his chin with his hand. "You see, men have never developed a true understanding of each other and that is why we never can stay in a state of peace. Wars have ravaged the people of Earth and have done great harm to our ecological system. We are headed for certain destruction with the technological warfare we have in our hands. Our ancestors see there is an immediate need to intervene. They come to enlighten us and help us see each other as we are. With this great illumination, man can evolve into the creature he was intended to be. Our Ancestors will finally bring about the peace that the majority of us so desperately want."

"How can they just show up and create peace? I mean, this all sounds great theoretically, but it seems like those who still want war will keep provoking it."

"People need to see that there is something bigger than themselves, that there is something 'outside' their own little world. When people everywhere finally see and hear from our Ancestors, their hearts will be changed."

"What in the world took them so long?"

"That's a good question, Zach, one that I asked myself. They wanted us to learn things for ourselves and they have tried to help us along the way. The reason they are coming soon is not out of want, but need; our need, not theirs. As wholly compassionate beings, they desire nothing more than to rescue us from ourselves." Bill said, clasping his hands together.

My forehead wrinkled from something he mentioned. "You said they have helped us along the way; how so?"

"Well, many of the unexplainable things that have happened throughout history, miracles as some are so fond of calling them, are actually the work of our Ancestors. There is technology that has been passed down and unfortunately lost; the Egyptian pyramids are a classic example of that. They've also left us guides for living right, basically golden rules, which you can obviously see throughout the history of every culture around the world. You're about to gain knowledge that sages and philosophers have searched for since time began. One nice thing is, you'll be able to record the upcoming events with photographs and video so there will be little doubt as to the veracity of your story. I have only two requests: you only use my laptop to do your work and you don't email or phone anyone until the end of your stay," he said firmly.

"Agreed," I said, wondering what anyone would even say if I called them with this news.

"Good. Now let's get back to the house as several guests are arriving who you'll definitely want to interview."

CHAPTER 7

Jogging back to the ranch house, I tried to keep up with my racing mind as I contemplated everything Bill had told me. While thrilled about the prospect of actually seeing alien beings for myself, plunging into this unknown realm had me simultaneously petrified.

When Bill and I approached the house, I saw several people already gathered on and around the porch. The diversity of the group made it feel like a mini-United Nations meeting. Within the first few minutes, I met two African gentlemen, one from Eritrea and the other from Kenya, before being introduced to a very petite woman from Laos and an elderly man from South Korea.

Across the front lawn, we briefly talked with a Mexican gentleman, dressed up in a business suit with his tie unloosed, speaking with two European women. Bill shared with us that these were most of the "out of town" guests who would be staying for the week, but that several local people from his native tribe and some other Californians would be coming up during the week.

I eagerly awaited my interviews and returned inside to retrieve a digital voice recorder where I stumbled upon the most intriguing and improbable of all the conversationalists. Hearing the two distinct accents inside the living room, I found an Israeli woman and a Palestinian man sitting on the sofa together, conversing as if they were old family friends.

Once inside my bedroom, I immediately noticed my laptop missing with a replacement sitting on the desk, and I barged into the kitchen to confront Bill.

"I need that laptop. I've got information on there I can't afford to lose," I said in a forceful yet hushed tone so the others wouldn't hear me.

"Relax, Zach, your cell phone and laptop will be returned in due time," he said, keeping his eyes on the coffee maker as he poured water into it. "The laptop you've been given has no internet access and no flash drive. We simply can't afford to have this story leaked prematurely."

"Well, I'm holding you personally responsible if anything is tampered with."

"Trust me. They're secure," he said, grabbing a carafe for some cream.

Still irritated that my valuables had been moved, I stormed back to my room and checked my belongings. Relieved to find my other things untouched, I sat on the bed for a minute to calm down.

I tried to understand Bill's point of view for the need for secrecy and even though I really didn't like others having complete control over my possessions, I had to accept that this was one of the little nuisances of the job. Grabbing my recorder, I headed back outside only to find that everyone had started walking around the ranch in small groups.

I caught up with the middle-aged Mexican gentleman who sported a thick black mustache. Even with a suit on, he looked as fit as a professional middle-weight boxer. I introduced myself using the few Spanish words I knew and to my relief, Pablo answered back in English and began to share his story.

"Well, it start for me years ago, in the mountains of Vera Cruz where I am from," he said. "I was outside my house, videotaping my *sobrinito.*"

"Your little nephew? I interpreted into the recorder.

"Yes, he is playing with my dog and right before the sun set, I saw a huge space ship flying near the volcano. The whole thing I capture on video."

"Have you showed anyone else this film?" I asked.

"Oh yes. All my friends and family. Not only that one. I got more."

"What, more videos?"

"Yes, yes. After the first day, I always carry a camera. And I now have a very big collection of sightings. It is become like, how you say, a hobby? *Mi abuela* thinks I am *loco*," Pablo laughed.

"Your grandmother thinks you're crazy?" I spoke into the recorder.

"Oh yes. A lot of my family think so. Many of them are very Catholic. It is very difficult to let go of their traditions. It is more easy for them to believe that people see the Virgin Mary in a tortilla than believe what I show them on video," he said, smiling.

"Have you shown these to any television stations?"

"No, but they already have plenty of videos. There have been sightings over Mexico City for many, many years."

"Really?" I said, surprised that I had never heard that news.

"Yes. That's one of the reasons I make it my life to try and contact the aliens. Then, all of the sudden, I get a letter from Señor Hunter telling me to come here. It was like an answer to my prayers," he said, seemingly still awestruck by the offer.

"Wait, you never met Bill before you came here?"

"I never know who he is before he write to me. He tell me the Ancestors explain how to contact me. That's how I know I need to come."

"That's amazing."

"I am very excited. I don't know if I can sleep tonight," he said, widening his eyes and gripping his hands tightly.

"Yeah…" I said as my thoughts drifted off and I wondered how exactly Bill might have been told about contacting me.

Strolling around the ranch and conversing with different people from the group, I discovered that many of them had not only seen UFOs, but had also experienced direct contact with aliens, as Bill described to me earlier. These common denominators had helped form an immediate bond between them, which in turn created an environment where they felt comfortable talking openly about these unique encounters with one another.

Later I met up with Emmy, the tiny, soft spoken woman from rural Laos, and learned she had a belief system extremely similar to Bill's tribe. She, too, held the aliens were our ancestors who had been with us since the dawn of time. Emmy said that her dead relatives had actually gone on to be with the "other" ancestors and helped watch over us when we were in danger. She believed that the Ancestors sometimes made themselves visible to remind us of their presence, letting us know that they were here for us. Even though we can't always see them, she emphasized, "It's a great comfort to know that they can hear our prayers." Emmy's beautiful opal shaped eyes lit up as she relayed how much she looked forward to when the Ancestors would usher in a "new day" for mankind and felt it would be soon.

Nobody at the ranch seemed to be able to pronounce the enormously long first name of a very dark skinned gentleman from Kenya, so we all called him Geb for short.

Having grown up at the base of the Aberdare Mountains, Geb told me that he saw alien ships for the very first time when he was left alone in the wilderness for a three day tribal ritual that celebrated the time a boy crossed over into manhood. After landing right next to where he slept, the "Ancestors" invited him to actually come aboard the aircraft. Inside the ship, they informed him that they would contact him from time to time to help him and his fellow tribe members find wisdom. In sharp contrast to Pablo's account of the Mexican culture, Geb's family and his tribe members had actually no problem believing his story and instead regarded Geb himself as a prophet. When I asked how he ended up here at Bill's ranch, he startled me by explaining that the Ancestors showed him how to initiate contact with Bill. Geb's focus changed, his eyes becoming watery as he shared how his tribe had sacrificed a great deal to raise the money so he could fly to the States to be here.

While Geb's story had a tangible feel to it, the middle-aged woman from the coast of Israel told me probably the most bizarre of all the stories I heard that day. Miriam surprised me from the beginning when she claimed that there are more U.F.O. sightings in her native country than in any other place in the world.

From here I somewhat expected to hear a story similar to Geb's or Pablo's, but ironically her account was much different. While never personally seeing an alien aircraft, she claimed to have conversed with alien beings ever since she was a teenager.

"My *safta* Naomi, who was the mother of my father, was very proud of her Jewish heritage. But she did not believe the orthodox rabbinical view of God. She felt there had been a great deviation from the original meaning of ancient scriptures. To her it was much more than semantics," she said in perfect English with a heavy Hebrew accent.

"*Safta* introduced me to a very esoteric form of faith, one that has been around long before Moses. Before Abraham even. When I was a teenager, she taught me that it was possible to travel through space, transcending boundaries of time, without even leaving our couch." She stopped, smiled slyly as if to gauge my reaction.

"Is this how you encountered alien beings?" I asked.

"Yes. My *Safta* and I started having these amazing adventures together. It's very similar to how people describe having "out of body" experiences. We would travel through outer space and come into contact with

extraterrestrials everywhere we went. By escaping this world and communicating with the Ancestors, we were able to attain a higher level of
consciousness. When I knew *Safta* would be at my house, I would get so
excited that I would run home from school, but she told me explicitly not
to tell anyone about these meetings, not even my parents."

"How in the world were you able to keep that a secret from anyone?" I
said, shaking my head.

Miriam smiled. "That's easy when you think they might put you in a
nut house. But even as an adult, I realized that most people would reject
the notion that crossing over into these dimensions is possible. Over the
years, I have only confided in a few people about my experiences, which is
one of the main reasons I'm so excited about our gathering here."

"So you can talk to people who don't think you're a lunatic?"

Miriam let out a laugh and said, "Yes, that's always nice, too. But more
importantly, after people around the world find out about this event, I believe it will give them the faith that such things are possible. It's my desire
to help others discover these great truths for themselves."

As I approached a twenty-two year-old blonde girl sitting alone at a red
picnic table, she looked up from the large book in her hand and invited me
to sit down. Enrolled in an archeology class back at a university in her native Finland, Irene informed me that she was trying to catch up on some of
her reading about recent excavations in Egypt.

"So you want to become the next Indiana Jones?" I asked.

"No, no. I definitely don't want to be an archeologist. I just find it extremely interesting. Especially this book. You wouldn't believe how much
these discoveries have to do with the reason we're all meeting here."

"I'm beginning to believe about anything."

"Would you believe that I'm the only one staying here who has never
seen a U.F.O. or alien beings?"

"Then how did you even end up here?"

"Well, since I was a kid, I just read every book I could get my hands on about the search for alien life. I felt like I was living vicariously through the other people's experiences and developed an intense longing to see these galaxy travelers for myself. Out of the blue, I got an invitation from Bill to come to the ranch and I intuitively knew that it was my destiny to be here. I am quite confident that this event will end up filling a huge void in my life."

$$\oplus \qquad \oplus \qquad \oplus$$

BREAKFAST THE NEXT MORNING PROVIDED a great opportunity for all of us to get to know each other better as we gathered around the long dining table. After becoming completely stuffed, I went outside to walk off my meal when I saw a silver SUV speeding up the gravel driveway. Once it slowed down and stopped bouncing, I immediately noticed the Department of Defense stickers on the windshield. The bearded passenger jumped out, waved at me and smiled. I barely resisted blurting out, "Ho, Ho, Ho" at Jack.

The driver got out and retrieved a briefcase from the back before walking directly toward me. While the stickers in the window offered a clue, his high and tight haircut along with the marine "hell dog" strut confirmed the military affiliation.

"Zach, I want you to meet one of my good friends, retired Colonel Appleton," Jack said.

"Nice to meet you, colonel," I said, trying to hide my extreme discomfort as the colonel crushed my knuckles with his vice grip handshake.

"Likewise, Zach. You can call me J.T," he said in a deep, southern drawl. "You're the writer, correct?"

"That's right," I said, faking a smile, but truly thankful that he had freed my mangled hand. At that point, I could only hope and pray to regain the use of it one day.

"Well, you are gonna have one heckuva story to write when we're through here," he said, grinning widely.

"It's definitely sounding that way already."

When Bill came over to join us, he embraced J.T. with a huge bear hug and it appeared the two were old friends. J.T. then asked Bill, "When are we going to see some fireworks around here?"

Bill hesitated before speaking and held his hands together. "I'm pretty sure tonight."

"That's fantastic!"

J.T then turned to me, pointing his thumb back towards Jack. "You know how many years I've been telling this old fart about alien aircrafts buzzing my planes? He always looked at me as if I had been sucking down martinis in the cockpit. Then, about five years ago, we we're flying together to Vegas in my Cessna when one of my little buddies gives us a flyby. You should have seen ol' Jack. Poor boy almost had a cardiac," J.T. cackled while Jack simply smiled in reply, nodding his head as if slightly embarrassed.

"What does our government know about all this? I mean, I've heard about all this Area 51 conspiracy stuff for years..."

"They don't know squat. I mean, there are people who work for the government who of course know aliens exist and all that. But as far as the government trying to cover up some event in Roswell, well, that just doesn't make a lot of sense to me. These aliens aren't collaborating with our government, if that's what you mean. They know better than to trust those rascals," J.T. laughed. "Heck, they're one of the main reasons The Ancestors are comin'."

$$\oplus \qquad \oplus \qquad \oplus$$

THE FLAMES OF A MASSIVE bonfire warmed us from the cool night air as we all assembled together for a late night barbeque. J.T. continued entertaining us with a myriad of stories when suddenly "the fireworks" started. Three huge cylinders of flashing light came soaring directly over our campfire in a straight line. The abrupt sighting caused everybody around me to begin yelling and clapping enthusiastically, while I sat stunned, unable to even move for a moment in my plastic patio chair.

Bill stood to inform us that we had just observed "a scout party" and we would see a fleet in the next day or two. Even though everyone else showed their elation, I felt my stomach drop before pushing my plate away. Trying to look 'normal,' I hoped the darkness concealed how all the blood had drained out my face.

No MATTER HOW MANY PILLOW configurations I tried, sleep proved elusive as I flipped restlessly from side to side. Several times during the night, my nerves forced me over to the window where I scanned the sky for any space ships that might be watching over us. I don't remember when, but exhaustion took over and I finally passed out. Waking right before sunrise, I felt I had been awake the entire night as I had slept so lightly.

Now sitting up on the edge of the bed, my anxiety level increased as I recalled having a nightmare about alien beings coming into Bill's house and how they were leering over us while we slept. While I wished I hadn't remembered the dream, pondering it only led me to question my decision to come to the ranch. As I tiptoed down the wooden hallway floors, I found the house quiet as no one else was up yet. Deciding to go for a walk and try to clear my head, I opened the front door softly in order not to wake anyone.

Just as the sun began to crest the distant peaks, I found a worn path and headed down through the woods. The same thought that had troubled me the night before kept replaying in my mind: *What was the real agenda of these beings? Did they gather us together so they could whisk us away for their lab experiments?*

This line of thinking rattled me so much I attempted seeing the situation from another perspective: If these aliens *did* mean us harm, they could have already abducted us. Besides, all the people I met at the ranch seemed relatively normal, minus their experiences, and none of them were harmed during any of their previous encounters.

For a second, I even contemplated what my peers would think of me. I also wondered if I would be stuck with some stigma, making it difficult to get other work if I became labeled as "The UFO Guy."

After traveling what must have been a couple of miles, I came to the edge of a tree line where I could look over a small canyon. Stopping to scan the wooded valley below me, I saw in the distance a ribbon of asphalt which I estimated to be around a forty-five minute walk.

As I stared down into the gorge beneath me, my thoughts became absolutely overwhelmed with the unknown dangers I might face later that night. While I hated losing my cell phone and laptop, I decided right then that the rational thing to do was cut my losses and leave while I still could.

Increasing the pace back down the trail, my heart and mind sprinted as I wondered if I would even see any cars on the road ahead so I could hitch a ride. A sudden noise caused my eyes to dart up the steep incline beside the trail.

Now treading slowly and light-footed, I attempted to remain silent when I heard a twig snap. Frozen in my steps, I held my breath and tried to listen over my pounding heart.

Am I being followed or is someone really watching me?

I clenched my fists and began walking downhill again with the resolve that I would not be deterred. About ten minutes later, I finally began to relax a bit when I heard another sound you don't hear in the city.

Cataclop, cataclop.

Stopping for a few seconds, I confirmed the hooves of a horse.

Great! I knew it; I am being followed.

Deciding to push on, I tried to find a place to get off the trail and hide behind some trees. I made it over a small ridge, facing back down the trail, when I was surprised to see a tall black horse with a large man in the saddle coming up the hill towards me. Realizing he could see me, I knew I couldn't hide now so I attempted to play it casual.

"Good morning, Bill!" I said.

"Mornin'. It's a beautiful day, huh?"

"Man, it's gorgeous out here," I replied, but my eyes immediately went to the rifle strapped to the side of the saddle.

Trying to pretend that I hadn't noticed the firearm, I quickly said, "Yeah, we don't exactly have views like this where I'm from."

Bill removed his Stetson straw hat and used his flannel shirtsleeve to wipe his brow before looking down at me.

"You trying to get away, Zach?" he asked point blank.

"Huh?" I stammered, guessing I looked as guilty as I felt.

"You know, get away and think. I try to do it at least once a day."

"Oh yeah. Definitely, I, uh, just..."

Bill cut me off, "I'm sure you are going through some real turmoil inside, not knowing what to think about all this. I mean, it's a lot to digest," he said gently.

"Yeah, it is."

"We've all had those doubts and even experienced some fear initially, Zach. But those tend to vanish. I can guarantee that you'll be glad you came in the end. "

His calm demeanor helped me settle down a tad, making me feel slightly foolish for my paranoia.

"Climb on up and I'll give you a lift? Coming down this trail is a lot easier than having to trudge back up it," he said, patting the back of his horse.

I grabbed Bill's extended arm, put one foot in the empty stirrup and pulled myself up onto his horse.

"I don't recommend walking out here alone, Zach. We do have our share of mountain lions and black bears," Bill added as we started back towards the ranch.

"Bears? That hadn't even crossed my mind. Note to self: Take hike on treadmill next time," I cracked.

We headed up the steep trail and I scanned the thick, unknown woods besides us. While I felt temporarily relieved to be on the safety of Bill's horse, I also recognized that the situation back at the ranch could quickly turn precarious.

CHAPTER 8

The clear blue sky had cleverly dissolved into a pink haze as the sun faded behind the horizon for the night. Soon a small convoy of cars and pickups began pulling into Bill's driveway with members from his local tribe. Even though Bill and Gloria had prepared plenty of food for dinner, complete with a roasted pig that had sat above a fire pit the previous day, everyone who had arrived brought coolers full of more food and drinks.

As the events that would actually unfold that night drew nearer, uncertainty set in. Bill must have noticed my constant pacing and instinctively headed toward me. Reaching into the cooler that lay open near our feet, he offered me a can of Mountain Dew. His enormous hand dwarfed the green soda can as he looked sternly at me. "Our Ancestors told us specifically to only drink Pepsi products."

I stared at Bill silently as I tried to process the strange request.

Unable to keep a straight face, Bill laughed loudly.

I shook my head and chuckled.

Bill had picked a timely place to reveal his wit and his strange little joke helped put me more at ease.

As everyone gathered to sit down and eat, a sleek, extended town car glided up the driveway. Darkly tinted windows matched the deep black paint job, making it virtually impossible to peer into the car. The chauffeur got out, hurrying over to open the back door for a tall, distinguished-looking man in a black suit and tie. Jack, Bill and J.T. got up and walked excitedly over to greet the newest arrival. While I inquired from everyone at the table, no one seemed to know anything about this mystery guest. As they all strolled back over to where we were all seated, Jack waved me over.

Jack said with a beaming smile, "Zach, this is Mr. Boris Wolff, a former ambassador to the U.N."

"Mr. Zach Miller, it's a great privilege to meet you. I have enjoyed your work for years," he said, reaching out to shake my hand. His accent told me Swiss German, but the abundance of hair products and a designer suit cried Los Angeles.

"Pleasure's all mine," I said, flattered that he had read my articles.

"Thank you, Mr. Miller. Our lives are about to be profoundly changed. I can think of no one else that I would rather have than you to record these events. We are certainly expecting great things from you. "

"Well, I hope I don't let you down, Mr. Wolff," I said, humbled by his compliment.

Gloria Hunter walked over to greet Mr. Wolff and he proceeded to kiss her tiny hand, making her blush.

Jack put an arm around me, whispering as we walked back to the picnic tables. "Mr. Wolff is a heavy hitter, Zach. He's respected around the world for his humanitarian efforts. He was actually one of the key players when the U.N. negotiated a peace agreement in the Congo a few years back."

"Never heard of him."

"Well, he's not exactly one of those self-serving political types who is always trying to get his name out there," Jack stated as we sat down to the feast before us.

As dinner came to a close, several tribe members walked out to their cars, returning with drums and now wearing full Native American regalia, complete with feathered headpieces. The wind began to pick up so we all sat, forming a semi-circle on one side of the immense bonfire, avoiding the heavy wall of smoke that blew steadily in the other direction. Once the drummers started beating in unison, I glanced around the group, noticing several people with closed eyes who appeared to be meditating.

We must have been sitting there for thirty minutes when I became edgy and wanted to stand. Just as I rose to my feet, I ducked my head as a massive orb streaked right over the ranch. Grazing the nearby tree line, it moved much faster than any military jet, yet strangely didn't create a sonic boom as it turned sharply and shot straight back up into the heavens.

Inhaling deeply in attempts to get my heart rate down, I squatted down onto my hind legs while continuously swiveling my head around to scan the horizon. For the next few minutes I waited nervously before seemingly out of nowhere, six orange triangles appeared directly overhead. Spaced evenly with one in the center, their symmetric positioning created a star shape as they hovered about a half-mile above us.

Feeling light-headed, I reached behind and pulled a chair underneath me and sat, clutching both of the armrests tightly. Even though the night breeze had grown chilly, sweat drenched the back of my shirt as I rocked anxiously back and forth. Several people near me bounced to their feet, thrusting their arms to the sky in excitement for what would come next while I remained seated, only managing to chew on what was left of my thumbnail.

As I watched the orange triangular ships descend, it was like peering through a kaleidoscope. Each vessel spun horizontally, rotating a full one hundred and eighty degrees, turning aqua green in the process. With every triangle now pointing toward the center, they converged until no visible gaps could be seen between the ships. At this point I couldn't say for sure whether it was still six individual ships or somehow they actually became one, but the end result was a perfect hexagonal shape.

Once the united spacecraft descended to only a few hundred yards above us, it came to a stop and began circling clockwise. This foreign machine appeared to be much bigger than our largest aircraft carrier, so it was uncomfortable having it hover over our heads. After about a minute, the ship began its quiet decent again, causing an avalanche of fear to slowly crush the air out of my lungs.

Suddenly halting only a couple of feet above the steel roof of the pole barn, the ship hung completely motionless before emitting a soft fluorescent light from its bottom, illuminating the area where we sat. Although in a semi-state of shock, my mind clicked on auto-pilot as I stood up and began making mental notes for my journal later.

Out of the barn, twelve beings came walking toward us, and I became instantly struck by the paradox of how similar these aliens resembled ones portrayed in many of the Hollywood movies.

A metallic ash scent now in the air left me confused as to whether it came from the ships or these alien creatures or both.

Giant egg shaped heads attached to diminutive bodies that stood no taller than four feet made them almost look childlike. Four long spindly fingers with an equally elongated thumb hung disproportionally from their small frames. Their tiny noses and mouths appeared like pinholes compared to their giant, slanted eyes, the black pupils and black irises making it impossible to tell what their eyes focused on.

While all of them had grayish skin, it appeared to vary in tone with each alien. The suits they wore were made of an almost transparent yet glossy fabric, and it looked unlike anything I had ever seen. Having always attributing those cinematic versions of aliens as simply the products of imagination gone wild, I now wondered if some of their stories were actually inspired from firsthand accounts.

Walking directly toward us from the barn, each of these beings selectively approached a few people. I noticed the African man Geb smile widely, unable to contain his excitement at what appeared to be a reunion with two of the aliens. His wiry arms moved around rapidly as I overheard the trio speaking in his tribal dialect.

The conversation between two other aliens and an elderly man from Bill's tribe resembled what you would expect from old friends. Trite things like, "How's your wife," and the, "Say hi to your family for me," which, if I had not been so astounded by what I saw, would have struck me as comical.

Bill Hunter conversed for several minutes with one whom I would later learn was the leader of the group. They both eventually began walking side by side toward the crowd and as I watched them pass by several people, my eyes went wide once I realized they were coming directly to me. Tensing up and having no clue what I would do, my feet felt cemented to the ground, taking away my option to run.

Closing within a few feet from me, Bill put one of his arms around the shoulder of the alien while his other arm extended out to me, saying, "Zach, this is Shanda. He asked to talk with you."

"Hello, Zach, nice to finally meet you," the alien said, as if he were right off of Main Street, U.S.A.

"Hi…" I stammered. Still feeling like I was caught up in a dream, I struggled to believe that this was indeed happening.

"Zach, we had hoped you would come and we're glad you are willing to bring our message to the world. Knowing you must have many questions, we hope, with time, to answer all of them. We will help you stay in contact and assist you in any way we can. Do you have anything you want to ask me now?" Shanda asked.

"Where are you from?" I said, surprised that my tongue could actually move.

"We are not from any place on your maps of the universe." Shanda's short reply made Bill chuckle. I stood silently, and Shanda said, "Why don't you see if you have more questions after I have addressed everyone?"

Bill then turned around and used his thundering voice to instruct everyone to gather into a large circle. Stepping to the middle of our group, Shanda began speaking in English and basically reiterated some of the things Bill had told me over the last couple of days. Not until after about five minutes into his dialogue did I even realize that while I could hear him clearly, it wasn't audibly; Shanda was communicating to us telepathically.

"My dear brothers and sisters, it is so good that we could all gather here tonight. Many of you know of our great plan for Mother Earth and her children. It's my desire that as you are hearing it again, your hearts will be renewed and encouraged at the hope that is at hand. The critical state of your planet will cause us to bring our plan to fulfillment sooner than we had designed. The men who have dominated the world with their powers and weaponry must come to realize it is time to lay down their tools of destruction and pick up the tools for life. Those in charge of the financial institutions who control the distribution of wealth must heed the greatest good for their fellow man and ensure that everyone has enough to satisfy their basic needs. Individuals who try to force others into their religious beliefs will need to be enlightened that we are all children of the universe. We desire to see our brother earthlings evolve into the race you were designed to be. Before Mother Earth is destroyed, we will help instill a new system, one that will create the harmony and peace you have all longed for. Meditate on the beauty of the simplicity: One world will become one family." Shanda paused.

"We will merge all government, financial, and spiritual institutions into one world structure. This in turn will finally create a world of unity where there is true equality for *all*." Shanda's emphasis on the last word caused all of us to break into applause.

Throughout my life, I'd heard a handful of people who truly possessed an oracle gift, but those other speakers now paled in comparison. Shanda's charisma, along with the sincerity in which he spoke, caused us to hang onto every word. The utterly captivating message not only stimulated our intellects, but touched our hearts. I finally saw hope for the troubles and tribulations that plagued humankind and the hope of ages stood right in front of me.

Shanda continued, "Naturally, there are those who will question our intentions and resist our ideas. Many of these people have held onto archaic principles and thoughts perpetrated by 'so-called' teachers and prophets of long ago. And while we have a deep compassion for those who maintain that humans cannot coexist, we will temporarily have to remove them before we can put our full plan into action. After they are transplanted to another planet and re-educated in the ways of The Ancestors, the ways of peace, they will later be reunited with the rest of humankind. We want to prepare the world now because this day is fast approaching. Share with your fellow men and women to have faith because world peace will soon be a reality. When you see The Exodus take place; rejoice! Rejoice because the new era is at hand. Take heart; we are always with you." Shanda finished by slightly bowing his head.

We were all silent for a moment before Shanda and his companions strolled back toward the steel barn. Just before reaching the large opened barn door, they stopped to turn around and face us. Gloria stepped forward to take several pictures of The Ancestors with the spaceship hovering in the background while another gentleman who had been videotaping the whole event also moved in to get some close-ups. Seconds after The Ancestors entered into the barn, the ship turned off the lights, leaving only the flames of the campfire to help us see. Without making a noise or stirring the air, the ship suddenly whisked straight up and vanished into the dark sky.

Unlike anything I had ever experienced, it left an incredible sense of serenity that pervaded our entire group. As many people turned and exchanged hugs, several of the women bowed quietly, weeping with joy. I now felt foolish that my fear had nearly caused me to miss the opportunity to witness the most amazing event of my life.

While always possessing a deep passion for the art of storytelling, I couldn't remember ever feeling so compelled to write. Charged with a new sense of purpose and meaning, I looked forward to the privilege of sharing this ground-breaking news story with the world.

As Bill walked my way, I eagerly jogged over to greet him. Not even knowing where to begin, I blurted out, "This is incredible, Bill. Thank you."

"It's my honor, Zach. I knew you would be happy to have been here."

"I'm so ecstatic right now, I don't know if I'll even be able to sleep to-night or maybe ever again. I can't wait to start writing about all of this," I shot off rapidly.

"I'm sure you are. You see how Shanda simply communicated with us through our minds?" Bill said enthusiastically.

"Yeah, that was amazing."

"Well, Zach, you can learn this art with some practice. You'll find you have access to your "guardian ancestor" basically whenever you want. When Shanda said, 'We are always with you,' he meant that literally."

"Wow! I would love to ask them more questions."

"Trust me, you'll think of even more than you have now. I have learned that they'll answer the right questions at just the right time. Before you head back to San Diego, I'll show you some techniques of how to contact them. It'll all come down to, 'If you simply ask, you will receive.'"

I stood there nodding, wanting to absorb everything Bill relayed to me.

"Now I know you'll be eager to write this story, but you must keep all of our identities and this location confidential."

"Sure, that's no problem."

"I didn't think it would be, but I needed to reiterate that. Look, why don't you walk around and take the opportunity to talk to some of the oth-ers you haven't met and get some of their stories while I catch up to Mr. Wolff before he flies to New York this evening. Let's meet up at the house later."

"Sounds good."

When I finally met up with Bill and Gloria later that evening, we ended up talking until well after midnight. Gloria shared the photos from her digital camera and we watched in awe at the replay of the day's events. In my room I felt exhausted, but too wired to sleep, so I picked up a pen and pad to record my thoughts. Writing for what seemed like only an hour, I was shocked to realize it was already four-thirty in the morning. I tossed the pad onto the floor and rolled over to crash out so I could start up again later that day.

The rooster's crow at sunrise didn't annoy me like it had the past mornings and even with only a few hours of sleep, I still felt completely rejuvenated and looked forward to the day ahead. Everyone else staying at the ranch was already awake and eating breakfast when I walked in the kitchen. Many of the eclectic crowd greeted me, some in their own language, but everyone looked my way and shot me a smile. I had come here not knowing any of these people, but now in a short period of time this monumental event had developed a connection between us that felt almost like family.

While sitting down to eat my breakfast, I enjoyed listening to everyone recall their favorite memories from yesterday and how Shanda's promises would impact us.

"Once we are free of the drug cartels that dominate my country, I am certain that Mexico will finally reach her potential," Pablo remarked.

"Yes. I know what you mean," Geb followed. "The warlords that control my local area in Kenya make it virtually impossible for us to get ahead. They even dictate who gets the water in my village. I'm greatly encouraged to know that they will soon be out of power."

Sitting next to Miriam was Ishmael, the Palestinian man. When he started to speak, everybody leaned forward to listen.

"While I had always hoped for it, I never imagined in my lifetime that there could ever be a lasting peace in our region. None of our leaders have been able to create a peace accord that anyone was willing to truly follow. That's because it was always about merely enduring each other. What the Ancestors want to do is different. They want to unify us. I now believe that our people will start see to each other as Miriam and I see each other – as brothers and sisters."

Many of them were leaving today so I gave each of them my contact information before saying my goodbyes and heading back to my room with a fresh cup of coffee.

It dawned on me that morning that I had started to burn out on my previous job because most of my writing over the years had increasingly revolved around the evils in this world. And after watching those vicious cycles of human tragedy continue to repeat themselves, I had been given no real reason to believe it would ever end. For the most part, I had been constantly bombarding myself and my readers with only the problems, without seeing any viable long-term solutions. Inspired by the events that transpired over the last few days, my writing was now fueled with more passion than I had ever experienced. Desiring this piece to be the most prolific work of my career, I immersed myself in the challenge to truly capture the totality of what I had just been shown, and what it meant for the human race.

After typing non-stop for almost two hours, I heard a gentle tapping on my bedroom door. Ute, a college student from Germany who I had only talked briefly with the day before, stuck her head through the crack in the door, asking if we could talk. Saving my work, I turned off the computer and we walked outside to the patio.

Pouring two glasses of refreshing well water from a crystal pitcher on the table, Ute handed one to me and held onto the other, saying she wanted to share a story that might help others around the world gain some insight about last night's event.

"About five years ago, I saw a U.F.O. as I rode my bike home from the university. I was very afraid and started pedaling as fast as I could. Unlike everyone else who I spoke with this week, I never wanted to see any spaceships or meet any aliens," Ute explained as she tucked strands of red hair behind her ears. "For weeks I went through periods of paranoia where I would be looking over my shoulder in town and staring out my window in the middle of the night. I started having strange dreams where I felt like aliens were inside my room observing me. In the mornings I would wake up feeling sick to my stomach."

"That's understandable," I said, remembering my recent emotional roller coaster.

"About a month later, I went camping in the mountains with some friends from school. I thought it would be good idea to get away, you know. During the middle of the day, they went for a walk while I stayed back to read a book." Her eyes became focused as she appeared to replay the events in her mind. "I was lying down inside my tent when I noticed an orange light above me, glowing outside the tent. I intuitively knew it was a U.F.O. and became so petrified, I didn't dare to look outside. I couldn't scream or call for my friends because I didn't want these aliens to know I was hiding in my tent. I'm sure that sounds silly that I thought I could hide under a nylon cover from extraterrestrials," she laughed.

I smiled back at her before she continued. "So then the light got more intense and seemed to be hovering directly over my tent when it suddenly stopped. After a few minutes, I heard footsteps outside the tent and was relieved because I thought my friends had returned. When I unzipped the tent, Shanda stood right in front of me and I almost fainted."

"How did you know it was Shanda?"

"He introduced himself to me. Told me not to worry, that they didn't want to scare me or harm me in any way."

"Why did he say he was there?"

"Well, he didn't say exactly, it's more like he showed me. This is the part of my story that gets kind of hard to explain because it's, well, kind of spiritual. It was the most incredible experience I've ever had."

"More than yesterday?" I said, surprised.

"Yes, because it showed me who I was. Let me try to explain. When I spoke with Shanda, we become enveloped in this globe of pure light. As I was in this light, I was able to see all that I was and all I would become. It showed me I am eternal. It is so hard to explain with words, but it helped me understand what my soul is and what my destiny and purpose are."

"And what is that, if you can explain it," I said, lightly rubbing my chin.

"Well, just to live a good life. You know, keep evolving. It was pretty simple, yet very profound and enlightening," she said, putting her hands together. "That's really not the part I wanted you to share with others, though. I want people to understand that it is reasonable to be apprehensive about things we don't understand. But when we finally open our consciousness and let our guards down, we can truly begin to learn. Well, you are the journalist, and so I know you can probably think of a better way to put that. I was just hoping my story might somehow help others."

"Absolutely. I think it'll prove very helpful for those who will naturally have the same fears you did. I had my own apprehensions about all this and honestly wanted to leave before yesterday."

"You did?"

"Yeah, but don't tell anyone. I have my machismo to protect," I laughed.

"Okay. It will be our little secret." She stood up, extended her hand and said, "Well, I have to catch a ride to the airport, but it was nice meeting you."

Shaking her hand, I replied, "Likewise. You take care. And thanks so much for sharing your story."

As I walked back to my room, the gears began turning on how I could weave her account into my article.

CHAPTER 9

Writing and editing for several days left me mentally drained so I decided to take a day off before writing the final draft. Joining Gloria and Bill in the living room after breakfast, I watched television with them for the first time since I had come to the ranch. It had been good to get away from all the noise of the world, but today's news brought us an update about a major earthquake that had just rocked San Francisco. Fortunately, the seven point two quake took place in the middle of the night and so far only a few casualties had been reported. I was startled to learn that this was the third significant earthquake to rock the Western Hemisphere in the last twenty days, the earlier two devastating Lima, Peru and Panama City, Panama.

After an hour of viewing the footage of damaged buildings and free-ways, Bill suggested we go for a ride. For a moment I thought he meant in a car until he dialed one of the ranch hands and told him to saddle up a couple of horses.

As we walked over to the barn, the tall black stallion waited attentively for Bill while a brown mare with white spots on her nose looked at me with less interest.

Holding the mare's saddle horn to help me get on safely, Bill said, "Zach, you don't have to worry about old Abby. She's the most mature, even-tempered horse I've ever owned."

"Are you sure you don't have a pony instead?" I replied, looking up at the huge animal.

"We'll be going pretty slow."

Chuckling to let Bill know I had only been kidding, I put my foot in the stirrup and hoisted myself up.

Bill patted the neck of his stallion before heaving himself up on its back. Turning to look at me, he said, "You're about to find out what makes this place sacred ground."

Shaking the reins while nudging his horse with his boots, Bill said, "Giddyup, Raven."

Abby followed obediently behind Raven down a narrow trail strewn with moss covered rocks. Riding through a nearby canyon, this path lead in the opposite direction of where I had previously tried to make an escape. Bill didn't say another word for a couple of miles so I simply enjoyed the beauty of the pristine landscape surrounding me.

The chirping of birds echoed through the trees and a light breeze blowing up the side of the ridge filled the air with a fresh wintergreen fragrance. Eventually a break in the woods revealed a dark blue lake in the valley below, bordered by a field of purple Owl's clover and yellow California Poppies. Springtime had also caused patches of Aspens to bloom brightly along the opposite slope.

We finally stopped after entering a grove of towering Sequoias, some of them appearing at least eight feet wide. Bill looked up and around, admiring the trees before speaking.

"Some of these Sequoias have been around way before Jesus Christ ever walked the earth."

"These are magnificent," I said, craning my neck back in attempts to see the tops of the trees.

"But this isn't why I brought you out here. We got about a half-mile more to go," he said before starting back down the trail.

As we rounded a sharp bend, the path opened up, revealing a boulder face about the size of a giant billboard. We dismounted from our horses and tied the reins to a nearby tree branch before walking up to the base of the rock.

Bill pointed to the petroglyphs engraved on the rock. "These carvings have been here for over two thousand years. Now look closely and tell me what you see."

Puzzled at first as to what I was supposed to see, the drawings looked self-explanatory. The crude lines revealed several Native Americans gathered around a campfire with two giant elk standing at the edges of the picture. Dead center above the campfire, a giant circle with lines extending out signified the sun. Or at least I thought it did.

"Look closer," Bill said after I remained quiet.

Moving nearer to the wall, what I had at first perceived as simply a rough sketch of the sun, I could now see a perfect triangle inside the circle.

"The ancestors have visited this place in their ships before."

"That's right, Zach. You are one of the few outsiders to have ever seen our massive history book." Bill said with his hands resting on his large belt buckle.

I moved closer so I could rub the cold granite with my hand, gazing deeply at the artwork.

"This is absolutely amazing. Can I get a picture of it?" I asked.

"That'd be fine. Gloria already has some back at the house you can use."

"Great. It'll really add a unique dimension to the story."

"Let's go back to the house because now it's time to *really* show you something."

Bill obviously enjoyed keeping me in suspense so I didn't even bother questioning him as we walked back over to our horses.

⊕   ⊕   ⊕

AFTER ENTERING THE PARLOR ROOM on the east wing of the house, Bill closed the door behind us, telling me to have a seat on the Navajo rug that seemed to spread out forever on the polished wooden floor. As I sat down facing the stone chimney hearth, my eyes were drawn to a large oil painting above the rock mantel, revealing a gigantic man sporting a deerskin wardrobe and with a striking resemblance to Bill.

"That's my great grandfather, Chief Barking Bear." Bill pointed at the picture.

"Great name," I said.

"I think he got it from being a legendary snorer."

"Nice," I laughed.

Bill grabbed a small drum off the mantle and slowly eased his big frame down toward the floor. Finally resting a few feet from me, he said, "I think this is the perfect time to show you how to pray to your guardian Ancestor. Are you ready?"

"Ready as I'll ever be."

"Okay. Now it's all about getting the right set of mind. You want to be receptive to the message your Ancestor has for you. I prefer to sit cross-legged like this and methodically beat my drum to pace my breathing and relax my mind. But you don't have to do that. You can just inhale and exhale deeply, and slowly. And as you sit there, try to not think about anything; just let your mind go."

"Is this where the peyote comes into play?"

"No jokes Zach. We gotta focus on absolutely nothing," he said, smirking.

Patting his drum softly, Bill began taking a series of long, deep breaths through his nose.

Rotating my shoulders in attempts to relax as much as possible, I followed Bill's lead and breathed in deeply, which reminded me that I now smelled like a horse. It didn't take long to discover that trying not to think about anything was extremely difficult. My attempts at this sort of meditation only made me more conscious that I was thinking about not trying to think.

I considered some of the many questions I wanted to ask The Ancestors, the same ones that had seemingly perplexed the rest of mankind for centuries. After sitting for at least thirty minutes in the warm room, I finally felt like I could start to focus on nothing, but it only made me ready for a serious nap.

Bill startled me when he spoke out loud and said, "Ancestor, thank you for joining us here. We thank you that you give us guidance and wisdom. Zach is searching for knowledge and we hope you can help him. Go ahead, Zach."

"I, uh, yeah..." I paused, peeking out one eye to scan the room. Bill seemed unfazed by my hesitancy and sat completely still with his eyes closed. Unable to spot anyone else in the room, I shut my eye again, hoping this would somehow help me to sense the Ancestor's presence.

"Well, I want to know what happens to us when we die."

Since I hadn't heard anything yet, I expected Bill to relay this answer to me, but then I distinctly heard a voice that sounded much like Shanda's.

In a smooth, soft tone, the Ancestor replied, "You never actually die – your spirit simply moves on to another level where you continue to grow."

I like that answer, I thought.

87

"What about all the different religions? Why does there seem to be so many different opinions about who God is?" I asked, wondering if he would even have an answer.

"Many religious masters were good teachers and many of their principles and dogmas can be helpful in life. There are certain ones who understood the essence of holiness. They recognized the reality that we are all gods. Unfortunately, many of their teachings have been changed and distorted over time, which is why they cause so much division. We must warn you, you will encounter opposition for what you now know is true. People will come against you and say all kinds of evil because of us. Practice compassion for all will come to see the truth one day. Remember, we are always with you."

After a few seconds of silence, I opened my eyes and Bill smiled at me while he unfolded his legs straight out in front of him.

"So, what'd you think, Zach? Probably not what you were expecting."

"Definitely wasn't sure what to expect. But that was really eye-opening," I chuckled. "I almost felt like I was going take a siesta before you started talking to him."

"Yeah, it can be a little 'too' relaxing. Sometimes it takes me forever before I can even establish contact and sometimes I can hear from them without even trying."

Taking in a deep breath, I reflected. "I liked what he said."

"Just keep searching, Zach. You'll find the answers you are looking for," Bill said, pushing himself up from the floor.

"Yeah, I don't think I'm going to add this into the story right now. To me, that was more mind-blowing than when we saw The Ancestors land right in front of us."

Bill laughed. "Whatever you think is best. We trust your judgment."

WHILE OUR CHANNELING SESSION HAD delivered a deeper understanding of the metaphysical, it had also given me a glimpse of how much the story would actually challenge the world-views that many held onto so dearly. Even with all the physical evidence we could provide, people had shown throughout history how stubbornly they held onto superstitions and fables.

Thinking of my own sister, I wondered how she would react at hearing the story and how it would impact her and other religious fanatics. Even though the information was a great deal to comprehend and misunderstanding was to be expected, I hoped it would ultimately help her and others in their own spiritual quest. Knowing I would be facing an uphill battle at times, I realized it would take great resolve to remain empathetic toward those who questioned the validity of my account.

I looked forward to future conversations with our Ancestor, something Bill liked to call "surfing the universe." The experience proved to be extremely invigorating, and I headed back to finish off my story with a boost of energy.

AFTER COMPLETING THE ARTICLE a few days later, I shared it with Gloria and Bill who both read it while I took a long walk around the ranch. They both told me they were well pleased. With their blessing, I emailed an agent friend who began working on a unique deal with a publishing company that would pay handsomely for exclusive rights to the story once I provided the video evidence. It took less than thirty-six hours to work out the deal with New Fountain Media and the story hit the major media outlets as I left the ranch on Friday morning.

Departing the ranch after almost a three week stay, I thanked Bill and Gloria for their hospitality and requested we get together soon. After Bill returned my cell phone and laptop, we shook hands and I noticed Gloria's eyes had moistened. As I reached over to embrace her, she momentarily buried her face in my shoulder.

Gathering herself, she said, "I made you something, Zach."

She held out a piece of titanium rainbow quartz about half the size of her small fist. "It will help you meditate and keep calm when life gets tough."

"I appreciate that, Gloria. It means a lot to me."

This time it was only Peter and I who began the long drive back south to San Diego. Once we made it onto Highway 5, he told me I could take off my blindfold and sit up front. Pulling into a gas station to refill and stretch our legs, I recognized some road signs and knew I would be home in only a few hours. I expected my answering machine to be full of calls from every media source I could think of and amused myself as I imagined Harry begging me to come back to the magazine.

Wanting to make the most of this great opportunity life had afforded me, I envisioned plans of speaking engagements and a TV talk show tour to coincide with places I had always wanted to visit. I also mentally outlined a screenplay in hopes of making still more money.

When our van finally pulled onto my street, I observed several cop cars lining the street and countless camera crews posted throughout my yard.

"Let the games begin," I said to nobody.

Sinking into my seat below the window line, I told Peter not to slow down and keep driving.

Not really knowing where to go or even what to do next, I finally instructed him how to get over to Vanessa's place so I could come up with a plan. Knowing full well how much attention the story could generate, I still foolishly underestimated the cost of my new-found fame. Somehow I had been naïve enough to imagine that I could dictate when and where I would speak to the media. Confronted by a lawn full of reporters, I realized I wasn't ready yet to talk to all of these people.

Over the years, I had tried to withhold resentment toward those in my profession who had invaded people's privacy in the pursuit of a story. Now forced to acknowledge that these bloodhounds would most likely ensure that my private life met an early demise, I felt a plague of bitterness creeping into every fiber of my being.

LOCATED IN ONE OF THE city's oldest neighborhoods, my sister's small stucco home was situated on one of the few streets in Southern California where everyone's yard has at least one big tree. As we pulled up to her house, a group of kids playing Wiffle ball out front scattered to the side so we could enter her driveway.

The front porch light still burned dimly mid-afternoon, meaning she had probably left for work before sunrise again. With her unpredictable schedule at the San Diego Police Department, there was no telling what hour she would return home, but I still lugged my bags up to her back patio. Despite the apparent vacancy, I knocked on her door before reaching for the spare key hidden under a neglected plant in a small clay pot. Slowly jiggling the lock open, I walked in and slid my bags across the wooden floors of her cluttered living room. Reaching out the back door, I waved good-bye to Peter.

I hastily turned on the TV and began flipping through the channels to see what kind of reports there might be on my story. When I saw CNN recapping the day's top news stories, I plopped down on a pillow on the floor and rested my back against the couch.

Apparently a terrorist organization had successfully detonated a bomb on a ferry boat right near London Bridge, killing at least thirty-six people the previous day, with a branch of England Islamic United claiming responsibility. Such stories had become so commonplace the past few years that it simply numbed the senses.

The newly appointed anchorman who ostensibly acquired his position through striking good looks and his ability to adequately read a teleprompter smiled awkwardly before going on to the next story. "There is still much uncertainty about the account of an extraterrestrial encounter released by New Fountain Media today." The camera broke to the scene outside my house, causing me to sit up and lean forward.

"Reporters are eagerly awaiting the arrival of Zach Miller, the former *Essence Magazine* writer who claims to not only have been an actual eyewitness of alien aircraft, but to have also made physical contact with alien beings. According to Miller, the aliens gave him a message of hope to all of humankind that they will come and help create a new world order where peace and unity will reign forever. New Fountain Media claims that later today they will release actual video footage of the event. As of now, experts are still examining the photos you have been seeing to check their authenticity. Government officials are making no official comment at this time except that they would like to interview Mr. Miller. For more information on the story, log on to our website at CNN.com." The anchor smiled smugly, no doubt pleased with his performance.

I heard the hum of an engine pulling up the driveway and hit the off button on the remote so I could hear more clearly. The faint squeaking of brakes caused me to crawl across the floor in the kitchen, before peeking out the window. Relieved to see my sister's Honda Accord, I wrestled to jar the window open and yelled her name so as not to startle her at finding someone waiting in her house.

"Zach?" she said, stopping as she rounded her car.

"Yeah, it's me."

"Oh my gosh," she said before hurrying to the house and meeting me at the kitchen door. "What's going on? What are you doing here?"

"I just got back in town and didn't want to deal with all the media in front of my house right now. I'm assuming you read the story."

"Of course; it's all over the news. Everyone at work was talking about it."

"So what did you think?"

"Well, I'm still just blown away. I can't believe my kid brother was there to see it."

I laughed and said, "Yeah, it still seems almost surreal to me as well. But it was such an amazing experience!"

"And you went to this ranch not even knowing what you would be reporting on?

"I had no idea. Once I got there and found out what was about to happen, I was petrified. I actually tried to escape out of there before it all went down."

"You did?"

"The more I thought about actually meeting extraterrestrials, the more freaked out I got. Fortunately as I was trying to leave, I got turned around and witnessed the whole thing. I wished you could have been there."

"Some news reporters actually called me at the precinct asking for a statement. I was wondering if anybody would show up here."

"Yeah, sorry about that. I don't know why I didn't expect the media to set up camp at my house. I'm gonna get my agent to set up a press conference after they release the video so I can answer as many questions as I can at one time."

"That sounds like a good idea," she said, unfastening her belt holster, and opening up a cabinet drawer to lock up her Glock nine pistol.

"Is it okay if I stay here for tonight?"

"Of, course. That's fine."

A knock at the door caused me to raise my eyebrows at my sister, as I wondered if the media had found me.

"Oh, that's probably Jason," she said and hurried over to the door.

"Hey, come on in. Let me introduce you to my brother Zach."

Jason looked surprised that I was there as I stood up to shake hands with him. Vanessa then informed me that Jason worked with her at the same precinct. A middle-aged detective, Jason certainly looked the part with his freshly shaven face, clean-cut hair neatly parted to the side, and casual-business attire.

"Hi, Zach, nice to meet you," he offered.

"You as well."

"Hey, that was some story you wrote," Jason said bluntly, and my sister shot him a look, attempting to get him to avoid the subject.

"What'd you think?" I asked.

"Well, I'd love the chance to discuss that with you more. But I think Vanessa wants to get over to the restaurant right now. Do you want to join us?"

"No, thanks. I'm gonna lay low and take care of some things."

"Okay, I should be back around ten," Vanessa said, edging Jason out the door.

"I'll probably be knocked out," I laughed.

Dialing my landline's answering machine to retrieve my messages, I ended up skipping past the ones from the New York Times, The Enquirer, and The Wall Street Journal. I finally stopped when I heard a deep voice say, "Mr. Miller, this is Alex Yelle from NASA. I would very much like to talk to you at your earliest convenience."

I saved his number into my cell phone and thought about all the different bureaucratic departments who would be clamoring to talk to me. Dwelling on this for a moment caused me to feel slightly paranoid that I might be followed by the F.B.I. and other agencies. *No wonder nobody at the ranch wanted to bring this story to the world.*

I called Johnny to see if he had the misfortune of dealing with the crowd outside my house and he picked up on the first ring.

"Johnny!"

"Zach, where are you, man?"

"I'm over near downtown," I said, trying not to reveal my address or my rising state of paranoia.

"I read your story this morning. What've you been smoking, bro? Johnny asked, laughing.

Comments like this reminded me I would now also be fair game to every comedian known and, even worse, people like Johnny who thought they were comedians.

"Johnny, I don't need comments from the peanut gallery right now. Let me cut to the chase. What's up with my house? Have you been by there today?"

Changing his tone, Johnny said, "Sorry about being so flippant; I didn't want to deal with that zoo over there. I drove by this afternoon and just kept going."

"I don't blame you."

"But man, I'm sure glad that you didn't listen to me and went up there. That was the most amazing story ever!"

"Well, thanks. It was hands down the greatest experience of my life."

"Yeah, well, when are you going to introduce me to these Ancestors?"

"Actually, that's a real possibility. I can teach you how you can contact them."

"For real? That'd be outrageous," Johnny's voice got louder.

"I need to ask another favor. Can I stay at your place for a couple of days?"

Hesitating, Johnny said, "I don't know, Zach, I don't want the press corps hounding me."

"Okay, I get that."

"Hey, you can make a killing on the talk show tour."

"Do you think Scooter's Scandals will invite me on their show?"

"Yeah, maybe. You'll have to say that you had an affair with an alien girl."

"Who said I didn't?"

"Oh man, I knew you had it in you," Johnny quipped, and we both laughed loudly.

"What's sad is that people would probably buy that story more easily than the truth," I added.

"Well, like they say, only in America."

"Alright, so can you check me in at the Hilton tomorrow around noon under your name and I'll just pay you back?"

"That's fine. I should be finished up with my web design for this furniture store by then. I'll call if I'm gonna be late."

"See you then."

$$\oplus \qquad \oplus \qquad \oplus$$

THE NEXT MORNING, A PICTURE of The Ancestors took up almost the entire front page of the San Diego Chronicle newspaper that lay on my sister's dining room table. The headline read, "Close Encounter of the Real Kind?"

"Do you want some bacon with your eggs?" She asked.

"Love some," I said.

Sliding the bacon onto my plate of eggs, Vanessa sat down next to me. She bowed her head quickly, saying grace for her food while I ate and continued staring at the photo.

"So, now that you see this, what do you think?" I said pointing to the newspaper.

"To tell you the truth, the more I think about it, the more confusing it gets."

"What do you mean?"

"While I hadn't really thought about life on other planets a great deal, but I always guessed it was possible. But when we were discussing it at the restaurant last night, Jason brought up some interesting points," Vanessa replied.

"Like what?"

"Well, if they brought us here, who created them?"

"I don't know, but... what does it matter?" I said, caught off guard by the question.

"Well, it's not very practical from the standpoint of design. The human body is a complex design, which is evidence of a designer. It's the same logic of why I don't believe in evolution and why I believe the Bible when it says that God created us."

I unsuccessfully fought back a smirk as I thought of a question that would stumble her reasoning. "What does the Bible say about extraterrestrials?"

"It doesn't." She paused and squinted at the ceiling. "Well, at least I don't think it does."

"Okay. And who created God?" I refolded my arms and leaned back.

"No one. He's always existed," she said it as if it were a matter-of-fact and poured some more juice into our two glasses.

"That sounds like a convenient answer."

"Look, Zach. I don't pretend to know everything, but there are some basic principles of the Bible that actually make sense if you think about it. I don't mind discussing these types of questions, and I hope you don't either because you can expect a lot more everywhere you go after that article."

"It's not like I have to convince anyone of anything. If photographic evidence and eyewitness testimony isn't enough, they'll see for themselves one day."

"You know, I still feel pretty new to my faith so I don't feel like I have that much knowledge, but something tells me that there is something very disturbing about all this. I mean..."

"What's disturbing is that the story throws a monkey wrench in your Christian view." I pointed my index finger at the table.

"Zach..." she said, rolling her eyes before taking a big swig off her juice.

"Look..." I took a short breath and consciously changed my tone.

"Like I told you, I was pretty fearful about meeting the Ancestors at first. But once I did, I was truly glad it happened. It was like, well, a religious experience," I said clasping my hands together.

"And *that's* what scares me, Zach," Vanessa said, looking directly at me.

"Look, you found something that makes you happy and that's great. I have found happiness and hope through meeting my Ancestors. I mean, I'm really excited about the prospect of them coming to bring peace on earth."

"I don't doubt you are excited and happy. I just want you to be careful..." The doorbell cut her off.

"That must be Jason and Pam. We're going over to Balboa Park." Vanessa said, putting down her juice and shuffling over to answer the front door. "Hey guys, come on in. Pam, this is my brother, Zach."

Pam had a cute, but round face and looked to be in her early twenties. Her short, red cropped hair and lightly freckled face, which lacked an ounce of makeup, gave her a tomboyish appearance that became magnified with her Giants baseball t-shirt and faded blue jean attire. I immediately thought it odd that she would be hanging out with two people almost twice her age and who definitely appeared much different than her. I learned she had moved here from San Francisco, and she had recently attended her first ever church service, which was where she had met my sister.

After my brief introduction to Pam, I turned my attention to Jason. "So, Vanessa was just telling me you have some issues with the story I wrote."

"Well, I personally don't doubt for a minute that you did interact with some alien beings. What I have a problem with is the message they gave you. I think there are some serious ulterior motives going on."

"You don't think they come in peace?" I said, folding my arms and wondering how he could jump to such a conclusion.

"No, I don't." He shook his head.

Thrusting my hands into the air and flicking my fingers outward for emphasis, I had to ask the obvious. "Well, why didn't they just zap all of us right there and start their reign of terror?"

"Because they want you to propagate their lie," Jason said with his hands resting on his hips.

"Their lie? Pfffttt…" I let out a small puff of air and slightly cocked my head to the side.

"Okay, let me back up. I think the aliens were telling you the truth when they said one day a huge population of the earth would vanish. But here's the part that I *believe* they twisted. My take on the scriptures is that Jesus will come and remove his people right before the worst period in the history of our planet."

"So wait, let me get this straight. Jesus just bails out on mankind and leaves those remaining so they can wait to be destroyed? That sure sounds like some loving God you have there," I said, staggered that this guy seemed to sincerely believe all the spew that came out of his mouth.

'Look, the Bible says that God does not delight in the death of the wicked, but wants all to come to repentance. It's not…"

"You know what?" I interrupted. "You can say all this and believe it because you have heard others say it, but none of you have *seen* Jesus. I saw The Ancestors. I talked with The Ancestors."

"He's got a good point," Pam spoke up. "I don't really see why it's such a terrible thing to believe in both God and extraterrestrials."

"Because Pam, the Bible warns us that demons come as angels of light. They may bring a ton of truth to the table, but when you really examine the context, it's a lie. I'll flat out tell you: I think these aliens are interdimensional beings who are none other than the legions of Satan."

"Oh, boy, is he for real?" I laughed, turning to Pam for an answer.

"I don't think I can convert you, Zach," Jason continued. "I do hope you would at least consider what your sister and I do for a living. We didn't come to some rash conclusion about the claims of Jesus and the Scriptures. We approached it like a detective and did our own investigation."

"Well, Jason, remember this: I am an investigative journalist. I take a similar approach to uncovering a story as you do on a case. I'm pretty sure that when you're building your case against someone, you always look for the eyewitnesses. Well, I am the eyewitness! Over fifty others experienced what I did! The videos and photos don't lie. I'd hope that'd be enough for you to *at least* consider things you might not understand yet."

"Zach, over five hundred people saw Jesus when he resurrected…" Jason said apparently ignoring what I just stated.

"Ahem…" Vanessa coughed. "Jason, we need to get going if we are going to find a close parking spot."

"Yeah, Jason, could you go ahead and send over some of that video footage of Jesus getting beamed up during his ascension to heaven when you get the chance?"

Jason shook his head, clenched his jaw shut and he kept his eyes on Vanessa as she walked between us. He clearly wanted to continue the debate, but Vanessa reached back and tugged on his arm.

"Well, I certainly look forward to reading more of your stories, Zach. I thought it was fascinating," said Pam smiling at me as she leaned forward to shake my hand.

Jason then turned on his professional demur and quickly said, "My disagreement with you is nothing personal, Zach," before offering a business-like handshake.

"Not a problem," I replied, but didn't mean it.

Watching the two walk out to the driveway, I could tell by Jason's hand gestures he desperately hoped to sway Pam to his opinion. Vanessa stayed back to tell me she would return in a few of hours and would give me a ride if I needed, but I told her it wasn't necessary and thanked her for letting me stay.

When she closed the door, I let out a deep breath of relief. The Ancestors had warned me this would happen. Still agitated with Jason's line of reasoning, I had no real desire to try to convince someone who wanted to hold on to their ignorance.

While still excited about sharing my story with others, I also recognized how tiresome it would be if that was the only thing anybody wanted to talk about with me. The real burden would ostensibly come from dealing with the skeptics and hearing the rant of those who always seemed to have a conspiracy theory for everything. Just as some still doubted that humans had actually visited the moon, they would say my cohorts and I had cooked up this elaborate tale. I knew I would need to make a conscious decision in the future to try and avoid any lengthy debates with skeptics, especially nuts from the religious right.

After calling a cab, I walked outside to wait on the sidewalk. Soon a red, white and blue taxi sped by me in a cloud of gray haze, filling the street with the sickening smell of burnt oil and antifreeze. Realizing his mistake, the driver suddenly hit the brakes. When he threw the vehicle into reverse, the transmission made a loud clunking noise. Now parked in front of me and planted firmly in his seat, the elderly cab driver glanced down at my luggage. His indifferent expression told me that the only energy he would be expending to help out was to push the button that opened the trunk. The heavy bags under his bloodshot eyes conveyed the end of a long shift so I happily lifted the luggage into the trunk myself and jumped into the empty back seat.

The cab jerked to a halt in the Hilton's semi-circle driveway where I waved off the bellman and paid the driver. Standing inside at the black, marble reception desk, Johnny nodded at me as I walked in. While hoping my hat and sunglasses would be a sufficient disguise, I deliberately avoided looking at anyone.

Once inside the tiny living room of my suite, I flipped on the TV and ordered a huge plate of nachos from room service.

"So Johnny, get a load of this breakfast debate I had over at Vanessa's this morning. Her church crew was claiming that I saw some demonic apparition."

"What? You gotta be kidding me."

"Seriously. Listening to this Jason guy sounded like I was watching one of those fruit loop preachers on a bad cable-access channel."

"Oh man, that must have been weird. But, really, what'd you expect from religious people?"

"Yeah, I guess I'm gonna have to get used to it."

"If it means anything to you, everyone I've talked to said they thought it was great."

Shortly after the server delivered our food, we both leaned toward the TV when a young female anchor announced that her station was about to broadcast my video footage of alien aircraft.

When the screen revealed the orange triangular ships rotating in the dark sky, Johnny's eyes widened and he exclaimed softly, "This is insane!"

"I've watched this clip a hundred times and still can't believe it."

"What? What just happened? I thought there were six ships?" Johnny's brow crumpled.

"I don't know, either. It's like they just fused together and became one gigantic mother ship."

"My gosh! How big is that thing?"

"I couldn't begin to tell you." I replied, shrugging my shoulders.

"It looks like a floating city," Johnny said, unable to move his eyes off the screen.

"Yeah, I was terrified the thing was going to land and crush us all."

"I don't see how anyone could doubt that this is definitely an alien air craft."

With the ship hovering above the pole barn, the clip abruptly ended as the anchorwoman returned to our screen. She then informed viewers they could expect more footage, stating her network would soon possess a video of actual alien beings and their message for the world, just as "writer Zach Miller had recently claimed in his groundbreaking article that chronicled an extraterrestrial visitation."

When they cut away to a commercial break, I shared some of the details of the story that I had left out of the article with Johnny. After my confrontation with Jason earlier at my sister's house, it was enjoyable recounting the event to someone with a receptive ear.

⊕   ⊕   ⊕

MY AGENT JOEL WHITTEN ARRANGED a closed press conference for the upcoming Friday at another downtown hotel, inviting a select group of reporters who were provided a short list of topics I would be willing to discuss. In case of a leak about the conference, we hired a security firm to prevent uninvited parties from bombarding me with questions I wasn't prepared to answer. Attempting to bring this story to the world on my terms, I hoped I could dictate to the media instead of vice versa.

A mid-size banquet hall had been arranged for the interviews, which turned out to be more than adequate to accommodate the twenty-one reporters and their camera men. While initially nervous before walking onto the small stage, once I got behind the podium I decided to just relax and have fun with it.

Before fielding questions, I informed them that they could expect to see the video of Shanda's speech released within the next week. I assured them that the footage would reveal my article had recorded his exacts words and nothing had been taking out of context.

A few rows back from where I stood fellow San Diego State alumni and Los Angeles Times writer, Kent Jones asked, "You wrote that these extraterrestrials have tried to help us along the way. How so?"

"Yes, I touched on that briefly in the article. Many of the so-called miracles of the past were actually works of The Ancestors. I'm talking everything from miraculous healings to methods of farming. You don't have to look hard to see they've passed on all kinds of technological innovations that helped us advance. For example, when you examine the ruins of Puma

Punka in Bolivia, you see that it would have been impossible for that civilization to build such a monument with laser-like precision on their own. There is actually a vast trail of evidence all over the globe that points to previous interactions with The Ancestors."

Raising his index finger before speaking, Boston Globe reporter Clint McConnell asked, "Have you been in contact with any of our government officials after this encounter?"

"No, but I'm glad you asked that. I'd like to be up front and say I don't mind cooperating and answering any questions they may have. While I've already stated in the article everything I know, I do reserve the journalist privilege of keeping my sources confidential. To protect the privacy of those who were at the ranch, I simply cannot and will not reveal any of their names."

Phyllis Cooke, a reporter for the San Diego Chronicle, stood up and asked, "How do we know that they have good intentions and aren't planning an attack?"

"Seems odd to me that they would announce their arrival if they are planning an attack. Kind of takes away the element of surprise, doesn't it?" I answered.

Cooke tilted her head quizzically in response, then asked, "But they also stated that they would be taking away a portion of the population to 're-educate' on a different planet. That could be construed as less than benign. Did they give you any indication of who those people would be?"

"You're correct. They said there are certain people who have been keeping the rest of humanity from evolving and that these people would have to be relocated, *but* they did say these same people would be eventually reunited with the rest of humankind. As far as who might be on that list, I have no idea, but I guess you could start with those sitting inside the California Correctional Facilities," I said shrugging my shoulders and some of the reporters laughed. "Phyllis, I'm not trying to dismiss your question because it's a valid one, but I wasn't given any more information than that."

"Why did they choose you to write the story?" John Holcombe from The New York Times asked.

"No idea. I'm just as good a hack as anyone, I suppose."

"A two-time Joseph Runyon award winning hack," Holcombe said, smiling back at me.

"Well thanks, John, but I'm not exactly sure. Being unemployed didn't hurt. But honestly, I think staying objective as well as open-minded is the key. We journalists get pretty cynical because we think we have seen it all. Doing this story reminded me of how much we don't know."

With her chin resting on her fist, Courtney Morris from the local FOX affiliate asked the million dollar question. "Did these aliens give you any indication of when they plan on coming back?"

"Great question. They said "soon" and obviously that's a relative term, but I do believe they are trying to start preparing us for their arrival. When that will actually be, I don't know."

After fielding a few more questions, I thanked all of them for coming, and more importantly, for treating me with dignity and respect. Wanting to be transparent, I explained that while I also had many more questions myself, it seemed reasonable to expect that many of those answers would prove difficult for us to fully comprehend.

Even with the conference over, I still didn't feel comfortable moving back to my house as I knew I could expect intrusions from reporters wanting an interview at basically all hours of the day. I had hoped that by calling the conference and answering questions upfront I could detract some attention away from myself, but experience told me that plenty of others would seek to get their own story.

On my way back to the hotel, I found a moment to call back Alex Yelle from NASA. Curious if they had any strange readings on their satellites over the Sierras that night at the ranch, I doubted if he could even disclose such information. Somewhat surprised that I hadn't already been called in for questioning by some government faculty, I assumed it would happen sooner than later. Desiring to be cautious, I took an extra fifteen minutes to find a payphone because I still didn't trust anyone working with the government. Fortunately a corner liquor store not only provided the almost obsolete phone, but sold phone cards as well. An elderly Russian clerk eyed me suspiciously through the glass front door as I leaned against the front of the brick building and dialed the Houston, Texas area code.

"This is Alex Yelle."

"Hey Alex. This is Zach Miller, returning your call."

"Great! Thanks for calling back." His voice changing from monotone to extremely excited.

"Mr. Miller, I work for NASA's Origin Program so I am obviously eager to speak with you. How have you been feeling since your encounter?"

"Well, uh, basically pretty normal except, I don't know, I think I've been more emotional at times, maybe a little more irritable," I said, trying to recall any other noticeable changes.

"Any nausea?"

"Only before the encounter."

"That's good. How about your sleep?"

"Well, you know I haven't really thought about that, but now that you mention it, just in the past week I haven't felt that rested after sleeping all night. The first couple of days I was going on full adrenaline, but maybe it's all catching up to me and that's why I have been so irritable. The last couple of nights I've dreamed The Ancestors were trying to contact me."

"Hmm… have you been in contact with the aliens since you left the ranch?"

"No, I haven't tried, but I was planning on seeing if I could re-establish some contact soon."

"Do you mean telepathically?"

"Yes, hold on a second," I said loudly as hip hop music blared from a teenager's car pulling into the parking spot in front of the phone. The music died when he shut off the engine and the young man shuffled inside.

"Mr. Miller, I have done research in these kinds of encounters for over twenty years. And there are certain patterns of side effects that tend to occur which you may want to keep a record of. I also highly recommend starting a journal and keeping it bed side so you can track what you saw in your dreams right after you wake up. You may find that they are actually contacting you while you are in a subconscious state."

"Thanks, that's good advice."

"Mr. Miller, off the record so to speak, many of us who work at NASA were positive it would only be a matter of time before we established this kind of contact with aliens. There are certain government officials who are in the know about extraterrestrials and the message you wrote about was actually one they have been aware of for a long time. As you can imagine, this message threatens many of those who hold dear to their fragile sense of power, which is why I am sure these aliens have never made an effort to contact them. While I'm not calling you as an official representative of NASA, I just wanted to let you know that you do have supporters over here."

"That's good to hear. It's definitely comforting to talk to others who believe you and know you're not crazy."

"That's one of the reasons I called. At the same time, you have to know that our public stance will be the standard," Alex's tone became robotic, "We cannot confirm nor deny this phenomenon at this point in time. Our team of specialists will thoroughly investigate these claims, but it is likely to take many months before we are able to distinguish the facts and reach a conclusion."

"Yeah, well, I had already expected that kind of rhetoric."

"You have one remaining minute on your phone card," a female voice interrupted.

"Well, my card is almost up."

"Okay. Do me a favor and follow up in a month or two to let me know how things are going. Shoot me an email at alexyelle-at-gmail-dot-com. I certainly want to be able to add your journal entries into my data."

"That's easy to remember so I'll reply back to you when I get the chance. And thanks for the support."

"Not a problem, take care."

Hanging up the phone, I hustled to grab a cab at the street corner. A gentleman who had been reading a newspaper from a bus bench stood up abruptly and started walking down the street parallel to me. Sensing he might be following me, I delayed my trip back to the hotel by taking a left down the next block, stopping into a coffee shop to see if he would come across the street. One minute later, he briskly entered through the front door. Turning my gaze quickly back to the register, I ordered coffee before jostling right past him to the exit as he read the menu on the wall.

Heading to the trolley train back to my hotel, I spotted him again the moment I reached the station. With the newspaper tucked under his arm, he never looked my way, but once the cherry red train came to a stop, he hurriedly stepped onto the same car I did.

Now sitting on opposite sides of the car facing me, he again unfolded the paper, pretending to read. Dressed casually in sunglasses, shorts and a striped polo shirt, his golfer's ensemble didn't give me a hint if he was indeed a government agent. For a brief moment I actually contemplated going over to sit next to him and turn the tables by following him. Instead, when the train came to my stop, I quickly stepped off in attempts to throw him off my trail and, with a bit of luck, to keep "them" from knowing where I was staying, if that was even a secret.

I wandered in the opposite direction of my hotel and entered a Marriott a couple of blocks down. Rushing into the lobby, I hopped into an empty elevator, went up three stories where I got off and ran down the hall to the staircase. Several housekeepers became alarmed as I entered their broiling laundry room where industrial sized washers and dryers banged out the musical harmony of a drunken punk band. Acting like a confused guest, I asked in Spanish for the exit and the women merely pointed down another hallway.

Finally locating the entrance to the loading dock, I nodded to a teenaged dish washer sitting on a crate with a smoldering cigarette drooping from his lips. Ignoring his stare, I jumped down a small set of stairs and ran through a parking garage before coming out on a back alley that led to my hotel. Before entering the poolside door of the Hilton, I looked around one last time to see if I could spot anyone following me, but felt confident that I had lost my trailer.

Relieved to be in my room, I collapsed onto the soft comforter atop my bed. I knew certain agencies would want to grill me, but I could only guess at their motives. Obviously helpless about the whole matter, I realized that I would just have to get used to being under surveillance. I couldn't think of a better time than to try to contact my Guardian Ancestor so I sat up, folded my legs into the lotus position, and tried to clear my head.

"Ancestor, please help me. I want to know who is following me and why?" I uttered. Straining to hear an answer, I felt intensely uncomfortable from sitting in this awkward position, and I lay back on my pillow.

I then distinctly heard a soothing voice say, "Zach, we have heard your prayer and have come to help. You will soon have your own personal vehicle to share our message of hope with those who will listen. Others will encourage you and your faith will continue to grow as they share their stories, providing more proof to the world of our existence. Rejoice, for the time is at hand."

When I opened my eyes, I instantly thought about grabbing my notebook. Rummaging for my pen, I began to wonder if I had been awake or in a dream state while talking with my ancestor. What did it matter: his message came back to memory as soon as my hand clutched the pen. While his words didn't really address the issue of those who might be following me, I still found them reassuring and would recognize later how they actually inspired my future plans.

CHAPTER 10

After my last contact, I became eager to share the intricate details of the encounter at Bill Hunter's property with those who wanted to know more and my agent booked a series of talk shows across the country. Most of the programs were devoted entirely to me and provided a great format to discuss the story. However, one particular show in New York caught me completely off guard as no one had informed me that we would be hearing the testimony of another guest. I had noticed the middle-aged man waiting nervously in the green room, but we didn't speak before the broadcast.

Like the other programs, the producers of the Maurice Coleman Show re-broadcasted the video clips of that night at the ranch while I recapped the highlights of the event and answered questions from the host.

I sensed that people were still in awe of seeing the footage so I followed up by saying, "Let me conclude that while I know viewing intergalactic space craft and extraterrestrials can overwhelm the senses, I certainly don't want people to lose sight of what's really important here. Their message is about us. With the help and guidance of our Ancestors, we can all change the course of history and finally become a unified planet, a unified people."

The audience applauded enthusiastically as my part of the interview finished and host Maurice Coleman smiled at me before swiveling back in his chair towards the crowd. Up on the two mammoth-sized TV screens to each side of us, his face took on a very pensive look as the camera closed in on him, and his voice grew increasingly serious.

"Our next guest has also had an alien encounter, but his story starkly contrasts with Mr. Miller's. I was personally taken aback when I heard his story and I warn those viewers at home, there are parts of this story that are extremely graphic, so you may want any small children who are watching to leave the room. Now, please welcome Richard Summerlane."

After hearing the host's warning about the man's account, the audience clapped politely, but now looked more rigid.

"Welcome to the show, Richard. Please sit down and share your story with us," Maurice said as he guided the new guest to sit down in a chair between us.

Sitting down slowly, Richard's eyes darted back and forth while his forehead had worked up a sweat before the intense studio lights even hit him. Casually dressed in a pair of jeans and a plaid button down shirt, he looked like your "average Joe."

Hesitating before he spoke, he clutched his hands to help keep them from trembling.

"Well, like you said, my story is much different from Mr. Miller's here. I didn't even tell anyone about it for several years until after I had seen a psychologist," he said in a deep, Bostonian accent. "It's caused me a great deal of distress and I actually ended up losing my job over it. My wife and I got separated, but right now we are working on getting back together."

"Please, start at the beginning," Maurice said, adjusting his suit coat before crossing his legs.

"I had gone on a fishing trip by myself one weekend up to the Adirondacks. And after going to sleep in the bed of my truck, I awoke to find several aliens standing around my truck just staring at me. They looked kinda similar to the ones Mr. Miller here talked about, except I never heard them say anything. The next thing I know I'm inside their spaceship where they laid me down on a white table. They started examining me with all kinds of instruments and then, uh..." Richard turned his head down to stare at the floor and rapidly tapped his right foot.

Uncrossing his legs and leaning forward, Maurice gently asked Richard, "How do you know this wasn't just a dream?"

"Well, I wasn't sure about anything when I woke up the next morning. For several years, I guess I tried to convince myself that it was an extremely bad nightmare, but it continued to traumatize me to the point where I started having problems sleeping, and concentrating at work. I finally broke down and went to a shrink. He's the first person I told about it, and he suggested I get hypnotized. During those sessions I found out that it wasn't a dream at all. It actually did happen to me and I had been trying to block it out all these years."

"Well, it's very courageous of you to come here today and share this painful memory with us. I understand that you've brought a video that documented the meeting with the hypnotist."

"That's right."

"Okay. Why don't we take a look over at one of the big monitors at this session that took place last fall at the Cambridge Psychiatric Hospital," Maurice said, spinning his chair around so he could view the screen.

The studio lights dimmed and the video revealed Richard lying on his back across a long, black couch, already in a mesmerized state and answering questions. While we could only see the dark outline of the hypnotist's head, his voice came through clearly as he attempted to elicit responses from his patient.

"After they put you on the white table, what did they do to you?"

Richard's body shivered on the couch as he recounted the next part of the story.

"They took off my clothes and started sticking metal objects into my ears and mouth. My arms and legs were clamped down so I couldn't move. They brought out this white hose and put it on my…" he paused. Embarrassed, he bit his lip before continuing. "Well, um, they attached it to me and started taking samples. It was the most painful thing I have ever experienced."

"Richard, why do you think they did this to you?" the hypnotist continued.

"They're beasts!" Tears began to streak his reddened face while we could clearly hear the hypnotist scribbling notes on a clipboard. The video clip faded as the studio lights returned to their normal level and the camera immediately switched back to the three of us.

Maurice paused several seconds for dramatic effect before asking Richard in a hushed tone, "Now, more than a year later, do you have any idea why these aliens treated you this way while the ones Mr. Miller encountered acted benevolent and offered help?"

He shrugged his shoulders before tightly gripping the arm of his chair. "No. I'm still as confused as ever. I completely believe Mr. Miller's account. I mean, obviously his story is far more believable, with all the photographic proof and everything. To tell you the truth, my story just still feels like a bad dream, but it really did happen."

Maurice then shifted in his chair, putting his hands together where the tips of his fingers slightly touched his chin and turned his attention to me. "Well, Mr. Miller, do you have any insight as to why Mr. Summerlane's encounter was so extremely different than yours, and do you feel like it somehow sheds a dubious light on the intentions of the aliens you reported on?"

"Well, I have to say that I'm dumbfounded at hearing his story. I can't say with certainty what happened to him, but I've heard that hypnotist don't always evoke events that actually occurred. To answer the second part of your question, I can only say from what I experienced, that I saw nothing but goodwill from The Ancestors. I believe the entire world will soon view them in the same light."

RETREATING TO MY HOTEL ROOM after the show, I couldn't stop thinking about Mr. Summerlane's alien encounter. While Richard's story didn't appear fabricated and was admittedly disconcerting, what I had said to the host Maurice was true: I could only rely on what I knew to be factual and had seen with my own eyes. Despite Richard's strange account, I prayed others would still see that The Ancestors did indeed offer us all hope.

The next morning I enjoyed French toast in bed courtesy of room service and reading the New York Times. As expected, there was an article about my appearance from the previous day on Maurice's show. After finishing the story, I pushed my half-finished food aside. Reading Summerlane's account had caused unsettling questions to arise and killed my appetite.

I tossed the paper to the floor and shuffled out of bed, heading over to the coffee maker on my dresser. A lone spoon next to my cell phone began rattling and alerted me the phone had been left on vibrate.

"Hello?" I said, wondering if I had picked up the phone, too, late.

"Zach, it's Bill," he said in his distinct, deep voice.

"Hey, where are you calling me from?"

"From home."

"On your home line?" I gasped.

"No, no. I have a prepay phone. This thing is disposable."

"Whew. That's good. I was pretty certain that I've been followed since I came back from the ranch, but I've been recently getting even more paranoid about it. My friend Johnny said earlier this week that someone had broken into my house, and went through all my stuff. And the other day in Chicago, I know for a fact that someone opened up my bags in my hotel room. It's been kinda weird, too, where I always notice a certain member of the audience who I get the feeling is not really there to see the show, but you know, just there to observe me."

"I'm sure your instincts are right," he said.

"Yeah?" I said slightly puzzled when Bill didn't try to subdue my paranoid state.

"Certain governmental departments are interested in your activities, but you have nothing to hide. You're telling a story, not trying to keep a secret."

"You're right," I said, hoping that someone was tapping my phone line to hear this. "I'm not trying to hide anything."

"Zach, the reason I'm calling you is because I saw you on the Maurice Coleman Show yesterday and I wanted to talk to you about it."

"That was bizarre, huh?"

"I was planning on telling you this, but since you were already on information overload, I figured I would wait. Now I don't know if this guy Richard's story is true, but this much I do know. There are evil ancestors. When you hear people talk about demons and evil spirits, this is who they're really talking about. These few ancestors have gone astray and are actually behind many of the problems we hear about."

"That definitely would explain some things."

"They have been battling with our Ancestors for thousands of years, but I assure you they will soon be defeated. When you hear people attribute evil to The Ancestors, understand why they see it that way—there are indeed wicked ones."

"My sister and her friend actually told me they thought Shanda and the other ancestors were demons masquerading as aliens. But now I can see how they could be confused."

"Exactly. I told you, Zach. We must practice patience and compassion with people. It takes time for us to change our way of thinking."

"Yeah, I see what you mean," I said, now gazing into a mirror mounted over the dresser.

"I hope that kind of clears things up for you."

"It does. I appreciate you calling because I plan on sharing this information on the rest of the shows I go on."

"Well, I knew this would be the right time to share that with you. I will catch up with you later."

When I hung up, I still remained perplexed about some things, but felt confident that additional pieces of the puzzle would come together and eventually everything would make more sense.

CHAPTER 11

Even though I flew first class and stayed in luxurious hotel suite, it only took about six weeks for me to grow weary of being on the road non-stop. The same routine of talk show formats only helped increase my distaste for the vagabond lifestyle. I never thought I would tire of reliving the greatest experience of my life, but after about the fortieth television appearance I almost dreaded answering the same redundant questions. While I truly enjoyed meeting people receptive to my account, it was still maddening when I encountered those who scoffed at my claims.

Out of all my critics, I gave Metro Magazine the award for publishing the "Most Ridiculous Conspiracy Theory" in regards to my story. Senior writer Stewart McKenna had the audacity to allege that I was in cahoots with film producers who staged the event simply to make a buck.

I had to laugh as my years of a healthy mistrust of anything Hollywood made the Metro article completely ironic. With the slightest bit of research, McKenna could have uncovered that during my talk show circuit I had already rebuffed some serious offers to do a feature film.

Even though I desired a bigger platform, believing that anyone in Tinsel town could maintain the integrity of my story proved difficult and I became leery about even pursuing it. Owning an inherent responsibility to make sure the spirit of the story didn't get watered down by their commercial interests, I knew I needed a format where I essentially had complete control. Tired of trying to convince those who didn't believe, I also desired an arrangement where I could focus my energy on sharing with those who were receptive to the message.

As I tossed around different ideas in my head from a hotel bed one evening, I finally had an answer to my current dilemma: I would start my own web magazine. This decision seemed like the best way to communicate in an unfiltered forum where I could control the information and elaborate on my experiences. I also wanted a way for others to share their own personal encounters, and a webzine seemed like a perfect fit. Concluding that this whole idea had been inspired from my last contact with my Ancestor, I found myself saying out loud, "Hallelujah, thank you, Ancestor."

Eager to get off the road for a while, the web concept put a new fire in my belly and I got extremely excited in anticipation of putting it together. Later that night, I talked with Johnny and he agreed to work on a web design for me. While advising me that I should go on a few more talk shows to get free publicity for the web site, Johnny also came up with the name: TheAncestors.com

ARRIVING HOME TO THE TEMPERATE climate of San Diego is always a welcome respite, especially after being soaked by the hot summer humidity

back east. As I pulled into the driveway of my split-level home that evening, I looked forward to finally sleeping in my own bed. I definitely needed a good night's sleep because the next day would be devoted to trying to straighten out a letter I had received a few weeks ago from my friends at the IRS.

Sitting at my coffee table cluttered with documents the next afternoon, I gave in and decided to call my former accountant. After dialing his number, I heard a familiar voice on the other end.

"Hey, stop dialing," she yelled.

"Vanessa? Were you just calling me?"

"Yes," she said laughing. "I heard you punching the numbers. Are you still on the road?"

"No. I'm finally home for a while. I'm gonna take a break from the talk show circuit."

"I've had so many people asking me if I saw this show and that, but I only saw the tail end of the 20/20 one because it was on late at night. So what's it like to be famous?"

"It's pretty weird to have people recognize you on the streets. Most of the time people stop and stare because they're not sure if it's me. But those that approach me are pretty respectable. I'd love to stop and talk to everyone, but I'd never get anything done if I did."

"I'm sure."

"So, how's everything with you, Vanessa?"

"Insanely busy. This latest case we've been working on is really wearing me out."

"What is it?" I said, not sure I really wanted to know.

"An eight-year-old girl was kidnapped and we suspect her mom's ex-boyfriend. It's totally heart wrenching because the girl has been missing for over two weeks. At least we've had some good leads in the past few days."

"I honestly don't know how you do your job."

"Cases like this are pretty brutal. The toughest part for me is when I start to wonder if I'm even making a difference at all."

"That's rough."

"Anyway, how have you been? I haven't talked with you in a couple of months."

"I've been a little busy myself. I just got back into my house last night, so I'm trying to get things back in order around here. I have all this money now, but I don't even have time to spend it. At least I'm gonna pick up a new Toyota Tacoma tomorrow morning."

"Good for you."

"Yeah, I got burned out doing the talk show circuit pretty quick, but my agent said the publicity generated even more interest for a feature film. I'm also starting up a new webzine."

"Well, I hope being so busy is the real reason you haven't called me in a while. I've wondered if my faith has made things weird between us."

Settling back against the couch, I rubbed my neck because she had pinpointed exactly why I had not wanted to talk.

"Yeah, well…" I paused. "Our views obviously clash. I mean, you'll always be my sister, but you can't try to sway me from what I've seen and experienced for myself."

"Zach, I'm really sorry. Well, sort of. I want you to know that I will always have your back and nothing will ever change that. I just don't want our difference in beliefs to drive a wedge between us. So I promise that from now on, I'll only bring up my faith when you ask me about it."

"Thanks."

"So, you wanna get together next Sunday for lunch?"

"Yeah, sounds good," I said.

"I'll be out of church by noon. Why don't I meet you at Ripley's downtown at twelve-thirty?"

"Twelve-thirty it is."

I was glad Vanessa had made the effort to call because she forced me to be straightforward about why I had been avoiding her. Now that we had cleared the air, I hoped she would keep the pledge not to bring up her outdated creed because I really did miss hanging out with her.

CHAPTER 12

Early Saturday morning, I went out to retrieve my mail and found the neighborhood dead quiet. Out of the corner of my eye, I noticed a white cargo van I had never seen before parked about half a block down the street. Shoving the advertisements back in the mailbox, I glared at the vehicle and instinctively knew that this was a surveillance vehicle.

With no real plan of action, I slammed the metal door shut and marched down to where the van sat, hoping to discover who was watching me and ultimately expose them. Approaching the driver's side, I immediately noticed the black curtains separating the cab from the back of the van. I went around to the back, but the heavily tinted windows only allowed me to see my own reflection. I impulsively tried to jerk open the back door. When it didn't budge, I yanked several more times, somehow expecting it to open with the next tug. I pounded on the door before slapping my palms onto the side of the van.

"Come out here!"

"Zach! What are you doing?" My neighbor barked as he charged toward me, wearing a bathrobe and slippers.

"I'm letting these guys know that I'm on to them," I yelled before banging even more furiously.

"Zach, stop beating on my son's van," he said, now standing face to face with teeth clenched.

I froze before turning slowly to face him. "Then, uh, why are these curtains drawn?"

"He has expensive camera equipment he sometimes keeps in there. Why don't you ask before you just come over here, waking us all up," he whispered angrily.

"Sorry, Matt," I said turning my eyes to the ground and I began lumbering back up to my house.

I almost turned around to tell him how someone recently had been in my house going through my things, but when several other neighbors came out to gawk at me, I just picked up my pace to get back inside. Right then I decided to call a realtor friend and put my house on the market.

$$\oplus \quad \oplus \quad \oplus$$

THE OUTSIDE PARKING LOT LIGHTS fluttered before finally coming on as I left the nearly vacant office supply store at dusk. While fumbling with my car keys, I heard the gentle click of a car door shutting, followed by footsteps shuffling right behind me. Battling the urge to glance over my shoulder, I didn't want to fall prey to having another paranoia attack like the other day when I "spazzed" out in front of my neighbors. As I drew near my truck, the pace of the footsteps quickened, and I spun around.

Stopping only about six feet behind me, a young, petite, Latina woman stood wide-eyed and holding her breath. One glance and I instantly knew she wasn't a threat so I turned back toward my truck.

"Excuse me, are you Zach Miller?"

I slowly turned back toward the bashful voice.

"Do I know you?"

"No. I'm sorry. I just thought I recognized you from the news. You are Zach Miller, aren't you?" she said revealing a beautiful smile.

"Yes, I am."

"I enjoyed watching you talk about the aliens," she said putting both hands casually in the back pockets of her denim jeans.

"So, you believe what you hear?"

"Oh, definitely. It makes total sense to me. Do you plan to write any more articles soon?"

"Well, I'm working on developing some projects right now. You can Google my website in about a week."

"I can't wait to check it out."

"Well... I need to load this stuff up and get going. Nice to meet you..."

"Gina Martinez," she said offering her hand. Looking directly at me with her soft, brown eyes made it difficult to look away.

"Zach Miller," I stammered and then laughed. "Well, you already guessed that."

"Hey, um, well, this is kind of awkward for me, but I was thinking, if you're not too busy sometime, maybe we could have a cup of coffee."

"Well... uh," I muttered.

"I'm sorry. I know your schedule is probably so hectic, and everything."

"Don't be sorry. I'm pretty busy, but we can still try to get together sometime."

"Where do you live?" she asked.

"Near Mission Valley."

"I live near San Diego State."

"You go to school there?"

"I do. I'm actually planning on starting my master's thesis this month."

"Oh, really? That's great." *Gorgeous and intelligent. Win, win.* I thought to myself.

"Here, let me give you my number," she said, pulling an envelope from her purse and tearing it in half.

"I'll try to give you a call," I said, putting the number in my back pocket and trying not to act overly interested. While she seemed to be cautiously flirting with me, I hoped I wasn't getting the wrong message.

As I drove home, I could not get Gina's endearing smile and beautiful eyes out of my head. It had been at least a year since I had been on a date, but I didn't remember being this excited about a woman since my college days. Feeling somewhat foolish about my schoolboy crush, I pondered if a relationship with a woman ten years my junior was really plausible. I also had to wonder whether I had simply imagined the attraction and if she merely wanted to hang out with a celebrity journalist.

It took all but three days before I called Gina and we agreed to meet for dinner at a Mexican cafe on the south side of town.

After greeting her in the parking lot, we walked together into the old, white brick building with a red clay tile roof. Since the cafe was located off the beaten path, I hoped I would go unrecognized, staving off any unwanted interruptions and allowing me the chance to get to know Gina more. Looking to get away from the blaring horns of the mariachi band that played on the patio, we headed toward the back until we found a quiet booth in the corner.

Gina talked to our waitress in perfect Spanish, which made sense when I learned that her parents were originally from Mexico City before relocating to Phoenix. Moving here four years ago to escape the Arizona heat, Gina had recently graduated with a double major in linguistics and behavioral studies. She laughed as she thought how possessing those two degrees could only lead to a job teaching the same subjects.

As our waitress brought us each a beer and a basket of freshly made tortilla chips with salsa, Gina asked, "So, how's a good-looking, successful writer like you not married?"

"Ha. Well, I've been married to the job for a long time. But I think even workaholics hope that one day Miss Right will come along."

She grabbed her beer and said, "Let's toast: Here's to finding Miss Right."

"Cheers," I said and tapped her beer bottle.

After telling me a little bit about her four brothers, Gina asked, "What about your family? Do they live around here?"

"My sister does. She only lives about a ten minute drive from here."

"What about your parents?'

"They both passed away."

"I'm sorry to hear that."

"That's okay. I feel fortunate to at least have very fond memories of both of them. My mom is the one who encouraged me to become a writer. She always enjoyed my storytelling and told me I had been given a real talent. We lost her to cancer my senior year in college."

"When did your dad die?"

"I was thirteen. He got killed in a high speed chase by a drunk driver."

"Was he a police officer?"

"Yeah, he was. I always wanted to become a cop until that day. It's kinda ironic that my sister ended up following his footsteps."

"Your sister's a cop?"

"Actually made detective about a year ago. My dad would have been proud of her."

"I'm sure your dad would have been proud of you, too, Zach. Hey, I need to run to the rest room. Don't eat my food if it gets here before me."

As I stared at my half-empty beer, photos of my dad's wrecked patrol vehicle flashed through my head. My finger nails dug underneath the label of the bottle, scraping it off piece by piece as those thoughts led to images of my recent car accident. For the last couple of months I had tried to rationalize and even minimize my crash by claiming it was a result of being too tired. A surge of remorse came over me, forcing me to concede that I was indeed guilty of the same crime that took my dad's life. Ashamed of my actions, I swore right then that I would never drive again after drinking.

When Gina came back to the table, I faked a smile, but she saw right through it.

"Hey, are you okay?"

"Yeah, I'm fine," I said, rubbing my now clammy hands across my jeans beneath the table.

Wanting to divert my thoughts, I quickly asked, "Hey, do you like sports?"

"Well, I know this is blasphemous since I am Mexican, but I absolutely hate soccer and boxing."

"Seriously?" I said, chuckling.

"Yeah, I know. I don't really like watching sports. I'd rather be outside riding my bike or hiking."

"I know what you mean, but I've been so busy lately. I need to make more time to get outside and enjoy this place."

Our waitress brought out two steamy plates and set them in front of us.

"You know this restaurant claims to have coined the phrase 'Holy Mole'," I said.

"Come on," she scoffed.

"Okay, I know that sounds corny, but try it."

Sampling her enchilada, Gina nodded before wiping her mouth with a napkin. "I stand corrected. This is the by far the best mole sauce I've had since I left home."

The huge servings proved more than enough so skipping desert was an easy choice. After I paid the bill, Gina asked me to follow her to Sunset Cliffs.

Arriving at the edge of a trail that led down to the bluffs overlooking the ocean, we strolled down to a couple boulders where we sat down to soak up the last ten minutes of the sunlight. With neither of us saying a word, we watched intently as minute by minute the edge of the world melted into a different color.

Almost completely dark now, the sandy trail contrasted enough from the brush, guiding us back to the lot. As we neared my truck, she turned around to give me a hug and thanked me for a great evening. While I didn't tell her, Gina's suggestion to come over to the beach had helped me forget the things that had been troubling me earlier at dinner.

As she put on her seat belt, Gina looked up at me and said, "I hope we can get together again soon."

"Sure. I'll definitely give you a call."

Watching her car's taillights fade over the hill, I started to think of something unique for our next date.

CHAPTER 13

Rocking rhythmically back and forth in my office chair, I slowly read over an email I had recently received from movie producer Barry Howard. Not only pitching me the most interesting concept on how to chronicle my encounter at the ranch, Barry was keen on the idea of having me directly involved with the creative side of the project. I had just started to email him my feedback when Johnny's phone call interrupted me.

Talking extremely fast, he blurted out, "Hey, flip it on CNN right now. "They're reporting on what the Vatican said about your story."

"This should be interesting," I said, turning on my small television in the study.

"We now go live to Chuck Saunders, our correspondent in Italy for a report on the Pope's comment about the topic of alien sightings, and what Catholics should believe about them."

"Thank you, Ted. As you can see, I'm standing right outside the gates of Vatican City, where a council of church elders is gathered to discuss this alien phenomenon that is apparently permeating every country and culture around the world. Many devout Catholics have been asking their local priests questions about the sightings and what it means to their faith, so as you could guess, this gathering of church officials to bring some conclusion on the matter has been greatly anticipated around the world." Looking down at his notes, the reporter read, "In brief, the official word from the Pope, and I quote, 'God has sent help in many different forms over the centuries. The scriptures implore us to always welcome strangers, for by doing this some people have entertained angels without knowing it. It is clear that the aliens are fellow creations of God and that we should in no way demonize these beings'."

Now staring back at the camera, he continued. "The latter part of this statement must have been in response to several Christian sects who have been labeling the alien sightings as demonic apparitions."

"Chuck, what is the mood there in Vatican City?"

"Well, Ted, it is actually quite festive. There seems to be one of celebration, as many here believe this is a time of signs and wonders from above. Several priests have told me that just like the sightings of Mary worldwide, they see these visitations as merely other ways by which God reveals Himself to people. What I have found so interesting is that many of the faithful seem to embrace the message of the aliens as essentially the same one the church believes in. They personally see it as simply a matter of semantics; they feel that what the aliens refer to as evolving is the same thing they teach about ethics. Basically for them it all boils down to how to better yourself as a person."

"That's fascinating, Chuck. It seems as though there are those among the Jewish and the Islamic faiths who also believe that these aliens are somehow Satanic and yet, at the same time, there are also highly esteemed representatives from those faiths who, like the Vatican, seem to embrace the aliens' ideology."

"That's correct, Ted. I recently spoke with a pastor back in the U.K. from a large Protestant congregation who basically came to the same conclusion as the Pope. So, just as you stated, there doesn't seem to be a consensus of opinion anywhere you go. We can only hope meetings like this continue to take place, to openly discuss the matter. I will have a follow-up report once I get more information."

"Thanks Chuck."

The camera cut back to the studio. "We will return to Vatican City once Chuck conducts those interviews, but right now, let's go to Wall Street to see how the stock market is doing...."

"That's wild. I wonder what Vanessa thinks about that?" Johnny said.

"I don't know, but I definitely plan on asking her," I replied, turning down the volume. "Hopefully this will give her a different perspective."

"So what's your plan for today?" Johnny asked.

"I'm still negotiating with a producer up in L.A. who has put together those programs on the Uncovering Life Channel. I'm firm that I have final say on the screenplay and be on the set for most of the production."

"That's awesome. I hope it all comes together soon. Surf's good; you wanna hit it?"

"I haven't paddled out in months, but I can write this proposal when I get back. "Meet me at Ninth Avenue in twenty minutes?"

"Can do," said Johnny.

"Oh yeah, I'll tell you when I get there about this incredible woman I just met. We've actually gone out a couple of times this week already."

"She got any friends?"

"Do you think I want to blow it by getting her friends all mad at me for introducing them to you?" I said, laughing.

"Good call. See you at the beach."

As soon as I got off the phone, I thought I recognized someone from the news story on TV, so I turned the volume back up.

"...in Paris where the negotiations are continuing for a prisoner exchange between Israel and Hezbollah. Some leaders from the European Union are here to mediate between the two and have said the talks have been progressing. Our sources say they expect to reach a settlement before the weekend."

"Well, I'll be. Looks like Mr. Boris Wolff is the man!" I said out loud. I flicked off the TV and headed to the garage to get my surf gear.

⊕   ⊕   ⊕

ONCE YOU SMELLED THE SWEET smoke pouring out of Ripley's Soul Kitchen you had absolutely no chance and your car would automatically pull over into the nearest parking space available. Known by the residents of San Diego for its southern-style entrees and hospitality, Ripley's was also loved because they featured local blues and jazz artists on the weekends.

Arriving earlier than my sister to beat the Sunday church rush, I grabbed a table near the window without having to wait. Vanessa walked briskly in at twelve-thirty and smiled brightly at the elderly hostess who had been working here ever since we could remember. Neither of us had to look at the menu because we both always ordered the same thing at our favorite downtown restaurant: a Barbeque Poor Boy Sandwich and a large iced tea.

"Hey, remember that time we went together to feed the homeless on Thanksgiving and you said you knew that guy pushing a shopping cart with all his belongings?" Vanessa asked.

"Tommy Garcia. He was a top-ten surfer before he started snorting his winnings away."

"Great news. I just saw him speak at church today. He shared how God got him sober and off the street. Definitely looks better than when we saw him."

"That's good. Glad he made it."

"He said he just got a job and found a little studio apartment."

"You know, I really enjoyed going down there with you and helping out."

"We should do it again this year," Vanessa said, smiling.

I inquired about the kidnapping case she had been working on, and she said the incident might be related to some other unresolved abduction cases. She thought it was a syndicate job that revolved around a child pornography ring, but spared me any gruesome particulars as our food had arrived.

Since I had skipped breakfast, I inhaled my food while Vanessa slowly savored hers.

As I updated her on the movie deal, Vanessa held the straw between her fingers and slowly drank from her glass before offering, "Hmm... that's interesting," as she struggled to find another euphemism.

Clearly wanting to withhold her thoughts about my movie's theme, she remarked "Looks like you got some sun. When have you had time to get outside?"

"I actually went surfing with Johnny earlier this week. It was the first time in ages. The waves were super fun."

Taking a quick bite off her sandwich, she pulled the napkin up to shield her mouth from me. "Did you feel out of shape?" she uttered like an amateur ventriloquist.

"Oh, I definitely got winded, but you know, the kid's still got it," I said, patting my biceps.

She chuckled and nodded her head. "Well, at least one of us got to play. I've been wanting to ride my mountain bike, but can never seem to find enough time to go out and hit the trails. I've been riding the stationary bike at the station's gym. At least I can catch up on news that way."

"Hey, did you hear what the Vatican said a couple of days ago about extraterrestials?" I asked as our waitress refilled our iced teas.

"Yeah, actually, I was just listening to a huge discussion about that on a radio talk show on the way home from work on Friday

"So, what'd you think? It doesn't look like the Pope thinks The Ancestors are from the pit of hell," I said, leaning back in my chair.

"Well, I certainly don't agree with everything the Catholic Church says. And I don't look to the Pope to form my theology. I look to the Bible."

"So, you don't think a group of priests, who might've just possibly read the Bible a couple times more than you, could come to a logical conclusion?" I cocked my head to one side and held my hands out, waiting for a response.

"I'm not saying that. I agree with them that they are creations of God. But like I told you the first day, Jason made some very astute observations when considering their nature and their message. I don't expect you to take a biblical view. All I've been trying to say is that I think you should be extremely cautious."

"The strange part to me is you Christians can't agree on anything. You must have a million different churches that all say something different."

"Well, there is some truth to that. But when you break down the fundamentals of our faith, any true church believes the same things. Like that Jesus was born of a virgin and he lived a perfect life. That God is triune— Father, Son and Holy Spirit," she said, taking the last bite of her sandwich and giving me a chance to interrupt.

"So you decide what a true church is?"

She grabbed her iced tea and took a big gulp, before continuing. "I just tried to explain that to you, Zach. We may not agree on everything, but there are the essentials that we do. You know what..."

"Hey, wait a minute," I said, cutting her off as I pointed to her brand new ring. "What's up with this?"

"Well, I was actually planning on telling you today," Vanessa gazed down, extending her ring finger out to admire the sparkling diamond.

"Jason proposed to me two days ago. We're getting married next September."

"What?" I shook my head as I chose not to feign my approval.

"What's wrong, Zach?" she said, biting her lip.

"I don't know. I mean, I didn't even know you were a couple. How long have you guys been dating?"

"Well, only about three months, but we have both prayed about it for a while and we have a real peace about it."

Folding my arms, I let out a breath and looked down at my plate. The waitress came by to give us our bill and I began twirling my straw around the bottom of my cup.

"Geez, Zach! Thanks for the 'Congratulations, I am really happy for you, sis' comments," Vanessa shot at me as soon as the waitress left.

"Sorry, it's just..." I paused.

"It's just what? Spit it out, Zach!"

"Well, it's bad enough with all your religious talk, but having to deal with both of you is going to be a nightmare," I blurted out.

"I knew it. I knew that was the whole reason you didn't approve of Jason. I don't have to defend him, but I will. I am blessed to have a man like that in my life. He is compassionate and caring. He goes out of his way for people..."

"Look, I'm sure he's a nice guy and all," I said, realizing I shouldn't have opened my mouth and wanting to backpedal. "I was just trying to make you see it my way."

"There lies the problem. It's the same old Zach. You want everyone to see things your way. Instead of being happy for me, you only care if it makes you happy."

"That's not..."

"Listen!" she cut me off. "I finally have a man who I know loves me just as I am, not what I can do for him. He is the first one in my whole life who hasn't tried to get me to sleep with him..."

"Maybe he's gay," I quipped.

Vanessa stood up so fast that her chair screeched as it moved backwards across the tile floor and the noise caused everyone at surrounding tables to look our way. Jerking open her pocket book, she threw some money on the table. "You're an egotistical jerk! Grow up already." Vanessa turned and marched toward the door.

I looked to the side and immediately felt embarrassed as a preschooler stood in his chair staring at me. While I regretted my asinine comments, I truly dreaded the thought of having a Bible-thumping zealot as my brother-in-law.

$$\oplus \qquad \oplus \qquad \oplus$$

WHERE THE BRIGHT MORNING SUNRAYS shining through my blinds had failed miserably to wake me, the doorbell proved triumphant. Grunting as I trudged down the hallway, I wondered when I would finally just disconnect this anti-sleep device.

"Zach, sorry to wake you," Vanessa said quietly from my doorsteps. "But my conscience has been bothering me since yesterday. I wanted to say that I'm sorry for making a big scene at the restaurant and calling you a jerk."

"Don't sweat it, Vanessa. I deserved it. I'm the one who should be apologizing. I don't even know why I made that lame crack about Jason," I said, rubbing my eyes. "Why did you drive over here? Why didn't you just call?"

"Because I got convicted about what I said and I didn't want to apologize over the phone. I felt I needed to say it in person."

"Yeah, well, you didn't have to. I wasn't mad at you or anything," I said, still puzzled as to why she would hassle with the commute over here before her workday.

"I didn't think you were, but I still felt bad about how things ended."

"Look, just don't go tell Jason what I said because I don't want him to kick my teeth in," I said, not thinking my comments would actually lead to an altercation between us.

"Zach, he would never beat you up. Make no mistake, he could," she chuckled. "He was a Navy Seal before joining the Police Department."

"Okay, things to remember: Don't start a fight with future brother-in-law," I said, using my finger as a fake pen and pretending to write in an invisible notepad.

Vanessa laughed before adding, "Back in the day he was telling me that he used to think he was pretty macho and got into his share of bar brawls. When his head was shaved a couple of months ago, he showed me a scar on the back of his head where he got slammed with a beer bottle over in the Philippines."

"Sounds pretty on-par for a Navy guy. Hey, you wanna come in and have some coffee?" I backed up and pulled the door all the way open.

"No, I'll get some when I get to the office. I have a feeling I'm in for a long day so I need to get on the road. So, if you'll just give me a hug, I'll feel better and let you crash out," she said with her arms extended.

"Of course," I said, reaching over and embraced her. "Thanks for making the effort to come by."

She smiled as she walked quickly over to her car. "I needed to do it. Have a good day," she yelled before ducking into her car.

"You, too," I hollered back and immediately wondered how that would be possible as she exposed herself to detailing heinous crimes committed against children.

While I brewed some coffee in hopes of jumpstarting my day, those plans ended with a newspaper folded against my chest as I fell back asleep on the couch. This time it only took a soft knock at the door to awaken me.

"Zach? Are you in there?"

I jumped up as I recognized Gina's muffled voice behind the door. "Just a minute," I yelled before rushing into the bathroom, gargling some Listerine, and throwing on some other clothes.

"Did you forget that I was coming over?" Gina asked as I opened the door.

"No, no. I just woke up earlier and ended up passing back out. Come on in."

The first couple of times Gina and I got together she rarely asked about The Ancestors, but the more time we spent together, the more the subject came up. I didn't mind the conversations focusing on my encounters because it seemed to help us get to know each other on a deeper level. Sitting outside on my back patio, Gina started to elaborate about when she had heard about the visitation at the ranch.

"The day the story came out I can't even explain how excited I became. I mean, things just seemed to start to click for me. I guess some would say I have kinda been a pessimist, just always seeing the negative things in life, but when I heard the message The Ancestors brought, I finally saw hope for the world," Gina said.

"I know what you mean. Before I went to the ranch, I had actually been going through a bout of depression, which was weird for me, because I'm a pretty upbeat person. Writing had become beyond tedious, more like a chore than something I loved. Some of the things I'd been reporting on definitely played a part in making me all bummed out. But this experience has given me a great sense of purpose; really, a new reason to live. It is strange though, because while I still feel like the world's spiraling out of control, I also feel there is immense reason for optimism."

"I grew up going to Mass every Sunday. And I guess it was good at teaching me right from wrong. But, I had all these major questions about life and I never felt that my parents' faith really answered them. But when I read what Shanda said, I felt a new awareness, and a deep desire to know more. When I saw you that first time in the parking lot, I felt it was our fate to meet. I almost let you just walk away, but…" Gina got up from her chair and came over and sat down next to me on the bench. "…I'm really glad I seized the moment."

I put my arm around her, giving her a kiss and said, "Me, too."

A pain shot thru my neck, causing me to pull away from her. I gripped the back of my neck, trying to massage a giant knot.

"Are you alright?"

"Oh, it's my neck. I've been bending over at the computer a little too much. It has been a lot of work trying to keep up with the webzine."

"Hey, I'd be happy to help lighten your workload."

"Be careful what you ask for."

"No, seriously. It sounds really interesting."

"If you're up to it, we could always use the help. Let me show you what I'm working on."

We got up and headed into my cluttered study where I showed her the numerous unopened emails and all the ones I had flagged that I intended to respond to later. I explained how I had received countless letters that were obviously fabrications, but was uncertain of the validity of others. Since one of my biggest challenges was deciding which stories were legitimate, I had played it safe by only publishing ones that seemed to relate to the message I had received, and those similar to the accounts of the people I had met at the ranch.

"Oh, you've got to hear this one." I pointed to the one I had put two asterisks by and began reading:

"Mr. Miller, thank you so much for bringing the truth to the entire world about our ancestors. It was a great relief to hear from such a distinguished journalist as yourself who could validate what many of us have known to be true for many years. My first experience with The Ancestors occurred many years ago in the Ozarks in

Southern Missouri. I've kept in contact with them ever since, and have been shown many wonderful things. The reason I am writing you today is to share something that was recently revealed to me. What I am about to tell you may sound unbelievable, but it indeed did happen.

"I was meditating in my back patio right before sunset when a spaceship appeared overhead. The next thing I knew I was being levitated into the aircraft. While I had seen UFOs above my property before, my experience in communicating with extraterrestrials was limited to channeling sessions. I'd never seen any of these beings or been inside a ship until this day. The Ancestors looked exactly as you described them in your articles; they then informed me that I had been chosen to receive a special message. I was taken above the earth and was able to view our planet in all its splendor. We must've been traveling faster than twice the speed of sound. They showed me everything from island chains and mountain ranges, to big cities and country farms. The Ancestors said that everything I could see was, in reality, mine; essentially, our planet was a gift to all of us. They also said that in order to keep the Earth alive, it is imperative that we listen to them. While this all may seem familiar to you now, what they showed me next came as a great surprise to me.

They explained that because man had continuously looked outside himself for help, he had not been able to evolve as he should. Whether it had been from other fellow men or even to some 'god,' humans have somehow failed to realize that we already had all the answers we needed. One of their goals is to help humankind see that we can progress by simply utilizing the power inside all of us. They said we needed to recognize our own "divinity," that we don't need a god because we are gods. We are the ones who can and will decide our own destiny.

Up until now, I have only revealed this to people in my inner circle of friends, but please feel free to publish it if you desire. I sincerely hope that it will be as beneficial to others as it has been for me.

Peace & Blessings to you,

John Richardson
Fayetteville, Arkansas.

As I finished reading the note, I turned and looked at Gina to see her reaction.

"That's amazing." she said, holding her chin.

"What's really wild is that I didn't even publish what my guardian ancestor told me the first time I prayed out at the ranch. He basically told me the same thing that John emailed me, so it helps solidify what I had already heard myself."

"Did you email him back and tell him you had a similar experience?" Gina asked.

"Of course—I was so pumped when I first read it. This is something I plan on putting in the webzine soon, but as far as some of these other stories I have read, well, like I said, some of them are so outrageous that it can become hard to decipher the authentic ones from the ones that are total fantasy. That's why it would be great if I could get someone else's thoughts about some of these."

"Why don't you forward all the emails over to me so I could give you my opinion?"

"If you insist," I said and quickly highlighted almost ten pages of emails before shooting them to her address. I turned off my computer and spun sideways in my office chair towards Gina.

"It's pretty funny when I read this stuff and think about how crazy they sound. I mean, I'm one of the last people who would have believed my own story if I hadn't experienced it for myself."

"I was thinking about all of this the other day. This is a really unique time in history, basically like this new age of enlightenment," Gina added.

"Or we're just finally rediscovering old truths."

Gina hopped up from her chair excitedly and grabbed my hand. "Come on; get your keys, but leave your wallet."

"What? Where are we going?"

"Shhh. It's a surprise."

Driving eastward for fifteen minutes, we eventually pulled down a badly paved road that ran along the border of Mission Trails Park. I had never noticed the windy off street before or the lone stucco building hidden down by the edge of the gorge. While the structure looked like it had been someone's home at one time, the driveway had been expanded into a parking lot that now held several other cars. Once we stepped out of my truck, I could finally read the small sign by the door that read: Esterios Greek Café.

"Zach, this is a family-owned restaurant that has become one of my favorites. They have amazing pastichio."

"I have no idea what that is," I replied as we walked up to the entrance.

"Well, it's kinda like the Greek version of lasagna. I think you'll like it. And by the way, lunch is on me today."

"Now you're talking my language," I said, making Gina laugh.

Sitting outdoors on a quaint brick patio facing the mountains to the east, Gina explained how she had been fascinated about the way I communicated with The Ancestors. Since she was extremely open to the idea, I offered to show her the technique of how to establish contact after our meal, which caused her to become so excited that she didn't even finish her lunch.

Arriving back at my place, we sat down on a rug in the living room and I began demonstrating everything Bill had taught me. After almost an hour, our efforts to make contact proved unsuccessful and Gina stood up and began pacing the room.

"Zach, what's the problem?"

"I don't know. I actually haven't tried it in a couple of weeks. Just try to relax. I'm not sure everyone can do it," I said, trying to think of what may be hindering our attempts.

"I want to experience what you did; I want to see what you have seen..." She paused for a second before sitting down on her knees and grabbing my hand tightly. "Take me to the ranch, Zach."

"I can't do that."

"Why, not?"

"Because it's not my call," I said firmly.

"Don't you care about me?" She squinted at me through her long eyelashes.

"I had hoped it was obvious that I do."

"Well, you have a funny way of showing it."

Gina had always come across as so easy going that her immature reaction caught me by complete surprise. When I didn't answer her, she flung her hands up in the air. "What is it then? You can't trust me?"

"Gina, settle down. You are aware that I've been asked to keep the identity of the others a secret."

"Yeah, well, it's not like I'm the K.G.B."

"Look, we can try again to contact The Ancestors on our own. Maybe we should go out to the desert."

"Out to the desert, huh?" She softened her tone and her eyes relaxed. Looking down at the floor, she began moving toward me until she grabbed one of the buttons on my shirt and twirled it in her finger. "Just you and me. Out in the desert. All by ourselves?"

Pulling her close against my body, I whispered in her ear, "That's right, just the two of us."

"Okay..." she whispered back and rested her forearms against my chest.

"But do you think I could ever meet the couple at the ranch? They sound like such great people."

"They are," I said pulling back my head so I could see her face. "Look, next time I talk to them, I'll ask if I can bring you up."

"You will?" She said in a voice rising with hope.

"Sure. I can't promise anything, but I'll ask."

"Thanks," Gina said, but then quickly looked at her watch. "Shoot! I need to get over to the library."

"You do?" I said letting my chin drop to my chest.

"Yeah, I'm sorry, but I'm so behind. Hopefully we can get out to the desert soon, maybe later this week," she said rapidly grabbing her purse off the couch, and headed for the door. "Call me later?"

"Sure," I said, and slowly ambled to the front door to give her a good-bye kiss.

$$\oplus \qquad \oplus \qquad \oplus$$

RETREATING BACK TO MY STUDY, I noticed I had received an urgent email from my film agent regarding the movie deal. He had been trying to call me for the past couple of hours, but my landline had somehow got knocked off the hook and my cell phone had been on silent mode. Hoping that he had been able to reach the deal we were looking for, I frantically dialed his number.

"Zach Miller! You are going to be a happy man. Very happy!" Joel screamed so loudly I had to pull the receiver away from my ear.

"It's done?" I stood up quickly, gripping the phone.

"Let's just say that with your signing bonus alone you can start shopping for a home over in La Jolla."

"Yes!" I pushed the back of my office chair and spun it around.

"And it only gets better. I got you a higher residual on the royalty fee and this is where you are really going to get excited: the studio already hired none other than Sterling Hames to collaborate with you on the screenplay."

"Joel, you are The Man!"

"And you are absolutely correct," he cracked, making us both laugh.

"Now, they also told me that if you and Sterling can hammer this thing out in the next couple of months, they will start production by the end of this year."

"That's what I like to hear."

"I'm renting out this rooftop bar downtown this Friday night that can hold about two hundred people. Tell all your family and friends and we'll do this right."

"That sounds great. How 'bout I call you Wednesday and give you a list of names?"

"Can you bring that by our downtown office instead? Because you need to sign quite a bit of paperwork. That is, if you want to get paid."

"I will see you around ten."

"Congratulations, Zach! You deserve it, buddy," Joel finished.

Putting the phone down, I thrust both fists in the air before screaming, "Woohoo!"

Too excited to know what to do next, I began pacing in circles and rubbing my hands together. I wanted to share the news with all of my friends, but I couldn't decide who to call first. My attempts to reach Johnny and Gina went unanswered so I just left them each a message to get back with me as soon as possible. Dialing up the *Essence*, a longtime friend and a longtime art director at the magazine answered on the first ring.

"Rebecca, it's Zach Miller."

"How have you been, stranger?

"Couldn't be better, Rebecca. Sorry I haven't called, but it's been kind of awkward for me."

"No worries. Well, you sure fell into the story of a lifetime."

"You're not kidding—it's been an incredible ride so far."

"I can't begin to imagine. So when are you gonna finally stick your head in here for a visit?"

"Well, I was actually pretty bitter when I left which is honestly why I haven't come around, but you know what, I'm actually starting to believe now that things happen for a reason. Listen to this, I'm about to sign a huge movie deal and I wanted to invite you to a private party we are having this Friday."

"Congratulations!"

"Thanks. I don't have all the details about the party yet, but I'll email them later this week."

"Okay. I can bring the hubby, right?"

"Of course. How's everything been around the mag? How's ol' Harry?

"Same. He's been actually been a little more uptight than usual."

"Ouch. That doesn't seem possible," I said, laughing. "Do me a favor and forward my email about the party to Ken, Derrick and Dave. And you know, if you want to, go ahead and tell Harry about the million-dollar movie deal. But please, do it subtly. Like plaster a huge sign on his door for me."

Rebecca laughed before saying, "Consider it done. Maybe you should run an ad about the movie on our back cover."

"Ha. That would be classic."

"Okay, I'll let the guys know about your shindig. It's good to hear your voice, Zach. I'm glad you called."

"Thanks. It's going to be great seeing everyone again."

After hanging up with her, I immediately thought about Jack Norstrent. I had only talked to him a few times since meeting up at the ranch, but I knew he would want the update about the movie deal finally coming together. I looked forward to catching up with him and hoped he could attend the party, since he lived in San Diego. Unable to reach him by phone, I decided to get efficient and just email everybody.

Eager to start celebrating, I went down to Murphy's, hoping to run into the regulars. While I only saw Chris and Todd, they promised to let the others know about Friday night's bash as I left early after only a couple of beers.

The next morning while I made breakfast, I listened to an excited Johnny on my voicemail, asking me to call him back.

Pinching the phone between my shoulder and ear, I said, "Johnny, I hit the jackpot! I'm signing the deal with Trident Productions this week. Not only that, I'm going to be working on the screenplay with the guy who wrote *Even Odds* and *Cherokee Run*."

"That is incredible news!"

"On Friday my agent's throwing a huge fiesta downtown at this really posh rooftop bar," I said, scooping up my scrambled eggs from the frying pan to a plate.

"This is just what you wanted. Congratulations, Zach."

"Thanks. I got your messages from the other day and last night, but I couldn't reach you yesterday. What was it that got you so jazzed up?"

"A couple days ago I went down the trail at Black's Beach on the full moon and decided I would try to contact the aliens, just how you explained it to me."

"Really? I was just trying to show Gina and it didn't happen. It was actually pretty weird, and Gina left here kinda frustrated. So how'd it go with you?" I put Johnny on speakerphone and began eating.

"Man, I had the most incredible experience. I actually smoked a little herb before I went down there, you know, so I could have that relaxed state of mind. And, well, it was just awesome. It's hard to even explain."

"Try me."

"Yeah, I know you can relate. So, I was sitting there on my beach towel, legs all folded up in the lotus position and trying to think about nothing, which like you said, is way harder than it sounds. I ended up staring at the moon for like twenty minutes. I kept asking The Ancestors to speak to me over and over and the next thing I knew I felt as if I was floating above the sand. I knew my body was still on the towel, but I felt as if my soul was kinda floating above my body. It's almost like trying to explain to someone who has never surfed how riding inside the barrel can sometimes seem like you're in slow motion."

"So like a total out of body experience."

"Exactly. But the best part was what I ended up hearing, which of course didn't make total sense at the time, but now it's happening just like he told me."

"What was that?" I said, leaning closer to the phone.

"Basically he said how he knew that deep down I really had been searching for a soul mate; that my heart desired true love. He saw a past partner coming into my life again that would satisfy this longing I had. He also said that love costs and that I may lose a friend, but gain a lover."

"Hmm... well, that's a lot different than what I had expected." I slowly took a swig from my orange juice.

"I know. I figured if I did hear something it would be some general message for all mankind, something similar to the one you got. But when I thought about it, a lot of it actually made sense to me. I mean, as much as I like to see myself as a 'player,' I'd really like to have a wife."

"Did you bonk your head while you were surfing?" I laughed.

"I know that sounds crazy coming from me, but since then, things have been coming together just like he said."

"What? You met your wife?" I said almost coughing.

"I think so."

"Wait. Let me get this straight. Mr. 'I'll never get married' is telling me he just met his wife. What's her name?" I said, waiting for the punch line.

"It's Jenny."

"Is she like Cher, where she doesn't need a last name?"

"It's Jenny, Zach, you know her."

"Jenny Fitzgerald? What? You mean, *Todd's* fiancée, Jenny?" I dropped my fork onto my plate and instantly felt a knot in my stomach.

Johnny's silence on the other end confirmed my fears.

"Are you out of your mind? Todd is one of your best friends, Johnny!" I shouted.

"Well, I was with her before he was."

"A one night stand five years ago doesn't exactly qualify that you were with her."

"Well, it must have meant something to her, too, because I saw her the other night at a pub and, uh… We kinda hooked up," he said reluctantly.

"Oh, man, you didn't." The growing lump in my stomach pushed its way upward and I threw my napkin over my plate.

"Hey, listen. I know it sounds weird, but we just started talking and we both felt that connection. I mean, the next morning, I just started pouring my heart out to her and she said she felt the same way. She is actually coming over here tonight."

Still not wanting to believe it, I asked, "Does Todd know about this?"

"Not yet. Jenny felt like she made a mistake getting engaged and I guess she plans to talk to him soon."

"What about you? Are you gonna say anything, like hey, sorry Todd, but I'm gonna marry your fiancé?"

"Zach, it's not like it's that easy for me. I was having my doubts about all of this, but I got the affirmation I needed this morning."

"Affirmation?" I said, shaking my head.

"Yeah, listen to this; I have it right in front of me. I never read these things, but fate just led me to this today:

"For Scorpios—Outstanding luck in love marks the beginning of this new chapter in your life. Past lover comes back to make you interesting offers now through this month. Faithful partners are Aries and Virgo."

"Guess just who happens to be Aries? Jenny. Okay, now listen to the last part of this: "Things will change and be better, but you've got to do the hard thing and ask for what you want at the risk of hurting someone's feelings.

"You see, Zach, this whole scenario is laid right out before me. It's not going to be easy, but I can see now that it was meant to be."

"Really? Well, something crossed my mind while you read that. If she is a faithful partner because she is an Aries or whatever, doesn't that seem pretty contradictory of her since Jenny will be leaving her fiancé for you?"

"Well, that's just because he's not her soul mate. Hey, it's a lot better if this happens now than down the road and there were kids involved."

"Pffttt...do you even hear yourself?"

"Hey, I supported you when you received your message. This is what I received and I'm going to go with it. I can't help but follow my heart."

"I didn't tell you to go smoke a joint before you did it!" I said, indignant that he tried to somehow group our experiences together.

"I've smoked weed a thousand times before and never experienced anything close to this. I know what I heard and it wasn't because I got stoned an hour earlier. You act like I haven't even really thought about it."

"Yeah, I know Johnny." I let out a deep breath and began to massage my temples. "I'm just bummed for Todd. I mean, we're supposed to be in his wedding. And just so you know, I saw him and Chris last night at Murphy's and invited both of them to my party so I wouldn't show up with Jenny on your arm."

The awkward silence that followed made me think up a quick lie. "Hey, I forgot but I gotta get back to my agent right away about some paperwork."

"Alright. Later," Johnny said, hanging up abruptly.

Johnny's disclosure of his contact experience made me wonder whether he had actually heard from The Ancestors or if it was merely his drug induced imagination running off a cliff. Some of the physical aspects of his story sounded similar to other accounts relayed through my webzine, but the message he had received left me baffled.

Why would The Ancestors try to help Johnny in a way that would simultaneously wreck Todd's life? I thought.

Needing to get an explanation, I put my cell phone on silent and took my landline off the hook before heading to my bedroom. Back in the quiet of my room, I called out, "Ancestor, who is speaking to Johnny?"

I sat straining to hear something for at least ten minutes, but only the noise of a garbage truck outside, stopping and going between houses, broke the silence. Soon the blades of a helicopter whirring above my neighborhood caused me to grow impatient and I went back to my living room.

Pacing around the house for another ten minutes, I finally called Bill to get his thoughts.

"Bill, it's Zach. I kinda got a problem."

"What's going on?

"One of my close friends tried to contact The Ancestors, but he got a strange message about finding his soul mate."

"Well, that's actually how I found Gloria."

"Really? Well, she wasn't engaged to someone else at the time was she?"

"No."

"And that's the problem. My friend thinks that The Ancestors have been leading him toward the fiancé of one our close friends. I tried asking The Ancestors before I called you, but I didn't hear anything. I'm worried this might even be a message from the evil ones."

"Well, I can sense your frustration. But remember when I told you that you will get the answers that you really need to know at just the right time?"

"Yeah."

"This is probably one of those things. Look, I hate to cut you off, but I got a sick horse we are dealing with."

"Oh, okay. I'm sorry. I'll let you go," I said hurriedly.

"We'll talk soon."

Hanging up, I stood there perplexed.

While I had wanted to get some immediate insight into Johnny's experience, the unexpected message I was about to receive would soon require all of my attention.

CHAPTER 14

Announcing on my webzine's front page that a feature film was officially in the works, I now needed to rearrange the webpage's design to create a way for viewers to get updates on the film. Hesitant to call Johnny to get his advice on making the changes, I ended up working on it by myself for over five hours without the desired results. After grabbing a snack, I returned to my study in hopes of getting it right. Staring at the computer for over fifteen minutes with no idea of how to fix the site, I finally gave in and shut it down.

Too tired to even take a shower, I went straight to bed, but soon my deep slumber twisted into an unwelcomed dream.

"Zach, I have come to warn you. The woman you are seeing is not who she claims to be. You need to stay away from her. She works for those who are against us, who seek to expose and harm our family. Be careful and be wise."

My entire body convulsed, propelling me upward into a sitting position. With sweat dripping off my forehead, I rolled over to the other side of my bed to turn on the lamp and reached for my journal from inside the nightstand. Right as I grabbed the notepad, I shoved it back inside and slammed the drawer shut. The last thing I wanted to do was write down what I just heard.

Stay away from her? The words pressed hard against my chest and began to suffocate me.

Lying motionless in bed, I desperately tried to recall anything about Gina's behavior that appeared suspicious. Certain oddities came to mind, like how she always declined when I had offered to come over to her place. And it definitely still puzzled me as to why she couldn't establish contact with The Ancestors. Even though I wanted to rationalize the dream as a figment of my own imagination, I intuitively knew I should heed the warning.

Calling San Diego State University's registry first thing in the morning, I discovered there were five Gina Martinez's, and all but four were unlisted. While I had wanted to confront her in person about my dream, I also acknowledged that if she had been able to fool me this long, she would probably stick to the same story. The next day, I devised a plan to uncover her true identity.

INVITING GINA OVER LATER IN the week for lunch, I asked her to sit down on my couch so we could talk.

"Look, I contacted the couple over at the ranch and told them about you. How you were someone I cared deeply for and trusted. But when I told them about how you wanted to meet them, well…" I smacked my lips together and turned my eyes downward to fake my disappointment. "They felt that at this time it wasn't a good idea to bring you out."

"Well, when would be good?"

"They didn't say. But they also advised me not to take you out to the desert right now. They said you needed to be ready."

"Ready? They don't even know me," she said, raising her voice a little.

"I know. I know. But they have given me good advice up to this point so I…"

"So what?" You're just going to listen to them? This is ridiculous," she said, shoving up the sleeves of her sweater.

"You just have to be patient and understand…"

Gina stood up quickly. "Be patient? When you're ready, you can call me." Snatching her jacket off a chair, she stormed off to the door. "Until then, you can go out to the desert and have fun by yourself."

"Gina…" I let out a deep breath, trying to appear frustrated.

The door slapped shut behind her, causing my windows to rattle. Rushing over to look outside, I watched as she carelessly backed out of my driveway and came close to hitting a car parked on the street. Fortunately she skidded to a halt just in time before speeding off through my neighborhood.

Jogging out to my garage and hitting the door opener, I kick started my Kawasaki motorcycle and gunned it out of my driveway. The bike's powerful engine allowed me to catch her just as she approached the nearest on ramp. Since she had never seen my motorcycle, it seemed unlikely she could identify me, especially with my helmet and goggles on. Heading south on the freeway, she didn't make things easy for me by constantly changing lanes and blazing by everyone in her path. While confident that she wouldn't spot me, I still stayed back behind several cars, trying to stay out of her rearview mirror.

Once we got into downtown, trying not to lose her became even more difficult with the constantly changing traffic lights. Gassing it through a cross street, I nearly got whacked by a truck that failed to stop at an intersection. When I finally ended up directly behind Gina's car at the next light, she made an immediate right turn into a tall office building shielded by darkly tinted windows.

Gripping my handlebars tightly, I clung on to the hope that she was still who she claimed to be. That hope vanished as I watched her tail lights sink into an underground structure with the warning sign above: Parking Only for Employees of Federal Bureau of Investigation.

Staring into the dark hole where her car had disappeared, I flinched when the impatient driver behind me laid on his horn and I stalled out my bike. I kept my gaze down on the gas tank and kicked furiously while the car finally weaved around me just as I restarted my engine.

After driving straight ahead for several blocks, I came to a dead end at the harbor and parked the bike next to the sidewalk. Aimlessly ambling over to an old, empty dock, I sunk my chest against a rail and squinted into the glare of the water. With a mixture of emotions raging inside me, the railing's aged wood crumbled in my tightening grip, leaving my palms covered in a mix of tiny splinters and powdered white paint. I thought I had found a truly special woman in Gina and, unlike past relationships, had started to give her access to my heart. As I wiped my hands off on my jeans, I started to wonder if Gina hadn't shown me her real personality, the part of her that I had really been attracted to.

Faced with the reality that it didn't matter now, I stepped away from the ledge and sat down on an empty concrete bench. A lone seagull in flight caught my eye and I momentarily admired its effortless glide; the bird then swooped down, splattering my shoulder with the remains of its digested lunch.

As I sat there ignoring the fresh white streaks on my jacket, it was now painfully obvious why Gina could not contact The Ancestors earlier at my house. Leaning forward, I rested my forehead in the palms of my hands as I tried to think about what information she had possibly discovered and how they might use that information against us.

CHAPTER 15

Throughout the week leading up to the big party I actually contemplated cancelling the event. I had looked forward to going with Gina, but discovering she worked for the Feds was a kick to the gut, quelling my desire to celebrate. Knowing I needed to go anyway since I had invited so many people, I could only hope the rooftop atmosphere would help change my mood.

Standing by the bar near the entrance of the club, I was relieved that Johnny walked in without Jenny as only minutes later Todd followed suit with a crew from Murphy's. Meeting me over at the bar, Johnny shook my hand and asked, "Hey, where's Gina?"

"I'll tell you in a minute." I said, ordering him a beer before pulling him aside to a vacant corner of the roof that overlooked the shipyard.

"About five days ago, I had a vision warning me about her. I ended up following her and sure enough, she pulls right into the FBI building. I haven't talked to her since."

"What?" Johnny said almost spitting out his beer. "Are you serious?"

Pursing my lips, I shook my head, "Yeah. Can you believe that?"

"That's crazy. Your instincts were right when you said you were still being followed."

"Yeah, and as much as that infuriates me..." I paused and looked around almost embarrassed to admit what I was about to tell him. "My heart just sank when I saw her go in that building. I was really starting to fall for her and now I feel like a total sap."

"Zach, you can't let this get you down. Look, you're going to be a multi-millionaire. Let me repeat that: multiple millions. You'll definitely have no problems finding another woman."

"Yeah, I know," I said, grudgingly.

"And more importantly, people all over the world need you to tell them about The Ancestors. You can't let this set you back."

"You're right, Johnny, thanks."

"No problem. Let's go get another beer."

Knowing what Johnny said was true, I desperately wanted to put this whole Gina ordeal behind me. Thankful that so many people came out to congratulate me, I put on a good smile for the rest of the night. Unfortunately, every time I saw a couple together it made me think about her, so I ended up at the bar doing countless shots and getting rowdy with several friends. Pretending to celebrate, I instead made a conscious effort to numb the pain.

The next morning I awoke in a hotel room with my clothes on and no recollection of how I got there. However, my horrendous hangover certainly reminded me of why.

On the dresser I found a note from Todd that read, "Zach, you are classic. The pictures I took don't lie and yes, you can expect to be blackmailed. Ha, ha. The valets have your keys downstairs."

Oh brother, what did I end up doing last night?

Pulling into my driveway moments after noon, I still wondered if the house had been wired by Gina. My suspicions finally drove me to turn my house upside down looking for any surveillance devices. Although I didn't uncover anything suspicious, for the next few weeks I couldn't help but look over my shoulder every time I left the house.

$$\oplus \quad \oplus \quad \oplus$$

NEEDING TO GET AWAY FROM the distractions of life, I headed out to the mountains east of San Diego on a Monday afternoon to be alone with my thoughts. The brilliant January sky had brought perfect seventy-two degree weather to San Diego and I knew the mild temperatures this time of the year would follow me as I went eastward. On the way, I thought about calling Bill and Gloria, but decided against it since I didn't have a pre-paid phone with me. Reminiscing about my time with the two of them brought a smile to my face.

Driving on a winding single lane road through the Anza-Borrego Desert State Park, I pulled over several times to see if anyone trailed me. Now in a fairly desolate area, the only two vehicles that passed me appeared to be four-wheel drive enthusiasts, but they had gone by so fast that it was difficult to say for sure. Unable to determine if anyone had followed me, I knew I could not accomplish my goal if I continued to worry about it. By escaping out into the wilderness for the day, I wanted to not only commune with my Ancestors, but hoped I could somehow establish visual contact as well.

Right next to the pull-out, I located a trail that led to a lonely canyon and hiked down about quarter of a mile from the road before settling in a small clearing. Resting comfortably on an old, army sleeping bag I had brought, I enjoyed the warmth of the sun as the dry desert breeze blew gently against my face. A patch of wildflowers that broke through the rocky soil left me astonished as to how they could even survive in such a parched environment.

Dragging up one foot at a time and folding them across my thighs, I stared at a lone barrel cactus a few feet from where I sat and began the ritual of taking deep breaths. The crisp air that funneled down through the Cuyamaca Mountains carried a hint of sage, helping me relax. Almost immediately after closing my eyes, I experienced a bizarre sensation that I had instantly been transported into deep space.

My mind quickly shifted from shock to awe as I drifted by unknown planets and their moons. Curious at first as to what galaxy this was, I then noticed my speed gradually picking up as I started gravitating toward an intensely bright light in the distance. The other stars in my peripheral began to grow dimmer, eventually fading out as I drew closer and closer to the vast, glowing sphere.

Somehow along the way I became cognizant that this was not merely an inanimate ball of gas that awaited me, but rather some kind of entity that had a life of its own. Retaining an almost magnetic pull on my soul, the light soon enveloped me in a cocoon of absolute whiteness and a state of complete serenity.

Although I saw no visible beings, I heard a soft, placid voice say, "My child, it is good for you to be here. We want you know we have selected The Chosen One who will direct the earth out of its current state of misery. You will recognize him because there never has been anyone who can do what he will do. We will empower him to bring about our plan, proving once and for all what you already know in your heart to be true. He is the One the world must listen to or suffer grave consequences. The time is at hand. Rejoice! He is in your midst."

Immediately after I heard this, I found myself right back where I had sat down, gazing over the desert valley below me. Excited about what I had just seen and heard, I didn't want to forget a single detail, but now realized

I had left my pen and notebook in the truck. Rushing back up the steep hill, the sandy surface caused me to slip, falling down face first with my arms stretched overhead. After sliding a couple of yards on my stomach and shooting off the trail into some shrubs, I slowly began to push myself back up.

What took place next must have certainly been quicker than the blink-of-an-eye, but somehow seemed to only happen in slow motion. A large rattlesnake uncoiled from beneath the shade of a rock, launching at me and striking my outstretched wrist.

Petrified from the attack, I laid there motionless, staring at the two puncture wounds as the snake quickly slithered away into the brush. Uncertain of what to do next, I hiked cautiously up the hill as my entire hand swelled, burning with pain. By the time I got to the truck, my wrist had swollen to twice its normal size. While I tried not to focus on the reality that the nearest medical facility was at least twenty miles away, my good hand trembled as I put the keys into the door. After hearing a no signal sound in my attempt to call 911, I flung my cell phone to the passenger side's seat and started up the truck.

Tiny rocks sprayed out from under my spinning tires, enveloping my truck in a huge cloud of dust and making it difficult to see. A large thud came from underneath the vehicle as I bottomed out in a deep rivet right before the tires hit the pavement and I could only hope that I hadn't just done some serious damage. Recklessly veering down the wavy mountain pass for about ten minutes, the next rest area had me hitting the brakes so I could pull over and vomit out my half-opened door. Yanking my t-shirt off to wipe my mouth, I took several deep breaths in attempts to keep my heart from punching through my chest. Now sweating profusely, I stumbled out of the truck and my vision blurred as I desperately looked down the vacant road in hopes of an approaching car. With my arm now almost completely numb, I knelt to both knees on the side of the road and cried out to my Ancestor, "Help me!"

Fearing at first that the venom had caused me to hallucinate, I rubbed my eyes as I watched the swelling slowly decrease in my wrist. Almost immediately my heart rate lowered and my breathing began to steady. The only traces that I had even been bitten were the two small red pricks on my skin.

I climbed back into the truck, and sat stunned by what had just transpired. After a few minutes, I finally felt comfortable enough to drive ahead, but I found it difficult focusing on the sharp curves in front of me as I continued glancing down at my arm to see if any of the symptoms of the venom had returned. By the time I arrived to an extended straight-away, my appetite kicked in and I engulfed two granola bars and a small bag of chips that were stashed in my front seat.

Constantly replaying all the day's events, I was eager to return home, and post these wild turn of events on my webzine. Unsure of what was more astonishing, the miraculous healing or the amazing vision I had received, I realized that both had happened for a reason and knew the story would certainly benefit my readers. Nearing my home, I wondered how we could actually recognize this Chosen One the ancestors had just spoken of and when he would choose to reveal himself. Regardless of how those details would eventually unfold, I knew the entire world was about to witness some incredible things.

CHAPTER 16

A perfect winter storm had produced a generous ground swell that hit our coastline Friday afternoon and I made it over to catch several good waves right before the sunset. The long swim had left me ravaged and looking forward to preparing a feast when I got home. Driving into my neighborhood, my thoughts of what to eat were soon replaced with serious concerns as to what was going on inside my home.

Parked in the street outside my house, three dark sedans with government license tags sat vacant while a tall, odd shaped van occupied most of my driveway. From the side door of the van, two sets of thick, black cables ran along the ground up to my house, keeping my front door slightly ajar. After parking beside the van, I slammed my truck's door and marched up the sidewalk before being intercepted by a towering man in a blue suit and tie.

"Zach Miller, I'm Ted Smith from Homeland Security," he said, quickly flashing me some identification, but stashing it away before I could even verify it.

"What are you doing inside my house?"

"We are in the midst of conducting a search. We shouldn't be more than a couple more hours."

"I guess the Bill of Rights doesn't mean anything to you guys?" I said, staring up at him as the veins in my neck bulged.

"Mr. Miller, we now live in an extremely volatile environment, as I'm sure you're well aware of. Terrorists of every kind threaten life as we know it and it is our job to prevent all viable risks. But if it makes you feel any better, yes, we have a search warrant from a federal judge," he said, presenting a yellow envelope from his suit pocket.

"How do you view me as a possible menace when I haven't even said or done one thing that would threaten anyone?" I said, pushing the envelope away.

"Please step inside so we can continue this conversation," he calmly stated, turning sideways to allow me to pass him.

Several men with special instruments were scattered throughout my house trying to get readings. Two had been specifically assigned to the contents of my desk and had consequently divided my personal computer into sections along the hallway floor.

"You guys are wasting your time. You're not going to find anything that I haven't made public knowledge already," I said loudly. Both of the guys in the hallway looked at me briefly before returning to focus on their task.

Turning back to Smith, I pleaded, "You never answered my question. How can you guys see *me* as a threat?"

"That's what we're here to investigate. We can't determine yet whether we view you and those you have reported about as a genuine threat to National Security."

I sat down on my couch and tried to take a more passive approach. "Well, everyone I have written about is all about peace."

"However, you have reported that these aliens plan to come and forcibly remove citizens from their homes, and your most recent posting is about a new leader arriving and taking control of our nation. It's only logical for us to consider such talk as hostile. You may have thought you were merely reporting on the events that you saw, but you have to understand that it would be easy to view you as a co-conspirator. So, the more you cooperate with us, the better your chance at leniency."

"Hey, I'm not guilty of anything. Last time I checked, freedom of speech was still part of the Constitution," I said, wringing my fingers.

Smith clenched his squared-off jaw line tightly and squinted at me through his thick, black frames.

"Look, there's nothing we can do to stop their plan," I continued. "What you may see now as hostile, you will later come to see as necessary."

"That's the kind of rhetoric we hear from religious fundamentalists and that, Mr. Miller, is exactly why we're here." He removed his glasses and casually cleaned the lenses with a tissue.

I buried my face in my hands and slumped over in disbelief at what was happening. Noticing in my peripheral that Mr. Smith had started jotting down something in a small notepad, I slammed my fist into the coffee table.

"Well, why did you wait until now? You let me go on more than forty talk shows, spilling my sinister message and you just wait? With police work like that in this country, no wonder 9/11 happened."

Apparently I had struck a nerve as Smith flexed his muscular jaw and took a deep breath through his nose before coolly affirming, "You, of all people should recognize that we're not dealing with an everyday occurrence. We've tried to be as thorough as possible. You've been under surveillance for some time now, Mr. Miller."

"Oh, thanks for the news flash. I'm on to your good friend Gina Martinez."

"You mean her?" He pointed down the hallway to a woman who had just come out of my study.

I jerked my head sideways and saw "Gina" in the hallway, holding one of my file boxes.

Glancing back at me coldly, her expressionless eyes reiterated that our relationship had been strictly business.

As she returned back into the study, Ted continued. "Not to alarm you, but we've been monitoring several foreign agencies watching you as well. You should be thankful we wouldn't allow anyone to take you out of the country."

"I would be thankful if I thought you had the right motives," I said, cocking my head.

"Mr. Miller, you have maintained the statement that you don't know the exact whereabouts of the ranch. It is imperative that we talk with the owners of this ranch, so please tell us all that you know."

"You can't contact them and neither can I," which was a lie, but I didn't feel like indulging this guy. "Besides, they couldn't tell you anything that I haven't publicly stated already."

"Let us be the judge of that, Mr. Miller."

"Well, I can't tell you because, as I'm sure you have read, I was blind-folded when I went up there."

"Just tell us what you know." He clicked his pen in anticipation of what I would share.

"It's northeast of San Diego. Possibly four, maybe even eight hours drive..." I paused and held my chin pensively. "Umm, yep, that's about it."

Smith shot a look at one of the other suits who had also started taking notes over at my dinner table. The man got up knowingly, reached into a black leather bag and pulled out a stun gun before walking over to stand behind the couch.

Leaning forward, Smith slowly rubbed his hands together before pressing a fist inside the palm of his other hand. "We would obviously prefer to do things the easy way here, Mr. Miller, but we can also...."

"So, what?" I asked, shifting in my seat as my eyes danced between the two men. "You're going to torture me until I tell you what I don't even know."

Before I could even say another word, Smith nodded at the man behind me who obediently plunged the device into my neck. The four point five million volts threw me to the floor, causing me to flop around uncontrollably and bang my head into a leg of the coffee table. As I writhed in pain on the rug, his assistant methodically reached into his bag again to retrieve a syringe. I didn't feel the injection, but the pharmaceutical cocktail soon had its way with me and I began talking with the agents as if they were a couple of old friends.

Naturally, the details of that discussion remain hazy and I don't recall how it ended. Awaking in the middle of the night from a cold breeze blowing through an open window, I found myself alone curled up on the couch. Crippled by an intense narcotic hangover, I found it took several minutes before my eyes could regain focus. The government thugs were long gone, leaving my house in the same order they had found it. As I looked around, I became suspicious that everything appeared a bit too nice and tidy. Maybe they got what they were looking for, but it seemed fishy how they had conveniently left my hard drive here.

Rubbing the back of my neck to ease my aching head, I could only wonder what I had ended up actually telling them. Somewhat relieved that I had previously encrypted everyone's email addresses, I also had to acknowledge the very real possibility that the FBI's experts could break my codes. Since all of my calls and letters had certainly been traced over the last several months, I felt fortunate at least that Bill and Jack had continued using disposable cell phones.

Rising sluggishly from the couch, I saw a business card propped up against the lamp that read: Ted Smith, Senior Investigator, Homeland

Security. Flipping it over, I read his short note: Thank you for your cooperation. Please call me if there is anything else you would like to talk about."

His cute remark made the pain on top of my head radiate down into my temples.

What a freakin' Nazi! I thought.

Walking lightly to the kitchen to grab a couple of aspirins, I contemplated any legal recourse I could take, but it was a snowball's chance in Haiti that I would ever be able to bring those guys to justice.

Moving down the hallway to my study, I turned on my computer, relieved to find that all my files seemed intact. Extremely uncomfortable as the painkillers had little effect, I pressed forward so I could swiftly relay on my web page what had just transpired here. Needing to ostensibly protect the identity of certain people, I avoided writing anyone directly and could only hope that all my friends who I had met on the ranch would read my message.

> This is a note of <u>warning</u> to those who have met me personally and who know the truth. I will not elaborate on why I am writing this but, against my will, I may have given away information that could possibly jeopardize your privacy and civil rights. I trust you know that I would never do anything to bring any of my friends into harm's way. I hope this note will reach you and give you ample warning.
>
> Sincerely, Zach Miller

The bright glare of my computer caused me to turn it off and I sat rubbing my temples, wondering if this warning would end up helping anyone. It seemed fairly evident that if the U.S. Government wanted to find someone, they had more than enough resources to do so. As I thought about the tyranny that my own "democratic" government had demonstrated to me, I began to dwell on all the injustices that tyrannical regimes around the world had exhibited over the ages. For thousands of years, the entire human race had been dominated by the iron-fisted few who held all the power.

Staring back up at my blank computer screen, I remembered what my Ancestor had told me about the chosen leader who would come and free us from this oppression. Those words proved encouraging as I thought about a world leader who would truly care about the interest of all people and could establish a lasting peace. He would promptly chase the current despots out of office and finally establish a righteous government.

DEVOTED TO WRITING ARTICLES OVER the next couple of weeks, I became increasingly determined by the many supportive responses I received. I allowed my work to consume me as it helped me not to dwell on the negative things that had happened to me recently. When I hadn't heard of anyone else I knew being harassed by the FBI or Homeland Security, my confidence somewhat increased that no one had been jeopardized by any of my inadvertent confessions. Instead of quenching my desire to share the Ancestors' message, the government intrusion only fueled my resolve to stand firm and push on.

My ongoing phone conversations with award-winning writer Sterling Hames proved to be invigorating. Extremely enthusiastic about the movie project, he had made plans to relocate to San Diego in six weeks so we could begin the writing. I offered him one of my extra rooms in the house I would be purchasing in La Jolla and he gladly accepted. Ecstatic that I would soon be working with him on an everyday basis, I looked forward to seeing him craft his art.

With the prospect of working on the greatest endeavor of my life, things were finally coming together. Like the calm before the storm, I couldn't foresee how quickly my world would start to fall apart.

CHAPTER 17

The loud echo of someone's voice caused me to rise from my study and hurry down the hallway. Knowing it had to be someone leaving a message on my answering machine when I approached the kitchen, I barely recognized the scratchy voice on the speaker and I picked up the phone right before he hung up.

"Zach," Johnny moaned.

"Buddy, what's wrong?"

"You didn't hear? Todd's dead. He shot himself three days ago," his voice broke and he began sobbing.

"What? No!" I gasped. The painful lump immediately constricted my throat and I couldn't utter another word.

After a couple minutes of shocked silence, Johnny swallowed hard as he tried to compose himself. "The funeral is tomorrow, but I can't even bring myself to go."

"It's not your fault," I said, trying to sound convincing, even though I really felt otherwise.

"Yes it is, Zach. Don't you see? It's really all of our faults."

"Johnny, we can't beat up ourselves because we weren't there to stop him."

"I'm not talking about that. I mean, if I wouldn't have listened to those aliens, I would've never gone after Jenny and none of this would've ever happened."

"Johnny, I'm not sure you heard from The Ancestors, maybe you..."

"That's bull! I heard them just like you heard them. Zach, you're just as much to blame because you're the one who told me how to contact them!" Johnny shouted.

"I'm the one who told you *not* to hook up with Jenny, remember! Don't blame me because you were so freaking blind you couldn't even see that it was wrong!" I yelled back.

Johnny sniffled as he sat silent on the other end for a moment. Now calmer, his voice still cracked, "I can see that now. I take full responsibility for what I did. But I was misled and you had a part in that, whether you want to admit it or not."

Gripping the phone tightly, I shook my head and clenched my teeth, so I wouldn't say something rash. While there had never been any drama or tension between us since becoming friends in high school, an unsettling resentment began to take root in my heart toward Johnny. He had made a flat out foolish and selfish decision, but his attempt to shift the blame on me for his actions made me livid.

"Where's the funeral gonna be?" I finally said.

"Somewhere near Dana Point? Call Lindsey for the details," Johnny said, letting out a deep breath.

Wanting to say the right thing, I asked, "Hey, are you gonna be okay?"

"Yeah," Johnny's replied in a hushed tone

"Well, I plan on going, so if you change your mind and wanna ride up together…"

"Man, I can't show my face around there. Todd's brother wants to kill me."

Given Todd's younger brother Dave's violent history, I could understand Johnny's concern.

"Okay, well…" I said, not knowing how to respond.

"I gotta get off the phone. Talk to you later."

⊕   ⊕   ⊕

THE MARINE LAYER BLANKETING THE canyons around my home was unusually thick the next morning and I wanted nothing more than to roll over and go back to sleep. While dreading the day ahead, I needed to hurry and meet up with my friend Mickey so we could carpool up to the funeral service.

Driving toward Todd's hometown of San Clemente, a coastal town about an hour north of San Diego, Mickey relayed some of his fond memories since first meeting Todd in high school. Even though they had gotten in a fist fight with each other their junior year over a girl, during the past ten years they had traveled together on numerous ski trips and fishing excursions, becoming close friends.

In contrast, I had only come to know Todd a few years ago, but had instantly liked him the day we met. Thinking back, I couldn't even remember a moment when I saw Todd exhibit a sour attitude or even talk badly about someone.

While I felt it was good for us to reminisce on the good memories we had shared with Todd, Mickey eventually turned our conversation back to why we were here.

"Man, I still can't believe he's gone. It all seems like a bad dream that I keep hoping I'm gonna wake up from," Mickey said, shaking his head.

"Yeah it still feels almost dreamlike to me. I only heard about it yesterday so it's like it really hasn't sunk in yet. I just keep wondering if there was something I could have done. I mean, I don't think anybody could've seen it coming knowing Todd, but…" I was still trying to form my thoughts when Mickey interrupted.

"You know, I've tried hard not to be judgmental, but Johnny really screwed up. He flat-out stabbed Todd in the back," Mickey said, grabbing the steering wheel tightly with both his hands.

Up until now, I had been looking at Mickey as he talked, but when the discussion turned to the subject of Johnny, I averted my gaze out the passenger window. "I know. But what can we do about that now? What's done is done."

"It's just so hard to understand. I mean, I never thought Johnny would do something like that."

"Yeah, me neither," I said softly.

"Well, he better watch his back. You know what I'm saying?" He said, and his jaw tightened.

"I just talked to Johnny yesterday and he said he thinks Dave may try to kill him," I said turning toward Mickey to gage his response.

"Who could really blame him?"

"But what good would that really do? Johnny feels horrible because of what happened and you know it's not going to bring Todd back."

"Well, it's not like I'm trying to condone it. It's just that I can't imagine the hurt and anger Dave's going through. He's jacked people up for a lot less, you know."

"Yeah," I said, remembering a night at Murphy's where some poor guy had made the mistake of staring at Dave's girlfriend for a little longer than he should have. Dave had nonchalantly slammed a beer bottle over the guy's head, and would have done even more damage if Todd had not intervened.

I wanted desperately to change the subject, but Mickey continued his rant.

"Johnny's got some serious bad karma coming his way. Some of Todd's friends may not actually kill Johnny, but I could see plenty of them wanting to kick his teeth in," he said.

"I think Johnny's gonna be lying low for a while."

"He should move out of the country," Mickey added.

"You know, as much as I hate what Johnny did, I have to remember he's a human being, like you and me. He made a huge mistake and he's the one who will have to live with this the rest of his life. I don't think railing on him is going to make anyone feel better."

While I didn't especially like having to defend Johnny, I knew dwelling on the "what ifs" and "whys" certainly didn't help anyone.

⊕　　⊕　　⊕

THE WARMTH OF THE SUN finally breached the heavy cloud line, but went completely unnoticed by those walking up to the historic Cathedral Basilica of St. Anne. The entrance led us through a corridor lined with white concrete columns, large arching doorways, and wrought iron chandeliers hanging from the ceiling. Instead of a calming effect, the cold, gothic architecture only magnified this tragedy.

Inside the main sanctuary, a twenty foot wooden carving of Jesus hung on an invisible crucifix, suspended midair high above the pulpit, made me want to look anywhere but up at the grotesque figure. An elderly lady in the front row cried hysterically as she leaned on Chris' shoulder and I instinctively knew it was Todd's mother. Sitting down immediately next to Mickey, I kept my gaze down as I continually wiped my wet face on my shoulder sleeve.

A middle-aged priest wearing a long, black ceremonial robe walked solemnly out in front of the congregation and stood beneath the Jesus statue. With everyone quietly focused up front, even the slightest sounds from the crowd echoed off the coved ceiling a hundred feet above us.

The priest began the funeral as if reading a script, flipping back and forth between Latin and English. Doing what all clergy do, he spoke favorably about the deceased, even though I'm sure he probably never knew Todd. A few minutes into his monotone speech, I don't remember anything he actually said. I didn't need to. No one needs a priest to understand that there is nothing more tragic than when someone like Todd takes his own life.

MICKEY AND I DECIDED TO forego the burial, and headed back to San Diego. Neither of us said a word until about half way home when Mickey suggested that we grab some grub at a fast-food drive-thru. On the cup of our soft drinks, a cartoon drawing portrayed an alien aircraft beaming up some hamburgers into a ship. I hadn't even noticed it until Mickey pointed to the animation and asked, "Your friends frequent this place?" he said, cracking a smile.

"They know a good burger when they see one," I said, which caused Mickey to chuckle. My little quip seemed to help lighten the mood that had been weighing us down all day.

"Hey, Lindsey told me you started up some webzine, but I haven't checked it out yet."

"Yeah, it's been really interesting, but way more work than I anticipated."

"So, do you, uh, see these aliens often or what?" Mickey asked, keeping his eyes on the road ahead. He backtracked to make his thoughts more clear. "To me, it's obvious you saw what you saw. I mean, who could really argue with all the photographic proof you have and everything. I've wanted to ask you some questions, but it's not like I've had the chance to really sit down with you after that all happened. Plus I didn't want to annoy you since everyone and their grandmother has wanted to talk to you. I'm sure you're tired of answering the same old questions."

"Well, it's a lot easier just talking to people you know, but when you tell the world the most bizarre sounding story of the century, maybe even in all of history, then everything that comes with being that storyteller can start to really wear you down. That's basically why I started the website, so I could control the format and, just like you said, not have to answer the same questions over and over."

"I'm sure it's annoying having to deal with people who don't believe your story."

"The religious fanatics are the worst. I've been called everything under the sun. I love all these Christians who preach love, then turn around and say I'm a blasphemer, that I'm the Anti-Christ. It's all pretty ridiculous," I said, before stuffing my mouth with more French fries.

"Yeah, Johnny told me your sister became one of those born-again Christians. That must make for a strange dinner atmosphere."

"Well, it's pretty odd, but Vanessa is cool. Don't get me wrong. We've definitely had our differences of opinion; a lot of people from her church think that The Ancestors are demons, which is strange in itself when you hear other pastors from Unitarian Churches, Episcopalian, you name it, say that they think The Ancestors are really God's angels. I think it's their way of trying to explain what they don't understand. Anyway, my sister and I have had some lengthy discussions and even though she is adamant about what she believes, we still have a great relationship. Vanessa's okay in my book."

"So, Zach, I have a question for you?"

"Shoot."

"What do these aliens say about where we go from here when we die?"

"I've actually had bits and pieces of it answered for me, but let me try to explain it as I understand it. It's kind of like we are this source of energy, I guess what some call the soul, and we're going through the universe basically picking up information wherever we are. Our spirit just keeps evolving onto higher levels. This stuff is kind of hard to fully comprehend and what I've learned I actually heard explained from The Ancestors, and by others who have told me about their contact experiences. It's something I'm still trying to learn more about."

Mickey's straw made a gurgling noise in the ice at the end of his empty cup before he added, "That's pretty wild."

"You'll have to check out my website so you can read all the different stories. A few weeks ago I published a story explaining how people can contact the aliens for themselves." I immediately regretted that I had brought this part up as it made me think about Johnny.

"Really? I'd like to check that out."

"Yeah, well, you should definitely be cautious about doing it and make sure that you're ready."

"What do you mean?"

"Not everyone is ready for it, and I'm not sure everyone can contact them, either. Hey, all this traffic must be for the Chargers game. Flip on the radio to see when the game starts." I said, trying to change the subject.

"Good call. I almost forgot that they were having the game on Saturday this week. They should have a good team this year."

"I haven't really had the chance to follow any sports lately, but I want to get back into it."

Bringing up football provided a great diversion because it helped me deflect my thoughts from what continued to disturb me. I still couldn't grasp what had gone wrong with Johnny's contact experience and it didn't jell with everything I had learned.

While his strange experience raised several questions, one left me especially confounded: how were other people supposed to even discern whether they were hearing from The Ancestors or The Evil Ones?

DURING THE FOLLOWING WEEK, MY bitterness toward Johnny was replaced by concern when he didn't return my calls about fixing my webpage. Frustrated by another unsuccessful attempt to reach him by phone, I finally decided to drive over to his apartment to find him. I had just prepared to leave my house when I heard the distinct sound of Johnny's eight-cylinder truck roaring into my driveway before rumbling to a stop. Peering through my front window, I watched him stumble dejectedly up the sidewalk so I turned around, tossing my keys back on the table and yelled for him to come in.

With his head down and not saying a word, he sat down on my couch, staring at the floor. As I crossed by the couch to the adjacent lazy boy chair, it smelled like I had walked into a cloud of hard liquor.

"Hey, I've been trying to call you. Did you get my messages?" I asked.

"Yeah, I haven't felt much like talking," Johnny muttered.

"Okay, so what's up?" I said, leaning forward and wondering if he would actually open up.

"I was already in your neighborhood so I figured I'd drop by to tell you that I'm gonna split out of here."

"What? Where?"

"I'm going to move up north of Frisco. I got a cousin who can let me stay at his place and help me find some work. I gotta get out of here."

"Well, are you going to keep your place or keep your stuff in storage or... is this like something you think is permanent."

"I plan on taking everything. If I need something out of storage, it's going to be a pain to get it if I have to drive down here."

"So, uh, when do you think you're moving?"

"In the next week. No sense on paying rent for next month," he said, keeping his gaze on the rug beneath his feet.

"That makes sense," I replied and nodded while trying to think of something to say.

"Jenny and I are through. She came over and said she just felt like we went too fast and I don't know, just needed to step back and be friends," he said bluntly. "And well, you know all the lame things you say to someone who you don't want to see anymore. I guess I should've seen it coming, but..." He let out a sigh of disgust.

"Hey, we all make mistakes."

"Yeah, well, this one just tops them all. It makes me feel like my whole life has been one big mistake." His voice began to shake as he continued. "I ruined the life of a great friend. I'm the one that deserved to die."

Johnny's confession shocked me to silence.

His eyes flooding with tears, he suddenly stood and headed to the door. "I gotta start packing."

"Are you sure you're okay to drive. You can stay here and I'll make some breakfast.

"Don't worry. I'm sober." he said before walking out to his truck, and I quietly followed behind him to the driveway.

Once inside the truck, Johnny leaned up against the steering wheel, placing his palms face down on the dashboard. Continuing to stare down into his lap, he began to pour out his heart.

"I had a dream the other night, Zach. It was so weird because I was like half awake, but the dream felt so real. I've been pretty tripped out by it and it's really the reason I haven't called. I heard a voice say that there was a way out from all this grief. It said that I could finally get the peace and rest I wanted. Since then, not a day has gone by that I don't think about going out to my garage, turning on my truck and just going to sleep."

Leaning into his cab, I grabbed him by the shoulder and tried to get him to look me in the eyes. "Johnny, listen to me, your mind is playing tricks on you. You need this to stick in your head: suicide is a permanent solution to a temporary problem. I know you feel terrible right now, but it's gonna get better."

Johnny glanced at me before turning his eyes down toward the floor.

"That's easy for you to say. You don't feel the pain I do. You don't have to live with the guilt that I have."

He paused for a moment before trying to sound more rational. "That's why I need to get outta here. Get a new start."

"Yeah, moving up there will help you get your head on straight. Time will heal this; you have got to know that. And listen, if you need to talk, I don't care what time it is, you call me. Just please whatever you do, don't go and kill yourself. You're my best friend and it would crush *me* ..." My hand weakened its grip on his shoulder as my voice began to break off.

He finally turned toward me, his bloodshot eyes welling up with tears again. "Thanks for always being a good friend, Zach."

Pausing to get a hold on my emotions, I tapped the hood of his truck as if I had come up with an idea. "Look, why don't we take that trip down to that fishing village in Baja for a few days that you mentioned."

Johnny nodded his head, but didn't say anything.

"Or, you know, just a quick surf session or anything you want to do." I said grasping for something that might temporarily distract him from this heartache.

Johnny merely attempted a half smile and turned the ignition.

As I watched him drive away, my trivial suggestions of how to help him left me feeling powerless. Biting my lip, I felt like I was watching a condemned house teetering on the edge of a cliff and wondered how long before the weight of Johnny's guilt would push him over the edge.

CHAPTER 18

My concerns about Johnny's state of mind continued to grow as he didn't respond to my emails or return any of my calls over the next week. When I finally did hear back from him, he had already relocated to Jenner, a small community near Santa Rosa, CA. Reluctant to speak to me, his voice still carried the disheartened tone from when I last saw him. I tried to lighten up our conversation by asking about the nearby surf spots I had heard about, but nothing I said could change his mood.

He asked me if I would pick up some mail and a paycheck from his last client in San Diego when I got the chance. Glad to do him the favor, I got his new address and advised him to call me after he had received it. While I knew he probably needed the money, I really wanted him to call back so I could know how he was holding up.

Around two weeks after I had mailed the check to him, I received a confusing message from Johnny who slurred so badly I could only make out half of what he said. He babbled something to the effect that he couldn't find enough work and how things weren't getting any better. Admitting that he couldn't shake off the guilt that he felt over Todd's death, he said there was no point of trying to go on. He wanted me to know that I was like a brother to him and he loved me, but when he started to cry I couldn't understand the rest of his message. After he abruptly hung up, I tried desperately to call him back, but continued to receive a busy signal after about five attempts.

An operator informed me that the phone appeared to be off the hook and I yelled, "Oh, no!" Clueless as to what to do next, I tried to call Vanessa's cell phone.

"Vanessa, I need your help! I think Johnny might kill himself," I said rapidly.

"What? Where is he?" she gasped.

"He's up in Jenner. It's a small town north of San Fran. Can you call the local police and tell them to go over to 134 Sycamore Street?"

"Are you sure you have good reason to believe he'll actually do this?"

"Trust me. He thinks he's responsible for the suicide of our friend Todd. He just left a voice mail that sounded like a 'goodbye forever' message."

"Oh my. Let me grab a pen." Her voice became anxious. After I gave her the address again, she hurriedly said, "Alright, let me make some calls. Keep trying to call him and see if you can email him or something. I'll call you back in ten minutes, okay?"

"Okay. Thanks," I said, hanging up, and re-dialed Johnny's number. I cursed my phone out loud every time I heard the obnoxious beeping of the busy signal. Unable to sit still, I paced back and forth across my living room while jabbing a small pillow from my couch with my fist. Fifteen minutes later my phone rang and I rushed over to it hoping somehow it would be Johnny.

"Zach," Vanessa said, "I was able to get the local police to head that way and check things out. They said they'll call me back after the patrol car gets out there. Were you able to reach him?"

"No, I guess the phone's still off the hook. I wish there was something I could do because it's driving me nuts just sitting here and not knowing."

"Yeah, I know. The police captain himself told me they would call me back once they know something. I'll tell you what. I'm going to come over and keep you company until we hear back."

"Okay. That sounds good…" I exhaled deeply… "It's been a terrible last couple of weeks. We just buried my friend Todd and I couldn't handle losing Johnny."

"Hey, nothing's happened. Let me tell you something. I'm going to call some friends from church to pray about this situation. So, you just sit tight and I'll be over as soon as I can."

"Thanks," was all I could muster.

Around thirty minutes later, my sister's car arrived and I anxiously walked out to meet her. Vanessa closed her car door and jogged over to inform me she hadn't heard anything from the police in Jenner. Seeing the concern in my eyes, Vanessa put her arm around me as we walked into my house. After we sat down on the couch, I shared some of the details of how Johnny had arrived at this desperate stage and how nothing I had said to him lately seemed to help.

"Zach, this is kind of hard to explain, but after I prayed about this, I had an overwhelming peace come over me. I have a good feeling that everything is going to be okay. I've never really experienced that before. I mean, usually, I just pray for something and, well, I leave it in God's hands. I really don't know what will happen, but I trust God that it will work out according to His good and perfect will. That might not make any sense to you right now, but I just…" Vanessa suddenly reached down to pull her cell phone from her pants pocket and looked at the incoming number. "It's from Jenner," she said.

"This is Vanessa Miller," she answered formally. After several seconds she responded, "Okay, thanks you for all your help."

After hanging up, she looked back at me. "Zach, they went out there and couldn't find anyone in the house. Apparently Johnny's truck was in the driveway, but no one responded to their knocks."

"They didn't go in the house?

"Zach, they can't just enter into the house without probable cause."

"They certainly can. They've busted into my house, went through all my stuff, drugged me..."

"What are you talking about?" she interrupted.

"Forget about it! You work for the man." I said, thrusting my finger at her before hurrying back to my study. Firing up my computer, I bought an airline ticket to the Bay Area and arranged for a rental car in less than five minutes.

Meanwhile, Vanessa remained seated on the couch for a few minutes before leaning her head into the doorway where I sat.

"Zach, talk to me. I know you're upset, but I have no idea what you are even talking about."

"Just forget it. I'm going to go up there myself," I said.

"Okay. I'll just keep praying."

"You do that," I said, concentrating on the map on my screen.

After printing out the directions, I turned around to where Vanessa stood silently.

"Look, I'm sorry, Vanessa. I'm just freaked out right now. I appreciate you coming over and helping as much as you could."

"I wish I could do more."

Her graceful response made me ashamed of my rudeness so I walked over and gave her a quick hug. "Look, I gotta pack a quick bag; my flight leaves in less than an hour."

"Call me as soon as you get up there."

"I will."

ALTHOUGH FORTUNATE TO GET A flight up north on such short notice, I was worried about driving in the Bay Area as I heard the traffic had been completely hectic since the most recent earthquake. With a copy of the city's newspaper under my arm, I boarded the plane with hopes of immersing myself in some local news stories and diverting my thoughts away from the possibilities of what I would face when I arrived at Johnny's.

Once airborne, the first article that caught my eye was a statistical report on the rapid increase of terrorist attacks in North America. While my head spun as I learned that over the last two years the occurrences had actually tripled, the second story I read caused me to be sick to my stomach.

Doctors everywhere were extremely perplexed by a new epidemic similar to SARS that was spreading like wildfire through central Africa. With no cure in sight, it was proving to be so unbearably painful that many of the victims were simply taking their own lives.

Instead of taking my mind off the prospect of finding my best friend's dead body, I was again confronted with the purpose of my trip. Folding the paper, I tossed it below my seat and began staring through the small window into the dark, empty sky. I wondered where in this infinite universe The Ancestors were right now and when they would finally come to deliver us from this wicked world. Flicking off my overhead light, I shut my eyes and tried to think about the positive things The Ancestors had told me.

While I had never tried to contact my guardian Ancestor in a public setting, I couldn't think of a better time to try since I so desperately needed their help. Fortunately, the seat next to me sat vacant and the flight attendants didn't bother me as I pretended to sleep.

Not knowing where to even begin, I ended up praying, "Ancestor, my friend Johnny is in Jenner, California and in big trouble. I'm worried he might kill himself. Please help him."

My guardian Ancestor's distinctive voice replied, "Zach, my peace I leave with you. Remember, I am with you always."

Desiring further direction, I kept my eyes shut and continued waiting another fifteen minutes, but heard nothing else. While his voice had always had a calming effect, my feet began tapping the floor rapidly as I now questioned how much The Ancestors could help in this situation.

The scheduled hour and a half flight ended up taking over five hours. San Francisco's infamous thick fog had slipped in and hid the runway, causing us to be held over in Reno.

I could have driven up here faster than this! I thought.

With the constant public announcements ringing through the terminal, sleep proved impossible during the layover and I ended up walking in countless circles over the next few hours. Once we boarded the plane again, an exhausted silence filled the cabin until we landed in Oakland at 3:45 the next morning.

As I threw my bag into a rental car, a surprising boost of adrenaline came over me and helped me to stay focused on the road ahead. Speeding up the freeway north of the city, I could only hope for a sympathetic highway patrolman if I got pulled over.

Once I got within five minutes of Johnny's cousin's home, the sun began to rise over a nearby peak, revealing a vacant countryside. With no houses within a couple of miles, I could see how this isolated area could have helped lead Johnny into an even deeper state of depression. As I remembered Johnny's message, how I was like a brother to him and that he loved me, my heart ached at the thought that I had missed the chance to say the same to him.

My pulse immediately spiked when I saw Johnny's truck parked outside a small brick house and I slowed down to pull into the driveway. Hesitating to step out of my car, I quickly surveyed the yard for any signs of Johnny before approaching the house.

The old wooden stairs squeaked as I gently trotted up the front porch and peered into one of the screenless windows. The agitated cawing of a crow in flight startled me before it settled on an old oak tree in the front yard. I glanced back at the bird and caught his beady black eyes staring me down as if I didn't belong here.

Turning my attention back inside, I noticed an almost empty bottle of bourbon sitting on the small, round dining room table. Next to it stood a tall, red water pipe, undoubtedly used to smoke marijuana. I scanned the rest of the house for any signs of Johnny and became alarmed when I spotted a pistol lying on the kitchen counter. The screen door lightly screeched as I cracked it open and reached through to the front door, but a deadbolt kept it from budging. Not wanting to break a window if I didn't have to, I walked around back to try my luck.

Coming around the house to the back patio, I saw the outline of a body lying perfectly still in a rocking chair. With his head cocked awkwardly to the side and his legs dangling off the edge of the chair, I held my breath as I approached the limp body. Afraid to touch his corpse, I found myself half whispering "Johnny." When his lifeless body didn't respond, I fell to one knee in front of him and groaned "No, Johnny!"

Johnny's whole body shuddered, causing the chair to jerk sideways and his eyes fluttered open.

"Zach?" Johnny said, straining to focus.

"Yeah, yeah it's me... Geez, I almost had a heart attack," I said holding my chest, and collapsed into the empty rocking chair next to him. I let out a huge breath. "You really had me worried from that message you left me yesterday."

Trying to clear the frog in his throat, he said, "Uh, yeah, hey, I'm really sorry about that."

Johnny began digging into the side of his neck to relieve a cramp that had I assumed had resulted from his night on the patio.

"You drove all the way up here to check on me?"

"Well, I tried to get up here as soon as I could, but my stupid flight got delayed because of the fog. From the way you sounded, I was worried you might kill yourself."

Johnny exhaled slowly as he recalled the phone call. "I'll tell you the truth, Zach; I actually wanted to and drank a bunch of Jack Daniels to get the courage to do it. Then I gotta gun out and must've stared at the barrel for like ten minutes. But I didn't want a leave a big mess for my cousin so I thought I would just hang myself, but then I couldn't find any rope. The more I thought about it, the more agonizing it became and I somehow ended up out in the woods stumbling around for about an hour. As I walked back to the house, I decided I would just park my truck inside that big shed over there and try to let the carbon monoxide put me out of my misery. So I went out there and tried to start up my truck, and man, I can't explain it, but the stupid thing wouldn't start. The lights came on, so obviously it wasn't the battery. I looked under the hood with a flashlight for twenty minutes and couldn't figure it out. I mean, I just did a tune up myself the other day. So I decided to get back in the truck and try to start it one more time and again it didn't start. I just sat there dazed and I'm not sure why, but I flipped on the radio. The first thing I hear is this super deep, gravelly voice. And I don't know how to even describe it, but there was something about how he was talking that just seemed to draw me in."

Johnny had retained a puzzled look on his face when recounting his trucks mechanical issues, but began to grin as he remembered the voice.

"The guy on the radio said, 'Maybe you're feeling like there's no hope. Maybe you feel like there's no point to living. Maybe you've done something so bad that you don't think there is any way to get rid of that guilt. I'm here to tell you, there is good news. Jesus Christ truly loves you; He proved it by dying for every single one of your sins and He will forgive you if you ask Him tonight.' It was as if God spoke to me through this man. And now that I think about it, I know it was from God."

Staring at him in disbelief, all I could say was, "So, what, God stopped you from taking your life?"

"I don't know how else to explain it. Why didn't my truck start up? Don't you see it, Zach? That was a miracle," he said, rocking forward and planting his feet.

My fatigue began to overwhelm me and I certainly didn't feel like getting into some huge debate about the veracity of his story. While I couldn't see how some motorized failure qualified as a miracle, I was nonetheless content for Johnny to believe that something supernatural had helped ward off his suicide.

Johnny had been staring off into the woods before apparently having some illuminating epiphany that caused his eyes to moisten. "You know what the real miracle is, Zach? That God would still reach out to me even though I'd been rebelling against Him my whole life. I got saved last night; I asked Jesus to be my Lord and Savior."

Unable to keep my mouth from dropping open, I sat astounded as his last words seemed even more absurd than his account about the truck.

Continuing his stare out toward the tree line, Johnny stood up silently for a minute before instinctively turning around and looking me right in the eye. "You still don't want to believe it, do you, Zach?"

"Johnny, no one is happier than me to see that you're alive. Whether it was God or good luck that kept you from taking your life, whatever. The point is, you're alive and I hope you never get depressed like that again," I said, hoping Johnny wouldn't go on some tirade about the hand of God rigging his truck. I fought off my temptation to remind him that his mass consumption of bourbon and weed would probably explain volumes about what had truly transpired last night.

Sensing I had no desire to go deeper into discussion, he quickly changed the subject. "Hey, we should go check out the surf. There a few good breaks like twenty minutes from here that I haven't even hit up yet. My cousin Frank's up at his girlfriend's in Eureka so you can use his board and suit. Let me go grab it and we'll throw the stuff in your car."

"That sounds good. But when we come back, I'm gonna pass out hard because I haven't slept in about twenty four hours."

"Don't worry, when that fifty-two degree water slaps your face, you'll be wide awake," he said, laughing. Naturally the thought of me becoming a human ice cube amused Johnny.

While he gathered some towels and wet suits, I thought about Vanessa and yelled through the screen door as I dialed her phone.

"Hey, I'm gonna call my sister and let her know that you're okay." I ended up leaving a brief message on her voice mail that Johnny was fine and in good spirits.

Johnny strode back with an oversized backpack on his shoulder and sipping a Red Bull soda. Spinning a set of keys around his finger, he asked, "Hey, did you get a hold of her?"

"No, but I left a message."

"Oh man, I would love to talk to her. Let's go out to my truck and get my stuff out of the camper," Johnny said, grabbing some towels off of a chair.

I followed Johnny out to his truck, but instead of going toward the back of his truck to retrieve the gear, he sat down in the cab and popped the hood open. We walked around to the front and after a brief examination, neither one of us could find anything visibly wrong with the truck.

"When Frank gets back in town, I'll have him check it out. He knows a lot more than I do." Johnny paused as if contemplating what could be wrong, muttering something under his breath before impulsively jumping back inside the cab. The ignition didn't even sputter before, but now the engine roared to life, causing Johnny to look over at me with a huge grin. I could only chuckle as there was clearly no explanation to why it hadn't started earlier. He hopped out, ran to the backyard and returned with Frank's board under his arm.

We spun around in the driveway and once we hit the asphalt, Johnny purposely burned his tires on the pavement allowing the truck to fishtail for a moment. Sticking his head out the window so the cold wind could blow directly into his face, he yelled, "Yeaaaaaaah, I'm alive!"

He pulled his head back in the cab and looked completely maniacal with his hair doing its best Albert Einstein impression.

Johnny looked over at me, beaming from ear to ear, and practically screamed in my ear, "Ain't it great to be alive!"

While his hilarious facial expression caused me to smile and shake my head, deep down I was extremely grateful to see Johnny being young at heart again and hoped he could maintain this positive mental attitude.

CHAPTER 19

Walking through a skinny trail along the edge of a cliff, we were greeted at the bottom by the stench of rows of rotting kelp stacked along the sand. As I put on my wetsuit, my eyes scanned the jagged black rocks that lined the beach, making for a daunting entrance out to sea. Hesitating at the edge of the water, I finally launched onto the surfboard to begin the paddle out behind Johnny. Once I made it into the lineup, many of the head-high waves provided short, but fun rides and we ended up sharing the reef break spot all to ourselves.

Johnny had not been kidding about the water being bitterly cold and I couldn't surf more than an hour. After retreating back up the cliff, I sat on the warm hood of his truck, enjoying the solitude of this empty beach and the lush landscape that framed the coastline.

With the gorgeous weather and beautiful scenery, Johnny had an easy time convincing me to stay for another day. My unexpected trip up north turned into a nice little respite from my work and gave me a chance to finally experience the Sonoma County coastline. Since the forecast called for more good surf along with perfect offshore winds, I wished I could have spent more time in this secluded setting, but I needed to return home and prepare to meet up with Sterling Hames in Los Angeles.

The next morning after breakfast, Johnny followed me outside as I went out to put my things in the rental car and head back to the airport.

"Hey, this has been great hanging out. When I get the chance, I'd like to come back up here," I said as I scanned the back seat, trying to remember if I had forgotten anything.

"Anytime, Zach. Thanks again for comin' to check on me."

"Hey, I'd do it again, but please next time, and I know this might sound weird coming from me, if you start feeling depressed, stay away from the bottle."

"You don't have to worry about me now, Zach. I'm good. My drinking days are over."

"Yeah, that's probably a good idea for a while. Just take things one day at a time," I said, surprised that he seemed so ready to give up drinking completely.

With a convincing smile, he declared, "From now on, I'm going to start living the clean life."

"That's what I like to hear," I said, hoping this wouldn't turn out like some rash New Year's resolution.

Glancing over my belongings one more time, I looked at my watch and said, "Well, hey, I gotta hit the road."

"Wait, I almost forgot. Give me Vanessa's phone number. I'd really like to talk to her."

After relaying the number to him, I drove toward the airport and imagined how strange it would be to actually hear a spiritual conversation between my sister and Johnny. I certainly had no plans to tell Vanessa about his drunken encounter with God and could only hope that I'd be able to avoid discussing it with her.

INSIDE THE AIRPORT TERMINAL AT a bustling local brewery, the steady hum of chatter fell quiet at the breaking news story on TV. Footage of a UFO zigzagging across the Palm Desert, CA sky displayed on several big screens before the network cut to a reporter's conversation with an elderly lady who had recorded the home video.

When she was asked if she was still shaken up by the incident, I was surprised when she smiled, maintaining, "Don't worry about me. I'm more than prepared for any aliens trespassin' on my property." With a gleam in her eye, the tiny woman lifted up a twelve gauge shot gun and the entire bar erupted in laughter.

To further discuss the event, they broadcasted a live conference call between a senior news anchor and the chief astronomer from the Jefferson Institute, Leo Herschel. While Herschel initially admitted that he found the footage puzzling, he seemed way too ready to dismiss the video as merely a natural phenomenon rather than an alien aircraft. He reasoned that we most likely had instead witnessed the planet Mars at close proximity during this time of its orbit.

The network broke to another story about a terrorist's trial in Las Vegas and the clamor immediately returned as strangers engaged in enthusiastic dialogues about the UFO siting on TV.

A college-aged woman wearing a Stanford sweatshirt turned to me. "It'd be so cool to see something like that."

"Yeah, it sure would." I said, laughing to myself

"I didn't think that astronomer's explanation made any sense. I mean, since when do planets move all over the place like that?"

"I was thinking the same thing."

"Hey, don't I know you from somewhere?"

"Oh, I get that all the time. I guess I just have one of those familiar faces," I said, smiling back.

"Yeah, people say I look like the actress Laura Ledger from Streetscape."

"Wait a minute; you mean you're not her?" I said, turning my head so I could get a different angle.

"I wish. I'm Courtney. Nice to meet you…"

"Johnny, I said, extending my hand. "Sorry, but I got a flight to catch. Nice talking to you, Ms. Ledger.

"Ha. You're funny. "

I leaned down to pick up my duffel bag, heading for the bathroom before she could connect my face with the news story. An extra-wide Anchor Brewing mirror behind the bar revealed my five o'clock shadow that had grown out the past few days and I hoped it would help keep me incognito on the rest of my travels. On the short walk out toward my gate, I thought about how fascinating it was to watch normal, everyday people in a normal, everyday setting react to a sighting. While I not only looked forward to sharing this barstool perspective, I couldn't wait to read all the new posts on my webpage about this video clip.

The next day in my study I became swamped with all the messages regarding the shotgun-toting Granny. Many people who had personal experience with The Ancestors commented that we should expect even more sightings in the near future and that "unbelievers" would be given more proof of extraterrestrials. Finding it impossible to go through all of the posts that morning, I decided to run some errands and read the rest when I returned. Back at the house, I hurriedly put down my groceries in order to answer my cell phone in time.

"Zach, This is Jack. How ya' doing?"

"Hey, long time, Jack. What's up?"

"Sorry I couldn't make it to your little shindig celebrating the movie deal. I had already scheduled a flight back east to look at an investment property."

"No problem. I figured something came up for you. But, hey, my phone might be bugged so…"

"I thought that'd probably happen before you even wrote that warning. Thank goodness for these disposable ones, huh? The Colonel feels like he's been watched for years because he became so vocal about what he saw when flying for the Air Force. You know what, they can come after this old codger if they want, 'cause I got nothing to hide."

"I like your spunk, Jack."

"Well, what could they possibly learn from us that they couldn't just see for themselves on Fox News?" Jack started chuckling.

"Yeah, I saw that lady's video from the desert last night. I was actually at an airport bar and everyone started getting really jazzed up."

"Did you see the footage they showed about ten minutes ago?"

"No, what? There's more?" I said, hurrying over to turn on my TV.

"Only a couple of our friends circling the House of Congress."

"What? How did I miss this?"

"They just had a special news break. I turned the channel five minutes later and it was all over the networks. Just when it seemed the story was starting to die down some, The Ancestors appeared again to let people know they better wake up."

"This is incredible," I said, even though I was only finding a series of commercials as I flipped through the major networks.

"Yeah, my old neighbor called to say he was watching it, too. You should've heard him laughing at his wife in the next room. She used to always mock us when we talked about ETs back in the day. Now she knows we weren't crazy after all."

"It's bizarre that there's still so much cynicism. Maybe I was being kind of gullible, but I thought once I wrote the story that those who didn't believe would be the minority."

"Well, I'll be the first to admit that it's still pretty mind-boggling to me at times. But I have definitely seen more people coming around. A few weeks ago I read an interesting article in the Wall Street Journal. A couple of career politicians went on record as saying that we should be ready to embrace the message of hope and peace The Ancestors bring."

"I didn't hear about that, but hey, you made me think about a news story I saw on TV where I recognized Boris Wolfe in the background. I think he was mediating a prison exchange between Israel and one of those Islamic militant groups, maybe Hamas."

"I heard about that from Bill. Mr. Wolfe is constantly on the front lines trying to broker peace deals in those trouble spots around the world. Besides that, he's on a super proactive committee about climate change and Bill told me he's also working to set up his own human rights advocacy group. The guy speaks like ten languages; he's amazing."

"That is impressive."

"Heck, if Boris was a citizen of this country, he'd probably be President. Well look, I just wanted to give you a call and let you know we think you're doing an awesome job with the webzine, and look forward to seeing the story come to the big screen."

"I'm actually going to L.A. tonight to start collaborating with a big-time screen writer. He thinks we can hammer it out in a couple of months."

"That's great news, Zach. Listen, if you need anything at all, feel free to call me."

"Appreciate that Jack; thanks for calling."

"Take care."

"You, too."

Nothing but a continuous cycle of promises to save on my car insurance or secrets to flatter abs flashed across my TV, so I hustled into my study to look for the new story on Fox's webpage. Waiting for my computer to start up, my phone rang again.

"Hey! I just got off the phone with Johnny," Vanessa blurted out.

"Oh, yeah… Hey, go to Foxnews dot com. They have some fresh footage of a unique aircraft flying over D.C."

"That could be a challenge because I'm driving down the freeway. Why didn't you tell me about how God saved Johnny's life?"

"Well, it seems pretty ambiguous to me of what actually transpired that night. Did he happen to mention an empty bottle of whiskey?" I paused for effect. "Hey, don't get me wrong, whatever it takes. No one's happier than me that he didn't go through with it."

"You just don't think God had anything to do with his truck not starting? That was all by chance, just a freak accident?"

"I don't know," I said, only half listening as the broadcaster came on the featured video to explain the events that occurred over the nation's capital.

While the UFO made a few loops around the National Mall and back to the Capitol, the shaky camera work made it difficult to determine if the craft was similar to the one that I witnessed at the ranch. Despite the amateur footage, this clearly was not anything man made.

"Vanessa, this is absolutely incredible. They are showing this spacecraft right now."

"Yeah, I saw the news story yesterday about that woman out in the desert," she admitted reluctantly.

"So, what did you think when you saw that?"

"Well, right now I'm wondering how my brother could ignore the fact that his best friend experienced a miracle from God."

I stood up and grabbed my head. "Wait a minute! I hadn't even thought about this. I actually prayed to my guardian Ancestor on the plane."

"What? Are you trying to say that an alien somehow kept his truck from starting?"

"Look, you are so ready to give your god the credit, but did you even consider that I might've prayed, too? You don't know the half of what I've experienced lately. A huge rattlesnake bit me out in the desert; I'm talking out in the middle of nowhere. I got so nauseated I couldn't even drive to a hospital. I thought I was going to die."

"Really, what happened?"

"I'm sitting there puking my guts out on the side of the road, as helpless as I have ever been in my life so I just called out to my Ancestor. Next thing I know, I am watching the swelling in my arm go down before my very eyes. I drove straight home feeling like nothing had even happened. What do you think about that?

Because to me, that's a miracle!"

"Umm…well, I… I honestly don't know what to say," Vanessa said, dumbfounded by my account.

Receiving another call, her phone beeped and gave her the perfect escape from having to answer my question.

"But hey, I gotta take this call. I'm actually getting ready to interview somebody."

"Okay, give me a call later. Let me know if you and Jason want to get a bite to eat," I said enjoying the prospect of watching Mr. Fundamentalist have all his neatly defined theological ideas go up in flames.

"Okay, I'll talk to you later."

This is amazing. I can't believe I didn't even realize it.

Not only had The Ancestors rescued me in the desert, they had also answered my prayers about Johnny. Overwhelmed with joy, I looked forward to talking with him soon so I could share this revelation.

CHAPTER 20

The American dream came true for me in the form of a three thousand square foot English Tudor home, minus the white picket fence and two point five kids. Overlooking the ocean from a hillside in La Jolla, it cost me most of my advance for my story. But at the end of each day, as I soaked in the cool ocean breezes and amazing sunsets, it felt worth every dollar. Sitting on my patio with a good glass of cabernet, I had to almost pinch myself as I wondered how I had fallen into such luck. Thank you, Ancestors!

Sterling Hames came to stay with me two weeks after I had bought the place. Despite his peppered gray hair and grandpa bifocals, he looked almost ten years younger than his fifty-five years. I soon discovered that this famous author was quite the character.

Every morning he started the day the same way: wake up before sunrise, do yoga for thirty minutes, and finish up with a thirty minute bike ride. While telling him that I admired his discipline, I purposely failed to mention how humorous he appeared in his hot pink colored spandex shirt and shorts.

His exercise ritual wasn't the only thing he practiced religiously. Like clockwork, he prepared and drank an entire pot of coffee by nine o'clock, and always followed that by brewing up a batch of green tea each day after noon. These routines seemed to help him stay focused and fuel his inspiration as he proved to be a writing machine.

By six each evening, he would stop and pour himself his first glass of wine. I think I saw him break this custom only once over the next few weeks when he had to drive to L.A. to meet with a producer. Extremely pleased that he had done an enormous amount of research before arriving, I found we rarely needed to talk about the project after dinner, but had some great discussions about life in general out on my patio. When the clock struck nine, I could count on him retiring to his room and I wouldn't hear a peep out of him until he walked in from his morning ride.

During one of Sterling's early bike rides around La Jolla, I got an email from Jack telling me that Bill Hunter needed to talk to me immediately. I sent Jack my new cell number and got a phone call within five minutes.

"Zach, I hope I caught you at a good time. I have some great news."

"It's always good to catch up with you, Bill."

"Now, don't go and publish what I'm about to tell you – this is strictly between us. But let me just put it this way: we're not going to have to worry about Homeland Security interfering with us anymore."

"What? How can this be?"

"As you can imagine, I'm not at liberty to give you the details, but there have been some serious changes going on inside the White House administration. Things are moving fast, Zach."

"Well, whatever, that's absolutely amazing."

"I knew you and a couple others you met at the ranch would be relieved to hear it.'

"I've tried hard not thinking about it since they invaded my old home. I didn't know if my place was bugged or what, but like I told Jack, it's not exactly like they would have discovered anything new."

"You're right. And I think that honesty is really paying off. Listen, Gloria and I enjoy going on your webpage almost every day. We're proud of all your hard work."

"Thanks Bill, I appreciate that."

"No, thank you. We can't wait to see the movie."

"The writer that I'm working with is a flat-out genius. I think it's going be better than I even imagined."

"That's great, Zach. We are going down to stay in the desert in our motorhome a couple of hours from you the next few months, so we'll have to try and get together."

"That'd be great. Please, please call me and let me know."

"We will."

Always a man of few words, Bill ended the call abruptly. Absolutely relieved to hear that I would no longer have to worry about being trailed by my own government, I sensed that people were starting to open up to The Ancestors.

⊕   ⊕   ⊕

ONE EVENING IN THE MIDDLE of the week, Vanessa and her fiancé Jason were finally able to make it over for dinner. Excited to see my new home, they brought me a unique, handcrafted, wooden vase for a house-warming gift, which they had bought in Mexico while visiting an orphanage. Joining us for dinner, Sterling entertained us with his presence until nine o'clock when he predictably excused himself and retired to his bedroom.

As we moved out onto the patio, Vanessa told me about their wedding plans at a small local church, followed by a honeymoon on Kauai. Besides their wedding, we kept up the small talk, such as which new restaurants we had recently visited, comparing notes.

While genuinely enjoying their company, I was tempted to ask Jason if he was aware about some of the things I had recently learned that made their faith obsolete. I was curious to see how he would respond and if he would willfully ignore these truths. Part of me desired to leave the whole subject alone, but after I finished the last glass of wine, I caved into my temptation, opening the proverbial can of worms.

"So, Jason, did my sister tell you about how I got miraculously healed from a rattle snake bite out in the desert?"

"Yes. Matter of fact, she did mention it."

"And what are your thoughts on that?" I said, twirling the stem of my empty glass in my hand.

Jason paused, glancing at Vanessa as if she had reins on him, before talking with some apprehension in his voice. "Well, that's pretty puzzling, Zach. I honestly was taken aback when I heard your story."

"Uh huh," I said, hopeful this kind of story would help them start being more open-minded.

"But then I remembered that in the book of Exodus, Pharaoh's magicians actually performed miracles as well. It's pretty clear that demons have supernatural powers and are able to do a lot of things that we don't understand," Jason said.

"So, these "demons," who you Christians say are trying to hurt us, turn around and help me by healing me? You have to admit that doesn't make a ton of sense, Jason."

Jason wanted to reply, but Vanessa closed her eyes and flattened her lips so he remained silent.

"Let me give you kids a little knowledge to chew over at your next church picnic. Because I know you're all about historicity and facts, let me tell you about some other famous Messiahs; you know, the ones that existed before Mr. Jesus. Like Krishna from India, Dionysus over in Greece, and Mithra in Persia."

Setting my glass on the table, I leaned forward.

"Interesting little stories. Each one had their own following since they were all born of a virgin, with a little star in the East. Along come three kings proclaiming them King and Savior. Sound familiar? Next thing you know, Mr. Messiah, aka the Son of Light, aka Alpha and Omega, has himself a little cult following. The best part is how all of them have the same crazy recurring theme; seems like every story has Mr. Messiah finding himself crucified at the end."

Switching to my best infomercial voice-over impersonation, I added, "But wait, there's more. Wouldn't you know it; all of them are miraculously resurrected!"

Jason and Vanessa looked almost shell-shocked so I knew I had them right where I wanted them.

"I'm glad you brought up Egypt earlier because maybe you have, or maybe you haven't, heard of a guy named Horus. Same story. Mr. Sun God. God the Sun. Whatever you like to call him. He is the original. Crucified – Resurrected – Legend. Only Horus predates Jesus by three thousand years, but who's counting. Can I offer you any more wine?" I said, unable to hide my smirk.

"Did you say three thousand years B.C?" Jason seemed stunned at this revelation.

"Indeed. Your friends over Encyclopedia Britannica will confirm it if you care to look it up."

"Well, Zach. That doesn't make any sense. Crucifixion wasn't even invented until around 1000 B.C."

"Jason, you're missing the point." I said, slightly embarrassed and wondering if I had remembered the date wrong. "Don't you see? Every society has had their Savior. I mean, I get it. Everyone needs hope. I understand why you guys want to hold onto what you believe in, but you have to see…"

Inhaling deeply to compose my thoughts, I tried to refrain from maintaining the sarcastic tone I was so fond of. "Look, there are good aliens and there are bad aliens. I've been shown that. And I can see how you would see extraterrestrials as 'demons' in light of what you have been told, but there is something deeper going on here. Something below the surface of what mankind has believed for so long."

I paused because I really wanted them to think about what I would say next. "The problem with Christians is that they take authority as the truth rather than the truth as the authority."

He stood up, now clearly agitated. "Look, Zach. We didn't come over here to get into a spiritual debate with you. Your sister implicitly told me not to ever bring it up. But let me break it down for you."

"Jason…" Vanessa said, grabbing his arm.

"Vanessa, let me finish," he said without looking at her. "I care about you, Zach – but I don't care what you think about me. If I brought all the evidence in the world that supports what we believe in, it wouldn't make any difference to you. This isn't a matter of intellect; it's a matter of the heart. Your heart is cold to God and if you keep heading down this path, you will end up in Hell."

"That's hell-arious, Jason. How can religion reform me when it's the biggest form of slavery there is!"

Jason shrugged his shoulders, let out a big sigh and walked to the edge of the patio.

"Zach…" Vanessa said, trying to calm me down.

"And Vanessa, I really love how you've worked on brainwashing Johnny the last few weeks."

"Well, if it makes you feel any better, our friend Pam that you met at my house stopped coming to church because of your story."

"You mean she started thinking for herself? Well, hallelujah!"

Vanessa shook her head, her face now reddening as I continued.

"Unlike Johnny. No need for anyone to try to talk logically to him now because all you get is, 'well, the Bible says this and the Bible says that.' Just like a freakin' robot."

"Maybe you should stop to listen to what he has learned," she said.

"Come on! You have no idea how much that infuriates me. You guys act like I'm the one who is blind here when you don't even see how much damage believing in this little myth has caused to your own psyche. I mean, how much more do I have to dumb it down for you..." I immediately regretted phrasing it like that as I saw Vanessa's eyebrows furrow.

"Nice, Zach. Thanks for a great evening!" she shouted and stood up. Turning around curtly, she walked out to the car with Jason.

I gradually pushed my pride aside and lumbered out of my chair to catch up to them before they could leave. Coming around the corner of my garage, I winced, realizing it was too late to yell out a warning as I watched Jason's car shoot up my driveway backwards. Anticipating that his car would bottom out on the awkward curb at the crest, my whole body tensed up right before I heard the crunch of metal grinding against concrete.

Gritting my teeth, I hated knowing it was my fault for turning our conversation into a full-blown argument. Disappointed that I had become overly zealous to prove my point, I couldn't understand why after thirty-three years I still insisted on cramming my boots into my big mouth. Even though I knew I was right, I walked back into the house, regretting that I had attacked their intelligence and ruining what had been a perfectly pleasant evening.

As I passed through the dining room, for some strange reason I paused to look in a mirror, remembering something my mom told me in high school. After I had complained to her about a friend who complained all the time, she told me to sit down at the kitchen table with her. Looking at me gently, she smiled and said, "Many times, the things other people do that we hate the most are actually the same things we do."

Only as I stared at my reflection in the mirror did it become clear to me. While I despised it when others lacked tolerance, I, too, was guilty of intolerance. Just as nobody enjoys hearing a recording of their own voice, I certainly didn't like this realization about myself, but mother's words had given me a much needed dose of humility. As I moved into the living room and sat down on my couch, I began thinking about ways I could make it up to Jason and Vanessa.

I INTENDED CALLING VANESSA THE next morning, but soon became side-tracked. My accountant called, saying I should expect to get audited by the IRS soon and instructing me on how to get prepared. Never known for my organizational skills, I took several days digging through unpacked boxes in my garage to find some of the required paperwork.

Later that week, an emergency phone call from the Colorado State campus hospital had me driving Sterling to the airport to catch a red-eye flight as his son had come down with a severe case of pneumonia. While I naturally hoped his son's condition would improve, I also hoped Sterling could return soon as we were close to finishing the fourth draft of the screenplay.

His departure at least provided the free time I needed to finally reach out to Vanessa. Not only wanting to apologize, I decided to make amends by paying for their entire wedding as an expression that I would embrace Jason as my brother-in-law.

My call from around lunchtime went unanswered, but I did receive a short text message stating she would be home around six o'clock. She sent a second text saying it was important that I contact Johnny A.S.A.P.

Left guessing as to what was so important, I walked out to the patio and called Johnny.

"Hey Zach, I was just about to call you. How are you doing?" he said in a raspy voice.

"Doing well. You sound a little under the weather."

"Yeah, I got some bad news. I haven't been feeling too good since we last talked. I've had a real bad sore throat and thought it was because it was getting cooler and I left the window open. But after about two weeks of having zero energy I got some tests run." He paused and let out a short breath. "I just found out my cancer's back."

I took a step back and sunk into a patio chair.

"I'm at a loss for words, buddy," I said.

"The doctor's waiting for the other results that will come back tomorrow and we'll know if it has spread to my lymph nodes."

Thinking of the place where Johnny got cured the first time, I quickly asked, "Can you get back down to that clinic in Tijuana again for some treatment?"

"Not likely to help if it's spread. But we'll start talking treatment options after tomorrow."

Starting to feel desperate, I said, "As soon as you find out tomorrow, call me. Let's get you to the best specialists in the country. I'll cover all of your medical expenses."

"Thanks, Zach."

I stood up as my mind began racing. "We're gonna fight this thing together. You can move in down here with me if you need. I got plenty of room. Scripps clinic is right down the street..."

Trying to slow me down, Johnny said, "Okay. I appreciate that. I just want you to know that I'm good."

"I know that. You're a fighter. You beat this before and you'll beat it again."

"Well, I definitely hope so. But what I'm trying to say is that I'm good either way. I'm okay with dying now, Zach."

"Johnny, seriously – don't talk like that."

"But I am serious. I know where I'm headed when I die so I'm good. Okay?"

His nonchalant tone had me completely rattled.

"But there's something else I wanted to talk to you about." Johnny continued. "Vanessa told me about the huge argument you guys got into. She admitted to me that she's still pretty angry about the way you treated her."

"Yeah, I'm actually headed over there when she gets off work to talk."

"Good. I was just gonna say that you shouldn't take her for granted. You're lucky to have a sister like that. Anyway, I know you guys will work it out."

"You're right. It's been on my mind for a week now. I just let the wine get the best of me that night."

"Another reason I don't miss alcohol." He chuckled. "Look, I'm gonna lay down and rest, but I'll call you when I get back from the doctor tomorrow."

"Definitely do."

"Okay. Have a blessed day."

"You, too."

After hanging up, I got the weird impression that I was more concerned about Johnny than he was. While I was stunned by the news of his cancer returning, it was his calm response that had blown me away. It simply didn't make any sense how he could maintain such a peace about him while facing the biggest storm of his life.

WANTING TO MAKE MYSELF FAMILIAR with what Johnny would be facing and maybe even give him some other options, I spent the rest of the afternoon devoted to searching the internet for the top rated Oncologists, types of different treatment, and survival percentages for those coming out of remissions. As I suspected, two of the best head and neck cancer specialists in the world worked out of Scripps hospital in La Jolla.

Emotionally drained by the end of day, I wanted more than ever to see Vanessa and texted her that I was on my way over. Only seconds after making my ascent up a steep freeway exit ramp near her house, I glanced down at the rush hour traffic and witnessed the largest pileup in history unfold. The whole world around me slammed into first gear as I tapped on the brakes and watched in horror at the endless line of twisted metal and shattered glass. As far as I could see, the entire highway had screeched to a complete standstill. The once constant hum of speeding vehicles had been replaced with the unnerving sound of relentless horns. An eerie cloud of black and gray smoke had consumed the airspace over the freeway, filling it with the sickening stench of burnt rubber.

Nearing the off ramp stop light, I merged right onto Mission Avenida and passed at least twenty more cars that had crashed along the street. While most had collided into other vehicles, one car had plowed over a small concrete barrier and through the large glass window panes of a boutique shop that lined the street.

Beyond baffled, I kept driving straight ahead in a state of shock. It didn't even cross my mind to stop and help anyone until an idle car in the middle of the intersection forced me to pull over. Getting out tentatively, I approached the vacant car from the passenger side. I noticed an empty infant car seat in the back with a diaper sitting in it before my eyes darted up front. An open purse and what appeared to be an extra set of clothes lay on the front seat. With the motor still running, I grabbed the door handle only to find it locked. I jogged around to the driver side to open it so I could turn off the ignition, but discovered that all the doors were locked.

Across the intersection, other drivers stood by their vehicles looking at me as if waiting for an answer. I turned my palms upward, shrugging my shoulders to signal that I had no idea what had happened. A blur of emergency busses began honking as they rushed toward us so I jumped back in my truck, driving up on the sidewalk and around the car to get out of the way.

Detecting something extraordinary was taking place, I quickly speculated that maybe terrorists had launched a cyber-attack, wreaking havoc on our electrical and computer infrastructures; even more chilling, what if they had possibly released a chemical gas into the air that so far was only affecting certain people. Realizing I was grasping for straws, I scanned through the channels of my radio, but heard no updates except about the massive traffic jams across the city.

As I continued going through a number of disturbing scenarios, an alarming thought ran through my mind: *What if this is the day The Ancestors were removing parts of the population?*

I hit the gas, driving as fast as I could to Vanessa's.

Only a couple of minutes later, I came upon a small pickup that had crashed head-on into a large oak tree across the street from her house. From the demolished front end and fractured windshield, I became concerned about the driver's possible injuries. Parking across the street, I jogged over to the truck, but with no traces of the driver or passengers, I impulsively ran up my sister's driveway.

Banging on the front door and yelling her name, I didn't hear anything to indicate that she was inside. Back behind the house, her new Honda Civic sat with the windows rolled down so I knew she had to be home. Finding the back porch door unlocked, I flung it open and shouted, "Vanessa, where are you?"

Not waiting for an answer, I walked right through her house onto the front patio, continuing to yell her name. With no response from her, I moved out toward the sidewalk to see if she had possibly walked down the street.

The sound of parents shouting their kids' names, pleading with them to return home made my heart jump and I sprinted up a few random blocks, frantically hunting for any sign of my sister. My hapless search led me back to the edge of Vanessa's front yard where a middle-aged lady ran up and grabbed me by the arm.

"My baby! Someone's stolen my baby!" she gasped.

Before I could attempt to reply, she turned and ran to another house across the street, screaming the whole way.

"Oh jeez…" I babbled.

Remembering now I hadn't attempted calling Vanessa's cell phone, I speed dialed her number and a chirping ringtone led me back inside to her kitchen. My shoulders slumped when I discovered the phone on top of the microwave next to her car keys.

Where is she? I thought.

Footsteps shuffling along the front patio caused a jolt of hope to shoot through my heart.

"Vanessa?" I yelled before an elderly man leaned his head around the half opened door. The man had been Vanessa's neighbor for several years yet I could never remember his name.

"Do you know where Vanessa is?" I asked, walking quickly toward him.

"They're gone. Vanessa. My wife. They're both gone."

"What do you mean, gone?"

"I was thirty feet from that truck when it wrecked right out front. I hurried over there and looked all around, but the driver vanished. Instead of calling 911, I just panicked and jogged up here to Vanessa's. But when I couldn't find her, I ran back inside my place and now my wife's not in her wheel chair. It was right then I got a bad feeling that it really had happened just like they told me," he said, looking down with darkened eyes.

"What are you even talking about?"

"I'm pretty certain that Jesus came and took them…."

"That's ridiculous! How do you know it wasn't aliens?" I shouted.

"Well, I don't. But I didn't see any spaceships. And I do know I've been playing a game with God for too long."

Glaring at him incredulously, I questioned the old man's sanity and shook my head as I walked past him. As I looked up and down the street one last time to see if I could spot Vanessa, the man yelled at me from behind.

"Look on the TV, you idiot! You'll see."

I shut my truck door and rolled up the windows, hoping the solitude of my cab would help me gather my thoughts. As I stared at the floor and chewed on my cuticles, the constant blaring of fire truck horns and ambulance sirens continued to unsettle me. While still hoping to discover that Vanessa had merely been down the street, I had to face the possibility that The Ancestors had taken her away.

If this was indeed what had occurred, why would they take a good person like my sister? This can't be what happened. I thought.

Starting to feel sick to my stomach, I knew I couldn't sit there for another second. I cranked the ignition and hastily popped the clutch, causing my wheels to screech before speeding down the street. While having no idea where to go or what to do next, I just knew I needed to get out of that neighborhood.

Expecting the nearby freeways to be completely gridlocked, I flipped my radio back on to see if I could find out which roads were unaffected, but immediately got the emergency broadcast system. I scanned the channels until I heard a report coming from the local CBS affiliate "...no one seems to understand what kind of calamity has hit the west coast of the United States, but it now appears that the incredibly strange events that we have been reporting on are in fact a worldwide phenomenon. We just received reports confirming that airports nationwide are shut down after numerous plane crashes across the country. Freeways and interstates of every major city are at a standstill as countless have apparently abandoned their vehicles. We are struggling to update these reports at this time because our own station, along with our affiliates, has missing personnel and..."

Crack.

The broadcaster's voice went silent as pieces of my radio now lay scattered along the floor of the truck. From the instant swelling in my right hand, I was convinced that I had just broken the small knuckle. Now fumbling around with my throbbing hand, I struggled to pull my cell phone out of my pants pocket and call Johnny. There seemed to be some kind of problem with the connection because not even his voice mail worked. Putting the phone down, I tried to work my way home through some back streets, but with all the turmoil around the city it took me over three hours to make the twelve mile trek.

The drive home had left me wanting updates so I headed straight for the TV. Non-stop news footage soon bombarded me with a constant collage of carnage, revealing the entire planet had been thrown into complete mayhem. With my arms pressed against my chest, I stood mesmerized by the disturbing images until my legs wobbled and I stumbled back into the couch. Frantic to talk to Bill, I tried called him several times, but there was now obviously a system wide problem with the reception.

Thirty minutes of sensory overload forced me to ultimately retreat back to my bedroom as I desperately needed to establish contact with my guardian Ancestor. Hoping to uncover what had truly transpired, I also wanted some kind of instruction on what to even do next. Patiently waiting for over forty-five minutes, I ended up screaming out loud, "Where are you? Why won't you answer me?"

As I sat alone on the floor, the cold, dense walls of silence now pressed in from every side, leaving me to wonder if I had been utterly abandoned.

CHAPTER 21

With millions of people unaccounted for, the subsequent anarchy caused governments worldwide to institute Martial Law. In the United States, only military vehicles were allowed on the streets after dusk and the President had suspended all civil laws.

For the first time in history, an overwhelmed news media faced too many tragic events than they could possibly report. Almost an entire week had passed and I still could not come to grips with all the madness that just seemingly grew by the day.

Skies all over the world were filled with gray ash as fires raged out of control. Inundated with people needing aid, many Metropolitan hospitals were refusing to take on more patients. More than half of telephone and internet companies reported service issues which only created more problems. With so many employees tardy or missing from every kind of occupation, the economy grinded to a halt and inevitably on Monday all the international Stock Markets collapsed.

The President made a couple of brief speeches during the week and tried to encourage everyone to pull together. While attempting to appear confident, no president could possibly have been prepared to face this kind of epic disaster.

Reports kept pouring in from around the globe about people who had vanished into thin air, but what seemed even more bizarre was that *all* the young children in the world had simultaneously disappeared. Parents everywhere diligently sustained their search for missing sons and daughters, but became more distraught with each passing day. As I scanned the adjacent lots from my corner bay window, the absence of kids playing and laughing in their front yards made the neighborhood feel like a ghost town.

Everyone had questions and there was no shortage of rumors as to what had actually occurred.

Naturally people speculated that this was the Rapture that Christians always talked about, but this idea only seemed to confuse and divide people. No one appeared to express more outrage over this suggestion than the remaining clergy of Christian churches who were adamant that the Rapture was bad theology.

Discussions among scientists indicated that no concept was too farfetched at this point. All kinds of ideas were being tossed around: from unexplainable changes in the earth's atmosphere, to mysterious gasses released from within the earth, to even the idea of alien abductions. While everything was open for debate, no one could provide any concrete evidence for any of these theories.

Of course, the majority of people didn't have the luxury to sit around and speculate all day as to the possible sources of this pandemonium. The steady stream of depressing news stories confirmed that most people were simply struggling to deal with the aftermath.

In certain instances, I saw the goodness of man as people united to rescue others, clean up wreckage and do whatever was needed to restore order. On the opposite spectrum, rampant rioting and looting persisted around the world, unveiling people's darker side. My affluent neighborhood was now no stranger to frequent break-ins and I kept a loaded pistol next to my bed.

Impossible to anticipate or even imagine such a far-reaching catastrophe, we had been tossed head first into the worst nightmare of all-time.

Several news organizations had tried contacting me during the following week, but I instructed my publicist via email to say I had no comment at this time. Even though I went on my website daily, I had yet to reply to the infinite messages I had received. Everyone wanted to know whether this was the day that had been prophesized about The Ancestors' arrival.

Several of the "regulars" on my webzine blogs, many of whom possessed far more experience with The Ancestors than I, boldly proclaimed this was indeed "The Day," that this very moment in history would soon initiate an influx of astronauts from outside our galaxy. Pleading for patience, they preached that hope was on the horizon.

Others questioned the aliens' motives and methods of suddenly expelling a vast portion of mankind when the obvious results would be so much pain and suffering for those left behind. They wanted to know why the aliens chose to leave all these wicked dictators in power and menacing thugs to still roam our streets. Why abduct so many people who were not hurting anybody? And how were parents supposed to even function while worrying about the whereabouts and welfare of their children?

While frequent visitors to the webzine, and new ones alike, kept calling on me for answers, I remained paralyzed with dread as a mountain of my own questions weighed down on me. My continued efforts to contact The Ancestors remained fruitless, adding to my frustration and fear.

With my mind filling with doubts, I wasn't about to post or even admit out loud what bothered me the most about the latest developments.

For the last year and half, I had felt like a beacon of hope for people everywhere. Wanting to enlighten others to The Ancestors' promise of deliverance, I had looked forward to The Day they would come and save us. Even though Shanda had told me that they would have to remove a population from the earth to "reeducate" them, for some reason I had not given it much thought about the ensuing consequences for us who were still here.

For six straight days, I never left the confines of my home, thinking that if I could somehow isolate myself for a while that I might be able to finally get a better grasp on the situation. While I maintained my attempts to reach Vanessa and Johnny, every unanswered call increased my anxiety as to what had happened to them. When contacting Vanessa's precinct earlier in the week, I had been informed by a female clerk that no one seemed to know the whereabouts of her or Jason. While the clerk had promised to contact me if they found out anything, I had yet to hear back from her.

Several times a day I tried emailing and calling Bill and Gloria, wanting to make sure they were okay, but even more importantly I needed some imparting wisdom from them. From the strange way his phone and voicemail sounded, it was unclear if my messages were even recorded.

Since Johnny's phone continued to have technical issues, this gave me a glimmer of hope that I possibly hadn't heard from Vanessa because she simply had problems with her work cell phone.

Late one afternoon, I finally drove over again to her house only to find it still empty with no signs that she had returned. I wrote her a note to call me when she came in, but as I slowly turned the key to lock her back door my heart sank because I somehow knew right then I would never see her again.

As I lay in bed that night, images of Vanessa flooded my mind: memories of summer afternoons riding bikes and skateboarding down hills; the glow on her face at her college graduation dinner; the time she leaned on my shoulder at mother's funeral. While trying to cling to those times spent together, I now grasped I would never have the opportunity to tell her how much she meant to me and I finally broke down and wept.

⊕   ⊕   ⊕

IT HAD BEEN JUST OVER two weeks since The Day, but getting up in the morning only became more difficult as watching the news revealed an ever increasing number of alarming developments. The most distressing update came as some madcap militant group had captured a nuclear power plant on the border of Jordan and Israel. They threatened to vaporize everybody in the area along with themselves if Zionists around the world did not meet their vague demands. Thoroughly repulsed after ten minutes of that story, I knew I needed to get out of the house.

Even though many of the fires in San Diego County had been contained, the air now reeked of burnt plastic and rubber. Weaving along back streets behind my neighborhood and looking down over one of San Diego's major freeways, I was staggered when I saw with my own eyes all the wrecked cars and trucks still stacked across several lanes. The Department of Transportation had ordered bulldozers and snowplows to push the vehicles into the fast lanes, freeing up at least one lane, but you could outrace the traffic in either direction on a bicycle.

Even though more phone lines were reportedly working at this time, I still had been unable to reach Johnny. Hoping he had not become more ill, I also wondered what his test results had shown. As I neared the local market, I momentarily thought about getting on the Five freeway north to go look for him, but I realized that the trip would take forever to get up to the Bay area and I had no idea if I would even find him once I got there.

As I rounded a sharp curve in the road, a lone hitchhiker wearing a light blue t-shirt waved his thumb at me. I glanced over at him with no thoughts of stopping at first, but something about the look in his eyes had me pulling over about a hundred yards past where he stood. While he seemed harmless enough, watching him in the rearview mirror as he jogged up to the car made me rather uneasy of whether I should actually offer him a ride. The thought that I hadn't reached out to a single person during this crisis caused a crumbling, stone wall of guilt to topple down on me and I hit the unlock button to let him in.

Appearing in his mid-fifties, he wore a nicely trimmed beard with gray streaks. Sounding slightly winded, the man huffed, "Hey, thanks for stopping. I've been walking for a while and I just need to get up the road a bit. However far you can take me will be fine."

"No problem. I'm just heading to the market at the bottom of the hill," I said before merging back on the road.

"Hope all the grocery trucks have been able to get the supplies in. Name's Gabe."

"Nice to meet you, I'm…"

"Zach Miller. I've actually been eager to meet you." Gabe cut me off.

Alarmed at his statement, I quickly reasoned he must be a reader.

"Seems you have gotten yourself in a little dilemma, Zach," he said slightly tugging on his beard.

"It's safe to say we're all facing some huge dilemmas right now," I answered, trying to deflect his comment, but the personal nature of it made me tense up.

"There is definitely no getting around that. But it just baffles me when I read those posts a few months ago on your webzine. Please explain how you could put your faith in these aliens to build a new world if they left you in such a mess."

Trying to remain calm, I stuttered, "Well, I'm sure…"

"And another thing that doesn't make sense. If you are a divine being who can control your own destiny as they claim, how is it that you would still need their help to make the world right? I mean, which is it?"

Extremely irritated that he somehow knew the same questions that had been troubling me recently, I now regretted picking him up.

"Well, if you'd let me finish. I'm sure there is a reason for both of those points, but right now I'm trying to give it time so I can understand the 'whys' and 'hows'."

"Excuse me for being so blunt, but I keep wondering why you've been ignoring the one thing that you must know deep down to be true. See, I've been watching you for a while now and I don't understand some of your decision making…"

"What are you freaking talking about?" I shot back. Thoughts flooded my mind about how this guy may have been stalking me and I nervously gripped the gear shift.

Gabe spoke calm, authoritative. "I've been sent here to tell you that this is your last chance. You need to come to God before it's too late."

I jerked the steering wheel toward the bike lane and slammed on the brakes. "Get out!"

"I will," he nodded, keeping his eyes on me.

Unhitching his seat belt, he slowly opened the door before placing one foot on the pavement. "But you need to know there's a reason you haven't heard from these demons lately. We've been binding them so that you can have this final *chance* to respond to God's offer of forgiveness. Understand that from here on out, the forces of darkness are gathering for one final push for the souls of men."

He exited the truck before I could reply and I now saw him in my peripheral, walking back toward where I had picked him up.

A half second later, he instantly appeared on the driver's side of my truck, causing my whole body to jerk sideways in attempts to distance myself from him.

"Zach, even after you have led so many people astray, God still loves you and wants you to come to Him." His voice firm, he looked at me with a piercing gaze.

The suddenness of his peering into my window petrified me, but as I regained my clutch on the steering wheel, a warm wind began to mysteriously howl through my windows and shake my truck.

"But woe unto you if you do not humble yourself before the Lord," his voice thundered.

As soon as he said the last word, I salvaged enough composure to kick the gas pedal and my spinning tires created a haze of light brown dust. Rapidly stamping the buttons to lock my doors and roll up my windows, I peeked at the rearview mirror and my eyes went wide. He was gone.

Hitting the brakes, my body whipped forward before slamming back against the seat when the pickup came to a halt. A nasty crunching sound came from my gearbox as I prematurely threw the truck in reverse and floored the gas. The tires squealed while swerving backwards about a hundred yards and I almost lost control until my back wheels bounced off the curve and up onto a sidewalk. Yanking the emergency brake, I jumped out and spun around in a full circle, but he was still nowhere to be found.

A slight embankment down into a ravine led me to impulsively jog down it to see if I could spot him. Passing only the tiny shrubs that lined the floor of the empty canyon, I soon realized there wasn't anything substantial down here to hide a grown man.

"How could he just vanish like that?" I whispered as I turned to walk back up to the road.

Once back in the seat of my truck, I hurried to close my door as another car approached from the opposite lane. I nervously hit the gas, launching my pickup off the curb and back onto the street. The other car slowed down and two women gazed at me, no doubt pondering what influenced me to stop on the side of an empty road. Making a conscious effort to avoid their stares as they passed by, I began scanning the sides of the canyon as if Gabe could possibly be somewhere down the way.

By the time I arrived to the grocery store, I looked forward to being in a familiar setting around normal people; something I hoped would ease the churning knot inside my stomach. Pushing my cart aimlessly down the first couple of aisles, I couldn't stop myself from looking back over my shoulder every few seconds and kept a Kung Fu grip on the handle to keep my hands from shaking. When I ended up in front of the beer section, I snatched up a twelve pack of Newcastle and hurried down the aisle. Once I found the hallway that lead to the bathroom, I ripped into the box and nuzzled three beers under my arms before pushing the door open with my shoulder. Hoping no one had noticed, I rushed into one of the stalls and began to guzzle down each beer.

My brief detour provided the desired effect as I ambled out of the bathroom slightly tipsy, but much more relaxed. Now I could focus on buying as much food as I could fit into my car so I wouldn't have to make another grocery trip for a while. It appeared that at least a few trucks had been able to make their deliveries, but the shelves still sat less than half full. Oddly enough, the beer and wine section remained well stocked, and I made another trip down that aisle and grabbed a few cases of beer.

The checkout line went almost halfway across the store as the two struggling cashiers were clearly undermanned. While I had avoided looking at people I had passed by in the aisles, I now noticed that almost everyone standing around possessed a vacant look in their eyes as if they simply anticipated impending doom.

Trying to distract myself from the ominous vibe that surrounded me, I browsed through the rack holding the tabloids and magazines. My eyes went quickly to the cover that featured Antonio Gonzalez, the US Ambassador to Brazil, along with several other dignitaries in the background. Picking up the magazine to get a closer look, I found the news article highlighting the United Nations efforts to help the world leaders join forces in this time of international turmoil.

The first paragraph quoted Gonzalez as saying that despite the many challenges the U.N. currently faced, he still felt extreme optimism and sensed that there would soon be a great turn for the good as the best minds on the planet were at work to help bring back a state of normalcy. He stated that one of the most pertinent tasks at hand was electing a new President for the U.N. General Assembly since a plane crash earlier in the week had presumably taken the life of Haya Al-Khalifalla. Asked to give his opinion on the most qualified candidates, Gonzales noted the early favorites as either Secretary General Reina Fuentes or the new European Union Ambassador, Boris Wolfe.

Back in the safety of my home, I sat down on the couch to eat a turkey sandwich and finish the rest of the article about the U.N.'s efforts over the last week. Even though I had been extremely impressed with what I had heard about Boris Wolfe, I wondered why he did not publicly mention his belief in The Ancestors. Maybe the timing wasn't right, but I sensed Mr. Wolfe chose to play it political and remain ambiguous about what he really believed.

Unable to finish the rest of the article as a lack of sleep caught up to me, I rolled over and passed out. Hearing someone whisper my name, I perceived that my guardian Ancestor was hovering above my couch.

"Zach, we need to warn you again about the evil Ancestors who are trying to deceive you. Do not be fooled as they want to distract you from fulfilling your great calling. Remember, the time is at hand. Soon we will reveal ourselves to the entire world and we will all rejoice!"

My entire body flinched violently, jolting me awake. I immediately noticed my arm and shoulder muscles ached as if I had been struggling to break free from the grasp of something, or someone. Sitting up quickly, I scanned my living room for any indication that someone might be in the house.

With dusk setting in, the living room lamps cast long shadows across the intricately designed rugs. The dim light emanating from the kitchen made me wonder if I had left it on and my eyes shot over to the blinking green light on the central alarm panel by the front door, revealing that it had not been triggered. This did little to ease my nerves, so I started to slowly roll my neck and take deep breaths in attempts to calm down. While most of my previous encounters with The Ancestors had given me a greater sense of clarity, this one had left me extremely perplexed. It also led me to re-examine my strange meeting earlier with the hitch hiker, which only compounded my confusion even further.

Dwelling more on these two conflicting messages began to completely overwhelm me and I felt like my head was going to explode. Convinced that I would go insane if I sat there for another minute, I jumped up in hopes to preoccupy myself with some trivial tasks around the house. Flipping on several lights around the house, I started to clean up and organize my small makeshift office. As I dug through a pile of unopened mail, I spotted a crate beside my desk that held a couple of books that my sister had given me. Vanessa had claimed these books contained facts that validated her faith, but I had always considered these mere opinions from born again Bible thumpers. While planning on throwing them away years ago, I was glad I hadn't because it gave me something to remind me of her.

I picked up the paperback, titled *Facts Are Stranger Than Fiction* before finding the next one strangely titled, *How Jesus Wrecked My College Keg Party.*

Tossing them back in the crate, I noticed a tiny orange book that had been pushed to the corner by a stack of magazines. Surprised to discover a pocket-sized Bible, I couldn't recall ever seeing one that compact and it struck me as odd that she would give me one with such small print.

The edges of a crumpled photo wedged inside the Bible caught my eye and I pulled it out to find a picture of my mother and Vanessa sitting on a car-sized boulder at Yosemite National Park. I was glad that I found this photo that captured our last vacation together a month before my mom became ill. The opened page also revealed a note Vanessa had written to me on the inside cover.

Dear Zach, my only desire is for you to see how real God is and how incredible it is to come into a genuine relationship with Him. If you take the time to read this book, I am sure that Jesus will reveal Himself to you through His Word and you too will know that God is good.
Love, Vanessa

Slapping it shut, I gripped it tensely between both hands. My eyes immediately looked up at a framed picture of Vanessa and Mom on my desk, but it soon became blurred through my watered eyes. As I placed a shaking hand over my face, a sense of pure desperation led me to do something I had not done since elementary school: I prayed to God.

"Lord, if you are real, if this book is true, please show me so I can know."

Looking down, I opened the Bible randomly and it fell to the book of 1 Thessalonians, chapter four, and my eyes went directly to the following passage:

> *According to the Lord's word, we tell you that we who are still alive, who are left until the coming of the Lord, will certainly not precede those who have fallen asleep. For the Lord himself will come down from heaven, with a loud command, with the voice of the archangel and with the trumpet call of God, and the dead in Christ will rise first. After that, we who are still alive and are left will be caught up together with them in the clouds to meet the Lord in the air. And so we will be with the Lord forever.*

Slowly folding the Bible closed, I sat there astonished at those last two lines. Knowing this was beyond coincidence, my soul stood confronted with the truth that God had indeed raptured His people.

More importantly, I could no longer deny that God had sent His angel Gabe for me to remember these words: "God still loves you, even after all you have done." As the profoundness of that statement breached my heart, I found myself sliding out of my chair and onto my knees.

The tender lump in my throat caused my voice to quiver before I finally whispered, "Jesus, I'm so sorry. Please forgive me." Absolutely broken by years of foolish pride, I collapsed face first onto the floor and began to cry.

After several minutes, I pushed myself up from the floor and used my shirt to dry my eyes. As I sat propped up against the wall, I felt drawn to flip the Bible open again and came across Psalm 130:

Out of the depths I cry to you, LORD; Lord, hear my voice.
Let your ears be attentive to my cry for mercy.
If you, LORD, kept a record of sins, Lord, who could stand?
But with you there is forgiveness, so that we can, with reverence,
serve you.
I wait for the LORD, my whole being waits, and in his word I
put my hope.
I wait for the Lord more than watchmen wait for the morning,
more than watchmen wait for the morning.
Israel, put your hope in the LORD, for with the LORD is unfail-
ing love and with him is full redemption.
He himself will redeem Israel from all their sins.

Now positive that God heard my plea for mercy and had forgiven me, this ancient prayer had become my own song. For the first time in my life I made no attempt to wipe away my tears, but simply allowed them to spill freely off the edge of my smiling face.

⊕   ⊕   ⊕

THE NEXT FEW NIGHTS I stayed up late devouring entire books from the New Testament. Books like the Gospel of John and Acts led me to not only grasp spiritual truths, but provided great comfort by reminding me that Vanessa and Johnny were in God's hands and I would see them again one day.

Even though I still wanted updates for late breaking news reports, and subjected myself to hours of heartbreaking accounts, that time proved useful as it taught me to pray throughout the day and develop a deeper compassion for others.

Rolling blackouts for the entire San Diego area left me without power for parts of the day, but also saved me from being completely mesmerized by the televised tragedies. Fortunately, *How Jesus Wrecked My College Keg Party* provided a well written story from an "ex-professional beer-drinker" whose life had been turned upside down from his search for truth. Initially challenged to examine his worldview by a Christian roommate, the author discovered his former party life paled in comparison to the spiritual high he now found in Jesus. While the ending of that book pulled on the strings of the heart, sitting down with *Facts Are Stranger Than Fiction* appealed to the intellect. The first chapters outlined archeological finds and secular history, showing why even scholars never doubted that the Bible was the most historically valid book in the world. The second half of the book took a philosophical approach, discussing things like the origins of morality and conscience, the purpose and the destiny of man.

Reading these books ultimately opened my eyes to how I had deceived myself over the years. I also came to realize that the aliens had specifically told me things I had wanted to hear versus those that I needed to hear. One scripture summed up why I had been so willing to listen to them: "The heart is deceitful and desperately wicked above all things; who can know it."

While all these resources helped fan the embers of my faith in Christ, I remained deeply concerned about what would happen next around the world and what these aliens would actually do. My sister had mentioned some of the horrible things that would transpire in the last days, and remembering parts of Armageddon stories only added to my fear. Although it was still difficult to digest, I now discerned Jason had accessed it correctly: demons were indeed masquerading as extraterrestrials.

Knowing I needed to warn people and tell them the truth, I proclaimed on the webzine my testimony of how I had been deceived by the aliens. I shared what had been revealed to me the past week and how I found true hope in becoming a child of God. For the next few days, I relayed new things on the webpage I had uncovered from my research that substantiated the claims that Jesus is God.

More than anything, I felt compelled to share this: Jesus had suffered an intensely brutal death to pay the penalty for our sins so we could be forgiven. His resurrection assured us victory over the power of sin, death, and hell. By simply putting our faith in Him, we could know for certain that one day we would be in paradise with Him. I could only hope that my previous beliefs would lend some credibility to what I now professed and that my new postings could somehow reverse the damage I had done.

CHAPTER 22

Over the next week, I contacted several news organizations about my conversion story, but oddly none of them were interested in doing an interview with me. While glad I could still use my webzine to promote the gospel, my efforts to share my testimony resulted in a deluge of backlash. Even though a few of the letters were supportive, most of the responses I received were extremely negative. Many of the regular visitors to the site had no problem voicing their sense of betrayal, sharing how disappointed they were in me and how I had basically let everyone down. Some were not as tactful in their word choice, deciding to use their creative skills to come up with new combinations of curse words for me.

Despite anticipating negative reactions, I continued calling friends to share what happened to me, hoping to at least start a dialogue. My attempts were frustrated by the persisting trouble with cell phone towers and my call to Sterling happened to be the only one that remained uninterrupted.

Intrigued by my account, he said he would be willing to read the books Vanessa had given me. When I told him I would no longer be pursuing the movie project, he chuckled and said, "Yeah, I kind of figured that." Relieved that he wasn't angry, I promised him I would mail out the books to him in the next week, but that he could just get the cliff notes from the webzine.

Retreating to the solitude of my back patio to pray for Sterling and his family, I became hopeful that the light sprinkles indicated that we would get some badly needed rain. The dark storm had moved in rapidly over the ocean, obscuring my view up the coastline. With the soft drizzle turning to downpour, I headed back inside, but stopped right as my hand grabbed the knob of the French doors leading into the kitchen.

Spontaneously turning my face to the sky, I raised my arms upward, allowing the rain to completely soak me. As I stood there enjoying the moment, the raindrops softened and I opened my eyes out over the sea below to catch a set of beautiful bright sunrays triumphantly breaking through the imposing black clouds.

AFTER GOING INSIDE AND CHANGING into a dry set of clothes, I tried calling Bill again and he completely surprised me by picking up on the first ring. He put me on hold and then said, "Look outside."

Pushing the living room curtains aside, I saw Bill stepping out of his old Ford pickup. He quickly grabbed an umbrella from the bed of his truck, waving at me before he hung up.

Ecstatic for the opportunity to share the Gospel with him, I rushed to open the door.

"Bill, good to see you!" I said and found myself actually trying to hug him. He put his hand out to shake mine and I ended up in an awkward position as his extended forearm kept me from embracing him.

"Hey, Zach, Nice to see you."

"I've been trying to reach you for weeks. Is everything okay?"

He moved across the room, sat down on the couch and removed his cowboy hat. "Everything is good on the home front. So Zach, what's this stuff about God and Jesus on the webpage?"

Not knowing where to even start, I said, "Yeah, I just put this thing together last week. Have you been able to check it out?"

"Yes, I took a look at it," he said, lightly tapping his hat.

"Well, you know me, I was extremely skeptical about religion and I understand how others can be…"

"What about The Ancestors?" he winced and fixed his gaze on me.

"Well, if you read the webpage, then, well, you know that I…"

There was another knock at the door and I jumped out of my chair, welcoming the break so I could think of how to tactfully explain this new development to Bill. I walk hurriedly over to the window and noticed a full sized limo with a driver standing upright near the trunk.

Opening my front door, I staggered back a step, amazed to see Mr. Boris Wolfe himself standing on my front patio.

"Zach Miller. It's a pleasure to meet again," he said, shaking my hand.

Unable to say anything at first, I shook his hand robotically.

After inviting himself in, he waltzed across the living room before relaxing in a chair next to the couch. "This is quite a nice place you have here. The sunsets must be spectacular."

"Mr. Wolfe, Zach was just telling me about his new postings on the webpage," Bill said.

"Is that right? I would very much like to hear more about this myself," Boris said, unbuttoning the top button of his black suit jacket.

Not many people had ever intimidated me, but Mr. Wolfe's presence made me stammer. "Can I...would you guys like something to drink?" I started toward the kitchen, trying to avoid their stares.

"No, no, Mr. Miller. Thank you, but I'm actually in a hurry. We have lots of work to do as you well know and we are counting on your writing talents to help bring the hope of a new, unified world."

His last statement gave me an instant case of indigestion and I wanted nothing more than to avoid talking about my change of heart with Mr. Wolfe.

Boris crossed his legs and held onto one knee with both hands. "Mr. Miller, I have talked to many people over the last year who have told me that your words have inspired them and given them good reason to be optimistic. They see that very hope being realized right now, even as we face so many challenges. You can make the difference and I'm sure you are eager to join our efforts in making things right in our new world," he said stoically.

"Boris..." I sputtered.

From the look on his face, it appeared that I had managed to stun Boris by addressing him by his first name. As I tried to regain my momentum, an unexplainable boldness came over me.

"I was wrong. I mean, I was dead wrong. I truly believe that the aliens are lying to us to keep us from putting our faith in Jesus."

"I don't believe it," he said.

Calmly calculating his next response, he paused for a moment as he tapped his fingers together methodically on top of his knee. "Mr. Miller, you may not know this about me, but I have been on the Interfaith Council for the United Nations for several months now. While I certainly acknowledge that Jesus made tremendous contributions to society, I've also witnessed firsthand the danger that comes from being so myopic to believe there are no other viable means to achieve spiritual harmony. I truly believe that like so many other people around the world, you are suffering from post-traumatic stress, which is clearly obscuring your vision."

"Actually, I've never seen things so clearly," I said, crossing my arms.

"Mr. Miller, please remember, you and I stood right next to each other and witnessed firsthand The Visitation. We were in no way ever in any danger, nor are we now."

"That's because they want to use us…"

"Insanity!" Boris shouted before clenching his teeth.

He then quickly grasped his hands together and uncrossed his legs as if to get a handle on the situation. "Mr. Miller, you've been told that there are evil ancestors and that they would try to deceive you. And now, going against all logic, you have chosen to listen to them."

"I don't see it that way now," I said, facing him and hoping he would see my resolve.

"Well, then. I do have to catch a flight to an important meeting in L.A., so I must be on my way." Boris stood up abruptly and buttoned his suit jacket.

I followed him to the door where he turned around to shake my hand and I obliged. "Zach, when you come around and start to think more rationally, please contact me so we can collaborate on some projects together."

"Boris, I can assure you, I see the light now and will tell anyone who will listen that Jesus is Lord."

"I see," Boris scoffed.

Without even looking toward the couch, he said, "Mr. Hunter, may I have a quick word with you?"

Bill stood up swiftly and walked by me, scratching his eyebrow so he could avoid looking at me. Before going through the door, he let out a deep breath and muttered, "I'll be right back."

As I watched from behind the edge of my curtains, the limo driver shadowed Boris with an outstretched arm to keep his boss under an umbrella. Bill caught up to them at the curb on top of the driveway and it came as no surprise to see Boris do all the talking. In fact, Bill didn't say a word. Standing still in the constant drizzle and holding his chin pensively, Bill continuously nodded to whatever the EU Ambassador said.

Lightning flashed across the hilltop behind them and I saw Boris duck into the back of the limo right before the thunder followed.

The stretched out car disappeared down the street and Bill slogged back down the wet sidewalk. Stepping back from the curtains, I hurried over to the kitchen table eager to continue my conversation without Boris' formidable presence.

"Look Bill, I know you are very open minded person. You gotta read one of these books I have right here. See, this one is called *How Jesus Wrecked My College Keg Party*. I know. Quirky title. But it's well thought out and extremely pragmatic. My sister actually left it for me years ago and you'll see why I believe this..." I stopped as I got close enough to see that Bill's damp face had lost its color. "Bill, are you all right?"

"Uh, yeah. I just need to use your restroom."

"Yeah, sure. It's right down there. There're some towels in the cabinet so you can dry your hair."

Hearing Bill's heavy footsteps echo down the hallway towards the bathroom, I quickly went over to my computer and flipped over to my webzine. Right after finding the recent message that I wanted to share with him, I heard a flush from the restroom.

When I could hear his feet shuffling back my way, I yelled, "Check this out, Bill. This is what I am talking about. This woman just wrote me about how she had been raised in a Christian home and how her mom told her that she felt Jesus would come soon and rapture His people out of here. Last year after she had gone off to college, she became enamored with my story about The Ancestors because she felt it was much more inclusive than her parents' religion. She said the moment all those people disappeared she instinctively knew that her mom had been prophetic..."

ZACH NEVER HEARD THE BLAST as the bullet instantly ripped through his skull, leaving his limp body to crash violently onto the wooden floor. Bill casually threw a hand towel he had used to deafen the gunshot into a garbage bag before stooping down to place the pistol into Zach's lifeless hand.

A burst of sunrays suddenly crashed through the French doors, stretching across the floor to cover Zach's body. Annoyed by the blinding light, Bill used his hand to shield his eyes and stood up quickly. He ripped the latex gloves off his hands one by one and stuffed them into the bag before replacing them with a new pair from his back pocket. Nudging one of Zach's legs to the side with his cowboy boot, Bill scooted into the chair and ran his fingers across the keyboard.

Dear Faithful Readers,

I have been under tremendous stress in these last couple of weeks due to the calamities around the world. My heart has been torn from the loss of loved ones and I must confess I've turned to drinking alcohol and taking pills in attempts to numb the pain. As many of you know, I have even been desperate enough to believe biblical myths while searching for some meaning of it all, but I now realize I was fooling myself. Nothing seems to alleviate the deep anguish within me, so I have decided to just go to sleep now and find the rest my soul longs for.

Sincerely,
Zach

Posting the letter onto the webzine, Bill left the computer on and again removed the rubber gloves. With the garbage bag in hand, he grabbed his umbrella before heading out to his truck where he stashed the bag into a plastic bucket in the bed of his pickup. After driving a couple miles down the road, he pulled behind a gas station and tossed the bucket into a dumpster while pressing his cell phone against his shoulder.

"Master, it's finished," Bill said.

The deep, German accent on the other line sounded satisfied, replying "Excellent. Well done, my loyal servant. Well done."

ACKNOWLEDGEMENTS

I AM THANKFUL FOR THE countless people who have crossed my path during this long journey, offering me feedback and continued support. Special thanks goes to Jennifer Allen, Chris Ahrens, Ashley Ludwig, Susannah Nelson, Anita Palmer and Brett Burner for their advice and guidance. I would also like to acknowledge Chuck Missler and Dr. Mark Eastman who helped inspire this story with their book Alien Encounters.

And all thanks goes to My Father in Heaven, who blesses me despite myself and loves me even though He really knows me.